# Step Into the Wind

BLUE FEATHER BOOKS, LTD.

*For K.C., you make my life beautiful; and for all of Mother Nature's wild ones who show us how to live life to its fullest.*

# Step Into the Wind

A BLUE FEATHER BOOK

by

# Bev Prescott

This is a work of fiction. All characters, locales and events are either products of the author's imagination or are used fictitiously.

STEP INTO THE WIND

Cover design by Ann Phillips

A Blue Feather Book
Published by Blue Feather Books, Ltd.

www.bluefeatherbooks.com

ISBN: 978-1-935627-75-3

First edition: February, 2013

Printed in the United States of America and in the United Kingdom.

# Acknowledgements

Life is bittersweet. How could it not be when its bookends are birth and death? People and animals come into our lives giving us sheer joy and then heartbreak when they go. Sometimes their passing leaves us so broken that we have to be strong enough to ask for help. Thank you, Laura, for helping me find the way through my darkness.

In the early hours of morning I spend a lot of time watching and listening to the wild ones who inhabit our meadow. Thank you for teaching me so much about living. Life is a gift to be cherished every second that we are able to hold onto it. To the eagles on *our* island, you especially, inspire me. I'm grateful to share this little piece of the planet with you.

To Emily Reed and Blue Feather Books, thank you for giving me a home to tell my stories. Thanks so much to my editors, Nann Dunne and Nene Adams. Your candor and patience helped make *Step Into the Wind* a better story, and me a better author. It was a privilege to work with you.

Finally, to my beloved, K.C., you gave me the world when you gave me your heart. Thank you for your unconditional love. I'll love you forever.

# Chapter 1

Alex Marcotte ran. She didn't dare look over her shoulder.

Tentacles of anxiety whipped across the back of her neck and grasped her throat, choking off her air. She tried to swallow but couldn't. She ran harder to get away. Her gaze darted around. She had nowhere to hide; it was the *place* that provoked her anxiety. Her clamoring heart rattled her insides. Despite the heat generated by her body's exertion, goose bumps broke out over her skin.

A voice barely registered above the chatter in her head. "Geez," Claire Durand said, "if I'd known we were going to sprint the whole way, I would've told you to run alone this morning."

Alex slowed and stopped to let Claire catch up. Up until this morning, she hadn't seen her childhood friend in nearly five years.

She tried to take a different view of the scenery around her. Glasgow, Maine, on the shores of Sebago Lake couldn't be a lovelier place to look at. Yet it terrified her to be back in the town where her childhood had been broken. "Sorry. I got lost in my thoughts."

"Really?" Claire was panting. "My guess is... you still run to escape... rather than to arrive... like most people." She put her hands on her hips and bent over to catch her breath. "You run faster than anyone I know." She gave a short laugh. "It almost killed me trying to keep up with you."

"I'm sorry. Do you want to walk instead for a while?" A strand of Alex's long black hair had come loose from her ponytail. She tucked it behind her ear.

Claire straightened. "If you don't mind."

"No." Alex took a step forward but let Claire set the pace. Her legs ached to go fast again.

"I'm glad you're home for the entire summer." Claire untied the long-sleeved T-shirt wrapped around her waist. "There's so much for us to catch up on. It's really good to see you again." She slipped the T-shirt over her head.

Alex's stomach knotted at the thought of the word *home*. She inhaled more oxygen than necessary to fuel her body. The lungful of air was meant for her mind. She focused on the morning calm that lay over the eleven-mile expanse of Sebago Lake. She and Claire walked along the winding dirt road that paralleled the waterfront cottages dotting its sloping shoreline.

A curtain of fog hung low over the massive stretch of the lake, shrouding it in a cloudy mist. From her vantage point above, Alex could make out the lake's islands because of their tall pines. The very tops of the needle-covered branches poked above the gray curtain.

"I'm not sure I can stay that long." Alex breathed in the moist, fragrant air laced with lilac, cedar, and pine. The melancholy cry of a loon in the distance pierced her heart and made her hurt for all she had loved and lost in Maine.

"You teach at the School of History at that university in southern California, right? I thought they gave you the entire summer off to finish that book you're writing. Your dad said something about wildfires?"

"Yes, the Maine wildfires of 1947. I'm really excited about it. Devastating wildfires are commonplace out west. There's a lot of history surrounding them, but not so much on the East Coast. A fire that burned entire towns and thousands of acres across Maine isn't something most people know much about. When my history students hear the words 'forest fire,' they always think of areas out west. The dean of the school believes my book will be an important addition to the history of wildfires across the country. I'm hoping it will get me tenure."

"Hmm." Claire slipped her hands into the pockets of her running shorts. "If you get tenure, you definitely won't be moving back to the East Coast. Now I really hope you'll stay the whole summer."

Unease filled Alex. She might as well get the truth out there. Claire would probe until she revealed everything anyway. "I won't need the whole summer to finish my research. You know the length of time I stay has nothing to do with the book."

The proverbial elephant stomped into the silence of Claire's pause. "Have you seen your father yet?"

"No, I got in late last night and slipped out this morning before there was a chance I'd run into him."

"You're staying in the main house. You know you're not going to be able to avoid him."

"I'm not trying to. I wanted to run first so I could get hold of myself before I see him."

"It's not going to be as bad as you think," Claire said. "Even though you haven't seen him in years, he always tells me whenever he gets a call or e-mail from you and his mood is happier on those days. He was really glad when he found out you were coming home."

"It would be nice if he told me that himself. I get a very different impression from him. My father mastered the art of passive aggressiveness a long time ago. I doubt I'll get any different treatment from him now."

"He doesn't know how to deal with you, especially because of how you still feel about your mother. He's been praying you'll go see her while you're here. I'm sure he's already told you her doctor said she probably won't live through the summer."

Alex glanced at her watch. "Seven hours and thirty-three minutes."

"What?" Claire asked.

"That's how long it took since I've been home before someone asked if I was going to see my mother."

"It is a main reason you came, isn't it?"

"No. I told you, I'm here to do the last of the research to finish my book. And my father insisted that he needed help with the camp because my mother's sick."

"Come on, isn't there some part of you that came home to see her one last time? Besides, he's been asking for your help for years during the summers, but we haven't seen hide nor hair of you until now."

Time's passage had created a chasm between her and Claire, Alex thought. The twelve-year-old girl she used to tell every secret to was now a woman who knew nothing about her, yet everything. At the bottom of the chasm lay the remains of what had happened to both of them the night her twin brother, Jake, died. Even if she had an answer to Claire's question, she wouldn't share it.

"I'm not ready to see my mother yet," she said. "As for my father, I came home this time because he sounded desperate."

"For what it's worth," Claire said, "he's been desperate since the day you left. Now he's struggling with the fact that your mom isn't going to be around much longer. It would mean the world to him if you finally reconciled with her."

Alex let the comment roll off of her back. Claire meant well. Over the years, the woman had become more of a daughter to her parents than she herself had been. Claire loved and cared about them, while Alex had grown cold toward her parents. Still, guilt for feeling that way crowded out her desire to tell Claire that she was tired of her parents' broken hearts mattering more than hers. There was no point in wallowing in that can of worms with Claire anyway. Claire never did see how her parents had contributed to what happened the night Jake died.

"Let's see how things go," Alex said. "For now, I need to help my father and make sure I don't come apart at the seams again while I'm at it."

"I thought you were getting better."

Alex shook her head, clearly not enough for Claire to notice. She felt pretty sure that *getting better* wasn't the right choice of words. Subsisting, maybe. "I'm holding my own." She gestured at the lake. "No matter what, this place will always be a part of me, the good and the bad. I miss being here, but as long as I'm away, I'm able to keep a lid on what happened to Jake, for the most part. Confronting my mother about it is a darkness I don't think I'm equipped to handle yet."

Her hands involuntarily clenched into fists and opened again—a telltale sign that her anxiety was on the verge of getting the better of her again. Ever since her plane had touched down yesterday, it loomed heavy in the background, waiting to make its predatory moves. *Breathe, Alex.*

"I know it must still be hard for you," Claire said. "Maybe finally coming home to the people and place you love the most is the best thing. Don't they say that to conquer your fear you have to confront it?"

Alex thought Claire couldn't possibly understand how it felt to slog through the anxiety and depression that had taken hold of her life like an anchor around her neck. Her former friend wasn't in a position to provide advice. Unfortunately, Claire had been front and center to her nervous breakdown and subsequent hospitalization after Jake's death at the tender age of fifteen. Even though they were strangers now, Claire knew her deepest secret. If she was going to get through even a week of being home, she'd have to use every ounce of patience she had.

"You sound like my therapist," she said. "I'd prefer that you didn't."

"I'm only trying to be a friend."

"I know. I don't mean to be short with you. Just give me some time to sort things out while I'm here." Alex nudged Claire with her elbow. "I'll do my best to try and find the nerve to see Mother. Okay?"

"Remember what you used to say to me when we were kids and about to jump off Hawk's Leap into the water?" Claire asked.

Alex recalled the thirty-foot cliff rising out of the lake on the eastern shore. Jumping from the top into the deep water below was a rite of passage and the means to be accepted into the "in crowd" for kids who spent their summers on Sebago. She nodded. "Don't let fear anchor your feet to the ground…"

Claire chimed in, and in unison they finished the refrain, "Or you'll never get to do anything fun. Just jump already."

Claire laughed. "You were the bravest kid in town."

The irony of her fearlessness as a child compared to being a grown woman afraid of her own shadow made Alex sad. Memories intermingled with the parade of theoretical horribles she had become so adept at conjuring. As an adult, she spent more time thinking about all the bad things that might happen to her as opposed to living in and enjoying the moment. Her mind became more anxious with each step. She needed to get control over her worries.

Alex closed her mouth and inhaled through her nose, letting the cool morning air of Glasgow, Maine, in late May fill her lungs. The sweet fragrance reminded her of more peaceful times when Maine was the only place she'd ever wanted to be. She exhaled slowly through her mouth and repeated the process, filling herself with calm by forcing worry out of her body with each exhalation. *I'm trying my best to be brave.*

"There's something you need to know." Claire's voice interrupted her efforts to find calm.

In the town of Glasgow, Alex could only imagine. "What's that?"

"Your father hired a camp manager. He spends so much time lately driving back and forth to the nursing home in Lewiston where your mom is that he decided he needed some help running the place."

"I think that's a good thing. For a long time, I hoped he'd get someone to help him. I may not want to have anything to do with the camp, but I do want it to continue to succeed. It's too important to the kids who come here every summer for it not to remain."

"The manager's James Bastone." Claire hesitated. "Your father hired him about a year ago. I know how you feel about him. But he's been a huge help to your dad and the camp."

Alex squeezed the bridge of her nose to pinch back an instant headache as they rounded a bend. The large rectangular road sign that signified the history of her family, the town of Glasgow, and her childhood came into view. The bold black letters on a green background read, "Camp Marcotte, 3 miles ahead. A place that holds the redemptive power of nature for all children. Established in 1921." The camp's slogan struck her as nothing less than satire. Her teenage years had been anything but redemptive, and now James Bastone was managing the camp.

"You're kidding, right?" she asked.

"No."

"Let me get this straight." Alex stopped. "The kid who was in every one of our classes from grade school to high school and who never missed an opportunity to bully Jake is now running my family's camp. My father is still so clueless. He might as well invite the fox into the henhouse and let it have whatever it wants."

"Your dad needed the help and James was there. Maybe this is James's way of making up for what happened. We were all just kids. Unfortunately, sometimes kids do stupid, cruel things. But they're still just kids. He's not like he was before."

"I find that impossible to believe. He was mean to the core." Alex bit back anger. "James and his cronies played a part in my brother being gone forever. My father should just sell the place if he needs that much help. Maybe James would be interested."

"Don't say such a thing! It would kill your father. You may have run from the camp, but he still clings to it, and he needs you. We all do. You're not alone in what happened to Jake. You never were." She gripped her elbow. "I can't imagine in a million years what it must have been like for you to have lost Jake the way you did, but we all went through it too. The camp has never been the same and neither has this town. We were all devastated. We shared the loss."

Tears caught in Alex's throat. *But not the blame.* She swallowed them, determined to keep her vow not to cry as long as she was in Glasgow.

She gazed at the lake. All the bittersweet memories locked below its surface would forever be imprinted on her soul. Forcing back the urge to panic, she caught herself holding her breath. She was standing in a wide-open space, but the conversation culminating in a discussion of James, her family, and selling the camp had backed her into a corner like a wounded animal. The all-too-familiar rush of adrenaline prepared her to bolt away. She tried to remain rational. Running at full speed was the only thing that would let her escape.

"I'd like to run the rest of the way," she said.

"Sure," Claire said. "I'm sorry I upset you."

"It's not you. Let me stretch my legs. That always helps me think."

"Okay. I'll meet you back at the camp."

Alex put one foot in front of the other, slowly at first until her muscles warmed. She picked up the pace, stretching her long legs. She imagined herself a race car, the engine throttle opening wide to accelerate. Her breathing became deep and steady. The myriad of thoughts and fears that clamored around her faded into the background. She was aware only of her body's movements and the sound of her breathing.

Attuned to the effects running had on her anxiety, she felt the adrenaline and cortisol being replaced by a cocktail of the brain-calming chemicals: serotonin, dopamine, and endorphins. Running was her drug of choice because it still worked, for the most part.

She glanced over her shoulder this time, not at Claire or anything tangible. Rather, to gauge whether the demons of Glasgow were still closing in on her. Something in the sky caught her eye. An enormous black raptor with a cloud-white head spread its wings and glided over her.

"Where did you come from, eagle?" she whispered.

As the eagle flew closer, it craned its head in her direction. Strange, she could've sworn it recognized her.

# Chapter 2

A couple of miles after leaving Claire behind, Alex slowed her pace. The impressive stone chimney of the camp's main building came into view over the crest of the last hill. Constructed from local granite, the chimney formed the backbone of the structure.

When she was a kid, she used to imagine where each stone must have come from, riding the giant glacier that had scoured the area before it melted and became Sebago, Maine's deepest and second largest lake. Since as far back as she could remember, she'd been the kid who sat alone, swinging on a hammock, gazing out at the lake and thinking about where and how people, places, and things had come to be. She'd imagined all the things that the ancient maple tree towering over her hammock and shading her from the sun had seen over the years. Her adolescent ponderings sowed the seeds that grew into her passion for history.

A white, vintage 1967 Ford pickup truck whizzed past her. Dust swirled around the truck as it slowed and came to a halt on the shoulder of the dirt road. Alex would've recognized the eighty-four-year-old driver and her canine passenger anywhere.

The white-haired woman leaned her head out the open window. "Well, aren't you a sight for sore eyes? Your father told me you were coming home. I see you still spend your time running your cares away."

Alex grinned widely as she jogged to the driver's side of the truck. There weren't many things or people from her childhood untainted by her family's tragedy. Sally Higgins, the local librarian, and her aging black Labrador Retriever, Buddy, were among the few.

"And I see you still have Hiccup the pickup and Buddy." Alex scanned the length of the truck. "She's still in great shape. Hard to believe she has so little rust after living in Maine her whole life."

Buddy wriggled and yowled like a puppy at the sound of his name. His tail thumped against the battered cloth bench seat.

"Yeah, well, the old truck still likes to back talk me with a hiccup every time I shut her engine down. Guess a little back talk is her secret to longevity. As long as Hiccup and Buddy stick around, I will too." Sally stuck a bony hand out the window and patted the side of the truck. "Like I always say, the most important things to take care of—if you hope to be around awhile—are your friends, body, mind, and ride. You do that, and they'll give you all they've got. How are you, girl? You all right being home so far?"

"I'm hanging in there." Alex slapped the edge of the open window. "It's so great to see you." Buddy barked. She reached into the truck and scratched the dog's gray muzzle as his tail wagged wildly. "Hey, good to see you too." She laughed.

"Hop in. I'll take you the rest of the way. I'm heading to the camp now." Sally pointed behind her to the pickup bed full of unfinished Adirondack chairs. "Your father asked me to deliver these early this morning. The kids are going to paint them, and we'll auction them off at the annual library fundraiser. Plus, he's all excited about me hearing some newfangled P.A. system this morning that *Mister* Bastone got in to play reveille."

Sally must've noticed her body stiffen at the mention of James. "You did know your father hired him, right?"

"Not until this morning when Claire told me." Alex shook her head. "I don't know what bothers me more, the fact that my father would have anything at all to do with James, or that he didn't bother to tell me he let him worm his way into the camp. If I'd known, I wouldn't have come back."

"Your father should've told you before you got here. I thought you knew." Sally reached out the window and stroked Alex's cheek. "For what it's worth, I'm really happy that you're home. Maybe we should check the barn for that old bugle you used to play. You can remind Bastone how it's supposed to be done and teach the kids to play it for themselves."

"You always had the best ideas." Alex put her hand on Sally's. "Still do. The kids would love it. For some of them, it's the only chance they'll ever get to pick up an instrument. It's inconceivable to me that my father would agree to a P.A system instead of having the kids make their own music."

"A lot has changed in the short time since Bastone took over managing the place."

"I guess I shouldn't be surprised by that." Alex ran around to the other side of the truck and slid in beside Buddy. He nudged her hand with his snout. Alex scratched him behind the ear. "You're such a good boy."

Sally jutted her chin in the direction of the glove box. "There are some smokes stashed away if you're so inclined."

Alex shook her head and laughed. "No thanks, Sally. I'm all set."

Sally gunned the engine and sent the truck forward. "Suit yourself. It's probably just as well. Your father still hasn't forgiven me for teaching you how to smoke cigars and cuss when you were little. I need to stay on his good side anyway. If you show up this morning smelling of cigar smoke, that's not going to work in my favor. I have an idea for the kids this summer that's going to require your father's buy-in."

Alex couldn't help feeling twelve years old again, riding shotgun with Sally while she schemed up her latest inspiration. The old woman was never in short supply of ideas, especially when it came to helping unwanted or injured animals in town. "What is it? Maybe I can help advocate for you." Buddy leaned against her and licked her cheek as she continued to scratch him under his collar. "I know, honey, I missed you too."

"Some dastardly person left a box of puppies at the town dump a week ago. Of course, Ralph, who still runs the place, called me right away to come and get them. The trouble is that they got away from old Ralph when he opened the box. All those puppies ended up running all over the road." Sally slapped her knee. "Ha! It was quite the sight. They were going in as many directions as the colors they came in. I'm guessing those puppies had several different daddies."

"Oh, no," Alex said. "I hope you got them all picked up safely."

"I did, but Sheriff Hall wasn't too happy with me blocking traffic with my truck while I was at it. He tried to tell me I couldn't park perpendicular across two lanes. Lucky for me, a crowd had formed because no one could get past my truck. Guess he decided against giving an old lady a ticket in front of all those bystanders when all I was trying to do was save a few puppies. I'm certain it was a political move on his part. The sheriff will be looking for donations to the policeman's ball in a couple of months."

"I'm sure he's figured out by now that it's not a good idea to cross you when it comes to helping animals. So what's your idea? I want in." For the first time this morning, Alex looked forward to the happenings at the camp. Who wouldn't with Sally, puppies, and little kids in the mix?

"I was thinking," Sally said, "that after Doc Parsons, the veterinarian, gives the puppies a clean bill of health, we'll do some fundraising and marketing to find them homes with some of the parents of the kids from the camp. We could have the kids make collars for the puppies and have a little puppy fashion show for parent's weekend. I'm betting more than a few folks in the crowd will fall in love and open their homes to a needy soul."

"I love it." Where her father was concerned, Alex could take issue with a lot of things, but his willingness to do something to help animals in need wasn't one of them. "I think my father will love the idea too."

"As long as he doesn't kowtow to Bastone on this, we should be fine. That's enough about me, what's been going on in your life?"

"I'm hoping to finish a first draft of a manuscript I'm working on by the end of the summer. Then it'll go to my editor. The book's on schedule to be published in the spring sometime. I'm writing about the 1947 forest fires here in Maine."

Sally slapped the steering wheel. "I am thrilled with that. Good for you, honey. I'm glad someone's not letting our history be forgotten."

"I was hoping you'd let me interview you about what you remember about the fires while I'm here. I'm also planning a couple of research trips to the archives in Augusta and Boston, but getting a description of the events from someone who was actually here at the time would be invaluable."

"In a heartbeat. You can ask me anything you like. It'll give me a chance to set the record straight about what those talking heads have been saying lately about how it could never happen again like it did in '47. I'll tell you, I think they're being naïve about that. Just ask all those poor folks out west whether it's possible for fires to still burn entire towns. They have access to all the same modern firefighting equipment we have here, but that doesn't always stop a fire before it destroys everything in its path. There are a hell of a lot more trees here in Maine to add fuel to a fire than they have out there in the desert too."

"What happened to make the '47 wildfires the subject of the news recently?" Alex asked.

"This past winter, we had barely any snow to speak of and it's been the driest spring on record. If the weather continues at this pace, the leaves will start turning to dust under our feet by early July. I'm worried about it. The air feels like it did then. The trouble is, people forget the olden times and doom themselves to repeat their past mistakes time and again. Just look at the silly things our politicians do, with the public's blessing."

Sally reached around Buddy and patted Alex's knee. "I'm so proud of you for becoming a history professor. You keep telling the stories of our past. It matters. I'll do anything you need to help you write your book."

"Great, thanks. Would it be all right if I stopped by the library in the next week or so?"

Sally turned onto the camp's long, winding, gravel driveway. "You stop by anytime you like."

In the light of day, Alex saw a fresh coat of gray stain on the cedar clapboards of the camp's main building. There were a few more bunkhouses now, and a new tennis court took up space in what had been part of the lawn. A line of trees still separated the camp from the lake except for the hundred-foot-long sandy beach and a small boathouse.

The white, two-story, saltbox house that she'd grown up in still stood across from the camp. It seemed smaller than she remembered as a kid. She wasn't sure whether it was because she now viewed the house through the prism of an adult, or that the camp, as always, took precedence over everything around it.

Sally parked next to a beat-up old Volvo. Alex wondered whether her father had managed to reach his goal of three hundred thousand miles yet on the only car she ever remembered him driving.

Just as she had always done, Sally threw open the driver's door before the truck came to a complete stop in the dirt lot in front of the main building. She hopped out while simultaneously putting the truck in park.

"I'll bet we have some old newspaper clippings from the time of the fire stashed away in boxes somewhere in the library attic that you could use." Standing next to the truck, Sally leaned over the seat and turned the key in the ignition to the off position. Hiccup rumbled and smoked.

Alex got out and counted out loud. "One, two, three, four…" She jumped at the loud bang that came at five. "Right on cue," she said. "Like always."

Sally winked. "There are still some things you can always count on, my dear."

Alex took comfort in knowing that Sally's pure heart was one of them.

"Would you mind giving Buddy a hand out of the truck?" Sally asked. "He needs a little more help these days."

"Sure. Come here, boy." Alex put an arm around Buddy's midsection and guided him down to the ground. He ambled off toward the lake. "He still loves the water?"

"Can't get enough of it," Sally answered.

"He always was the smartest and sweetest dog in town." Alex went around to the back of the truck and unlatched the heavy truck-bed door. "I'd love to look at whatever newspaper clippings you have about the fires. Sometimes the best stuff I've found has been in dusty old boxes that haven't been opened in ages." She reached for a chair. "Let me get those."

Her father's voice came from behind. "Hello, Sally, Alexandra. That won't be necessary. We'll see to them."

The moment Alex had looked forward to and dreaded had come.

Sally patted her arm.

Alex turned to see her father, Daniel Marcotte, with James Bastone standing beside him. Flanking them were the three men who had kept the camp's buildings and grounds in tip-top shape since long before she was born. They were reliable fixtures in the camp and in town.

The short, thin man, Chuck Sheppard, still looked the part of the wise old Mainer whom everyone turned to in a crisis. He smiled warmly at her. Bob Kilns's belly was bigger than she remembered. He still wore his signature suspenders that kept his trousers snug against the rounded paunch. He gave Sally a nod then studied the ground and didn't make eye contact with Alex. Martin West barely acknowledged Alex or Sally. He folded his arms across his chest. He wore the same gruff expression as he'd had when she was a child.

Alex smiled at the three men, thankful that their presence provided the opportunity to avoid her father and James a little longer. "Good to see you, guys."

"Glad you're home, kiddo." Chuck motioned to Bob and Martin. "Let's get these chairs out of the truck and give Alex and Daniel a moment to catch up." The three men went about removing the chairs while James remained in place.

Alex gathered her courage and looked into her father's face for the first time in years. He'd never looked quite so tired, not even during the time they had buried her brother. His shoulders slumped. He'd lost weight from his tall, thin frame. His formerly salt-and-pepper hair had turned a pure silver gray.

Daniel smiled. Behind the expression, she read a blend of hurt, disappointment, and love. "I'm glad you could take time out of your busy schedule to come help me with the camp this summer." He put his arms around her.

The distance between them felt like miles despite their embrace. Alex didn't mention she had no intention of staying the whole summer.

He didn't give her the opportunity to say so anyway. As was his custom, he jumped right into the camp's business rather than focus on her. "You and Sally are just in time to hear our new P.A. system."

Even though Alex had tried to prepare for dealing with her father's passive-aggressive approach to communication, their first thirty seconds together felt like a subliminal punch to the gut. "Sally told me it would replace having the kids learn how to play reveille themselves," she said. "We used to love taking turns playing the bugle to wake up the other kids. Remember?"

James laughed. "You were always the best little bugler when we were growing up. Times have changed, though, and the camp needs to keep up with the times. Kids aren't interested in that sort of thing anymore."

"If you gave them half a chance to play the bugle, they might actually like it," Sally said.

"I doubt it. It's all we can do to get them to put their phones and electronic games away long enough to look at the lake, let alone enjoy it. They could care less about playing the bugle."

"Maybe you should try harder?" Sally said.

James smiled at her. "Perhaps." He looked Alex up and down. "Being a professor suits you. You look great."

Unlike Chuck and the others, James's appearance suggested he should be on a yacht instead of a summer camp for kids. He wore perfectly pressed trousers, a silk shirt, and designer eyeglasses. He was every bit as handsome as she remembered. He'd always used his looks and charm to win people over. Those he couldn't win over, he bullied into submission.

Alex wondered how much her father was paying James for him to afford that kind of wardrobe. "Flattery never got you anywhere with me when we were kids, and it still won't. I'm jetlagged and a sweaty mess from my run. I hardly believe I'm all that much to look at. And I agree with Sally. Give the kids a chance to try playing the bugle."

"You still don't see yourself the way others do," James said. "Honestly, you were a great musician as a kid. Do you still play the ukulele?"

James always had a knack for saying things in a way that left one wondering whether he meant a compliment or a put-down. Knowing James the way she did, this was a stab at her. After what happened the night her brother died, there were plenty of people in the town, including James, who'd whispered behind her back and no longer looked at her favorably.

Bob Kiln was a perfect example. While he worked to remove the chairs from the bed of the pickup, he was obviously taking great pains not to look at her or get too close. Alex had no doubt that Bob would have plenty to say to his wife later about the town pariah who'd finally come home.

She wished she could think more quickly on her feet and come up with something subtly off-putting to say in response to James. Her thoughts were interrupted by the enveloping notes of a pitch-perfect, surround-sound recording of reveille.

James pointed toward the sky. "That's what I'm talking about. It's so much better than the awful honking of a ten-year-old playing the bugle for the first time. God, I wanted to poke my eyes out every time I heard a kid torture that song." He glanced in the direction of the lake, and his triumphant expression changed. He lifted his hand to shade his eyes from the morning sun rising above the vanishing fog. After the last note played, he said, "I thought I told those wildlife people not to step foot on our island without me being present."

Alex glanced at the lake. Buddy was playing at the water's edge. He barked at a duck as it swam by. On the island owned by the camp, about eight-hundred feet directly across from its shore, was a man in dark clothing. He knelt over what appeared to be a large duffel bag. A bright red toolbox stood beside him. Ropes hung from the tallest pine tree, and the tangle of branches obscured who or what was in it.

Daniel looked through the eyeglasses hanging from a chain around his neck. "I spoke to them yesterday and gave my permission to be on the island. All they said they'd do was check on the eaglets."

"Eagles are nesting on the island?" Alex asked. "Since when? That's wonderful."

"Sure is," Sally said. "The pair showed up last year and built a nest. The wildlife people think they may have laid some eggs, but no one ever saw any eaglets afterward. Then the pair showed up again this year, and it looks like they have two babies. I think it's the best thing that's happened to this town in a long time. Our very own pair of nesting eagles."

"With all due respect," James said, "the rest of the story is that those wildlife people blame us for last year's alleged failure even though they never bothered to investigate whether there were any eggs in the first place. It's folklore. If they have their way, they'll shut down the island without a shred of evidence that it's even necessary to keep people off it. We've used it every year since the camp's beginning. Our alumni—who donate a lot of money—won't be happy if they aren't able to camp and picnic on the island like they always have."

"You mean to tell me that donations are more important than these eagles coming back to the area?" Sally glared at him.

"Of course not, but those tree-hugging types can be completely unreasonable. That's why I have to make sure I stay involved to act as the voice of reason for this camp. I really wish you had done as I asked, Daniel, and not given them permission without talking to me first. As manager, it's important that I be involved in all decisions about the camp." He squeezed Daniel's shoulder. "It's necessary for us to succeed. I'm doing this for you."

Daniel seemed confused. The look on his face suggested that he struggled to find a recollection of the conversation with James. "I'm sorry."

Alex looked from her father to James and back again. How could her father let James talk to him like that? "This is still your camp, Dad. Whether you remember the discussion or not, you can give permission to whomever you like."

The confusion on his face turned resolute. "James has done a tremendous amount for me when no one else has, especially my own daughter. I trust his decisions, and I should've remembered."

"I'm going out to the island to have a word with them," James said. "Daniel, would you like to come with me?"

"No, I'd prefer it if my daughter pulled some weight around here for a change. She'll go with you." Daniel addressed Alex. "Please, go with James and take his lead as to whatever he thinks is best."

Alex held her tongue. Her options were limited. She didn't know how to insist that her father treat her with respect. Besides, standing up for herself would be much easier said than done.

She couldn't possibly undo, in an instant, thirty years of his way of dealing with her. His treatment of her was like a wave that she got caught up in and couldn't swim out of. Her logical brain was smothered under the weight of too much unresolved heartbreak. If she argued with him, he'd dismantle her as if she were still a child. The worst part would be having James and everyone else front and center for the show. Intellectually, she knew her father had no right to demand that she do anything. But the broken child inside of her spoke louder than rational thinking. She chose the path of least resistance. "Fine.

# Chapter 3

Zoe Kimball placed her palms on the rough bark of the lofty white pine and gazed up into its green branches. She wished she didn't have to wear climbing gloves so she could feel the trunk against the skin of her hands. She still couldn't believe she got paid to climb trees. She zipped her Maine Department of Wildlife and Fisheries canvas jacket all the way up to her throat to keep out the morning chill she suspected she might encounter when she got to the top of the seventy-foot-tall tree.

"How old do you think the eaglets are?" Her colleague, Rob Loren, asked when he passed her a handheld radio.

Zoe slipped the radio into a pouch clipped to her climbing belt. "The neighbor who's been watching the eagles estimated that the first egg was probably laid on Easter because that's when the mother stopped leaving the nest. She's stayed put ever since except for the short times her mate swapped places with her. So they should be about three weeks old."

"A perfect age for banding."

"Yep, they're big enough for their legs to hold the bands but still small enough for me to handle." Zoe took a step back and gazed up at the single arborist's climbing rope looped over a large branch about three quarters of the way up the tree. One bottom end of the rope was connected to the other part in a series of three specialized knots rigged to allow her to ascend and descend the rope in a controlled fashion.

She clipped the carabiner on her harness to the loop formed by the first knot and locked it in place. The second was a rescue knot for safety purposes, and the third was a climbing knot, also known as a Blake's Hitch. She could slide the climbing knot up and down the length of the rope with her hands as necessary to control her pace—up to ascend and down to descend. If she took her hand off of the knot, it would hold her in place along the length of the rope.

She leaned her weight on the harness to test the strength of the branch she had chosen for her climb. "That ought to work." She bounced a couple of times for good measure to make sure it wouldn't break.

"I really like the new slingshot you brought along," she said to Rob. "That's the highest branch we've ever been able to tie off on from the ground. Nice work."

"Yeah, I'm happy with it. It's the Big Shot Line Launcher from WesPur Climbing Equipment. You can see why it got such great reviews. It sure saved us a lot of time. You'll still have to use your throw bag at the top of the tree, though." Rob finished packing the slingshot back into its case. "I'm surprised Bastone didn't insist on being here this morning. The last time we talked to him, he was adamant about being out here when we weighed and banded the eaglets."

Zoe couldn't help the grin that spread across her face. "He doesn't exactly know we're here."

"Seriously? You do this all the time, and someday, it's going to catch up to you." Rob gestured at the shore. The island where they stood was covered in fog. "You'd better hope this soup holds long enough for us to do what we have to and get out of here before he catches us. For someone who loves her job, you sure like to take risks that could jeopardize it."

"Don't worry, I went over his head and spoke with Mr. Marcotte, the owner. He gave me permission." Zoe attached the steel foot ascender to her right boot and climbing rope. "Besides, technically, we don't need permission."

"Yes, but we're supposed to be good public servants and get it anyway. That's the commissioner's policy. Remember?"

Zoe put on a climbing helmet with face shield and neck guard and adjusted the straps. "You worry too much."

"You don't worry enough," Rob said. "And you look a bit like Darth Vader with that thing on."

"You're a real laugh riot. As for Bastone, I can't have him breathing down my neck while I'm trying to climb a tree." She made a disgusted face. "He oozes schmooze. I'm afraid I'd slip right out of this tree if he were hanging around. You wouldn't want me to fall and get hurt, would you?"

Rob rolled his eyes. "You could climb this tree blindfolded with one arm tied behind your back while angry mom and dad eagles buzzed you with their talons and beaks. I doubt seriously that James Bastone would somehow hinder you."

Zoe lifted her right foot off of the ground and clipped the rope into the slot of the foot ascender attached to her boot. "Maybe not, but I don't like him." She put her weight on her right foot and used her arms to pull herself up the rope. Her right hand slid the climbing knot higher as she went. Her body moved easily, and she repeated the process until she was about eight feet up. She reached down and grabbed the rope hanging below her and tied a slipknot loop into it. The loop was for safety in the event that her climbing knot failed to slow her descent. The safety knot would prevent her from slipping off the bottom of the rope.

"There are a lot of people you don't like, Zoe," Rob said. "You still have to deal with them."

She pulled herself higher. "Not when I'm in the trees."

After several efficient pulls on the climbing rope, she reached the underside of the branch that her rope was looped over and leaned her weight into the harness to rest. She yelled down to Rob, "I'm ready to tie the rope off onto the next highest branch I can reach. I should be able to do it on one of the branches just below the nest." She removed her climbing gloves and slipped them into the pocket of her jacket.

She reached into a pouch on her climbing belt and took out her throw bag. On her second attempt, the small, heavy bag, which was attached to a thin line of tightly threaded rope that fed from the pouch, looped perfectly over the target branch about twenty-five feet above her head and came back down to her. She pulled up the end of the climbing rope hanging below her—the part she had just ascended—tied it to the thin line of the throw bag, and pulled until it went up and over the higher branch and returned to her.

She unfastened the throw bag line and stowed it back in the pouch. With the rope now looped over the branch above her, she tied the same series of knots in it as she had from the ground and clipped her carabiner to the second loop. She made a new slipknot for safety and tested the branch's strength before unclipping the first loop from her carabiner. After unclipping it, she was ready to climb higher.

"The rope's good to go," she reported. She retrieved her climbing gloves and put them back on. "I'm climbing again."

"Be careful when you get toward the open part of the tree near the nest," Rob yelled up. "The parents are getting more agitated the closer you get to it."

Two enormous black and white raptors circled the tree, swooping in and screeching loudly when Zoe neared their babies. Being so close to them left her in no doubt as to their size. Their six-foot wingspans cast an ominous shadow when they passed over her head. She was thankful for the thick branches preventing the eagles from getting too close to her until she reached the nest in a more open part of the tree. Then she'd have to work fast and rely on the heavy canvas jacket and helmet to protect her from being sliced open by their razor sharp talons if they got brave enough to swoop on her.

Zoe spoke to them. "Aren't you two menacing with all that huffing and puffing? If you leave me alone, I promise to work quickly to put your little ones back safe and sound after I send them down to Rob for a quick exam. Keep in mind, I'm a friend and you're going to need me more than you know this summer." When she reached the second branch just below the nest, she took the two-way radio out of her pouch and depressed the Talk button. "Is it as loud down there as it is up here?" She released the button.

"Yeah, you would think their world was coming down all around them," Rob answered. "If all that squawking doesn't get Bastone's attention, I don't know what will. The fog's dissipating fast too. It's almost gone. Stay toward the left of the nest if you can. The branches are thicker there. The parents won't be able to reach you as easily."

"Got it. I'll let you know when I'm ready to send the first eaglet down." Zoe replaced the radio into its pouch and navigated her way through the branches to the edge of the nest.

She had to climb a couple of feet above the safety of the branch she was anchored to. Being at the nest was the most dangerous point, and she loved the rush. Standing on the anchor branch, she peeked over the edge of the nest. Two gangly gray birds bobbled around in front of her. Their small down-covered bodies were wildly out of proportion to their almost full-grown beaks and talons.

"Hello, my little lovelies."

The wide-eyed eaglets backed away from her to the other end of the four-foot-long nest. The larger of the two tripped over a duck bone in the process and squawked at her as if she had somehow caused the mishap.

"Don't you two have faces only a mother could love?" Zoe crooned.

The smaller eaglet spread its long, skinny, awkward wings and flapped them defiantly.

"Hit a nerve, did I?"

The eaglet held its ground while its larger sibling moved farther away.

"I hate to tell you this, but you look more like pterodactyls than majestic raptors. Maybe I should call you Terry and Dac. Hmm?" Zoe tied a safety anchor to one of the thick branches and pulled herself up so she could slide her butt up onto the edge of the nest. The average eagle's nest was about five to six feet in diameter and could weigh more than a ton. This nest looked to be about average size, giving her no concern over whether it would hold her weight.

The panicked parents screeched and circled overhead.

"Okay, Terry and Dac, let's not dawdle up here. Mom and Dad aren't too happy with me." Zoe picked up a twig and used it to move the stinking remains of a fish and a goose aside. She also thought she recognized what probably used to be a groundhog. "That is one funky smell."

She edged closer to the eaglets and sat still for several long moments, allowing them to adjust to her presence. If the helmet she wore hadn't made her look so imposing, she figured she'd probably have more success.

She pulled out the radio to call Rob. "I'm on the nest and safely anchored in. I'll send the first eaglet down shortly, probably the larger of the two. The little guy looks prepared to put up a fight."

"That's a surprise. I thought the smaller ones were easier to handle."

"That's usually the case, but sometimes it's the tinier ones you've got to watch out for."

"Sort of like Chihuahuas and you?" Rob asked. "Maybe that's your issue."

Sitting in the hefty nest with her legs outstretched in front of her reminded Zoe how short she was. Maybe her Maker hadn't been feeling too generous with building supplies on the day she was made. Her barely five-foot-tall frame left her the smallest person in just about any crowd of adults.

"Funny, Rob," Zoe said. She laid the radio down.

When she looked up, she took a moment to take in the scene. A scant layer of quickly fading fog still blanketed the lake below. A cloudless blue sky spread out above her. To the northwest, the snow-covered peak of Mount Washington rose well beyond all the other mountains around it. There was no place else she'd rather be. She might be the smallest person around, but when she was in the trees, she was at the top of the world.

She turned her attention to the two eaglets. "All right, little ones, time for you to meet Rob. He can be a bit snarky, but don't worry, he's harmless. He's just going to give you a once-over."

Zoe took off her climbing gloves and placed them into a second pouch clipped to her harness. She'd have to handle the eaglets gently so as not to harm their feathers or wings. Bare hands would go a long way toward being more careful, but it did mean that her skin and flesh would be exposed. Department rules required the use of gloves when handling eaglets, but she wasn't much for rules. Particularly since she was more than capable of determining her own safety needs.

If the parents went after her, she assumed they'd strike her from behind and aim at her head. The helmet, face shield, and neck guard would take care of that scenario. The eaglets were still uncoordinated enough for her to avoid their talons and beaks for the most part. Not wearing gloves was worth avoiding the possibility that she'd harm one of them by accident. Besides, finding leather gloves small enough to fit her hands so that she still had dexterity was always a challenge.

Zoe picked up a bone that still had some meat on it and held it toward the eaglets. "Come on, little ones. It's snack time."

The larger eaglet appeared to take some interest. It took a couple of steps toward her. She remained still despite the angry parents swooping close to her. She hoped the eaglet would stay focused on food as opposed to its parents' angst long enough for her to grab it.

When the eaglet leaned toward the duck bone, she dropped the scrap and placed both hands on either side of its body to hold its wings closed so it wouldn't hurt itself. Just as quickly, she slipped the eaglet under her left arm and held its feet together with her left hand. "I think you'll be Terry."

Like a kitten held by the scruff, the eaglet didn't struggle with its wings and feet trapped in her grasp. Using her free hand, she quickly retrieved a large canvas bag from the pouch on her harness and placed it over the eaglet. Then she zipped it shut, picked up the radio, and depressed the Talk button.

"Rob, get ready for the first eaglet. I'm sending it down now." She put the radio down and carefully lowered the eaglet in the bag via a second rope secured to her climbing belt.

Rob's voice came from the radio. "Got it. I'll let you know when I'm finished."

Zoe eased closer to the remaining eaglet. "Hello, little Dac."

It spread its wings and peeped at her.

"Looks like the fog is clearing." Zoe sat still in the bowl-shaped nest at the top of the tree with one of the greatest creatures on earth. She didn't think there was anything more she could ever need in this world, definitely not people and all the drama they stirred up.

The sound of reveille coming from the camp on the main shore across from the island intruded on the morning quiet. "Don't worry, Dac. I'll make sure you have a voice in all that human cacophony down there." She continued to sit quietly, taking in the absolute calm that came from being in the tops of trees with the wild ones.

The radio crackled to life several minutes later. "We're done down here," Rob said. "The eaglet is male and weighs a healthy two pounds."

"Okay, I'll pull it back up now." Zoe hoisted Terry back into the nest and released the eaglet gently from the bag. It shook itself off and stormed away from her toward the other side of the nest. She quickly grabbed Dac more easily than she would've predicted. Perhaps their time in the nest together had given the eaglet a false sense of confidence, causing it to let its guard down.

Like she'd done with Terry, she placed Dac into the canvas bag and lowered it down to Rob. When the line went slack, Rob's voice came again from the radio. "I have the eaglet. Unfortunately, it looks like company is on the way. A boat with two people just left the camp and is headed to the island."

Zoe removed the small pair of binoculars she carried in the deep cargo pocket of her pants. She flipped up the face shield and lifted the binoculars to her eyes. She recognized the man in the boat as James Bastone. He sat in the bow, and a tall, lean woman with long, dark hair pulled back into a ponytail operated the boat. She wore an expression even grimmer than Bastone's.

"Here we go. Let the people battles begin," Zoe said under her breath.

# Chapter 4

Alex motored the nineteen-and-a-half-foot Stingray powerboat across the lake's smooth surface to the small, sandy beach on the back side of the island. Operating a boat was like riding a bike. She'd done it so often as a kid it seemed like second nature now. It even felt good to be on the lake again with the breeze generated by the boat's movement brushing her skin. She gave the throttle some gas for momentum before turning off the engine. The boat glided up onto the shore and came to a gentle stop in the soft sand.

James stepped carefully over the front of the bow onto solid ground. Alex suspected he didn't want to get his shiny loafers wet. He glanced back at her briefly. "Let me do all of the talking. If it's who I think it is up in that tree, you'll find out quickly that we're dealing with a raging, radical environmentalist. I thought wildlife biologists were supposed to be meek and mild. Zoe Kimball is a damned pit bull."

"Good, I'd love to see you bitten on the ass by a pit bull," Alex muttered.

"Did you say something?"

"You shouldn't be anywhere near my family's camp, and you know it." The words tumbled out of her mouth and her insides shook. "How could you after what happened to Jake?"

"We don't have time to get into this now, but you know as well as I do that what happened wasn't my fault. It was your brother's—"

Alex cut him off. "Don't."

"Don't what? Say the truth?"

"You have no right to even speak Jake's name."

"And you don't get to judge me. When you ran off to the other side of the country to escape, I stayed. I was here for your parents. It's because of me that your family still has this camp."

Alex glanced around at the place she knew better than any other, yet it felt alien to her. Part of her wanted to fight to find her way back.

The other part gave up because the idea was too daunting. "Let's just get this over with."

"That's certainly my preference." He turned and stomped off.

She followed him over the uneven land through wild blueberry bushes and sweet ferns, enjoying the fact that his shiny shoes and pressed trousers were scuffed with mud and dirt at each step.

When they reached a clearing, a man in a long-sleeved, dark-green work shirt with the Maine Department of Wildlife and Fisheries logo over the left breast pocket held his arms stretched over his head to take a bag lowered from above. The logo on his shirt was comprised of the letters "DWF" embroidered over a patch containing the images of a trout and white-tailed deer. It reminded Alex of how much she missed the wildness of Maine.

She gazed up into the tree and saw a large nest with two ropes hanging over the edge. There was no sign of a person other than the bottoms of a pair of boots facing out over the rim of the nest, suggesting that someone sat inside it.

"I thought we agreed you'd let me know when you were coming back to the island," James said to the man, his tone more accusatory than questioning.

"You'll have to take that up with Zoe when she comes down out of the tree." The man unzipped the bag and placed his hands inside. "For now, this eaglet is going to be demanding my full attention once it realizes it's out of the bag, so to speak." He removed a foot long, docile gray bird from the bag.

Sure enough, the little bit of freedom and the sunlight shining down on it appeared to rejuvenate the eaglet. It wiggled and squawked. The man wrestled with it and asked, "While you're here, can one of you give me a hand?"

James recoiled a couple of steps. "I don't think so."

"I'd love to." Alex knelt in front of the man, who held the eaglet with its wings pressed to its sides. The eaglet wiggled and turned its head in her direction when her shadow settled over its body. It squawked at her.

The eaglet didn't look anything like what she expected. Its awkward gray body had no resemblance to its stunning parents. Yet its eyes were an entirely different story. In them, she saw a brave wildness and sheer will to be free that left her envious. Its power tugged at the part of her that used to be fearless.

"I think this bird likes you," the man said as he turned the eaglet onto its back, slid it under an arm, and held its feet together. "Thanks for the help. I'm Rob, by the way." The eaglet stopped wiggling against him.

"Wow, that's amazing how calm it is being held like that," Alex said.

"Just a like a cat held by the scruff. Makes it feel secure under the circumstances." The eaglet's parents screeched and circled overhead. "Mom and Dad being so nervous certainly doesn't help, though. If you want to see real calm, please hand me the piece of leather that looks like a little helmet. It's lying on top of the open tool box there." Rob jutted his chin in the direction of the box.

Alex got out the hood and handed it to him. "Looks like something from medieval times."

"Yeah, it does." Rob placed the leather hood over the bird's head and eyes. Its body went limp. "We use these hoods to keep the birds calm when we're examining them. Eagles aren't afraid of what they can't see. It's only us humans who are afraid of the dark." He pulled a pair of calipers from his pocket and held them to the eaglet's beak to measure the length. "I often wonder why that is."

"Maybe it's because being in the dark forces us to look inside ourselves," Alex said. "For most of us, there aren't many things scarier than that."

"I never thought of it that way. Makes sense. Animals have pure hearts. They have nothing to be afraid of in that regard. Humans, on the other hand, not so much. We're a messy bunch, every last one of us." Rob gave her a kind smile. "I didn't catch your name."

"I'm sorry. I should've introduced myself. I'm Alex Marcotte."

"Mr. Marcotte's daughter?"

"Yes."

"Nice to meet such an observant and lovely woman." Rob cocked his head in the direction of the bird pinned under his left arm while he held its feet together with his right hand. "I'd shake hands, but as you can see, my hands are kind of full right now."

James cleared his throat. "Can we keep whatever it is you have to do moving along here? I have an appointment in an hour, and I'd really like to speak with Ms. Kimball."

Rob raised an eyebrow at Alex. "You bet, Mr. Bastone. Alex, can you hand me those pliers and the red metal band next to them?"

Alex did as requested. As much as she disliked the sound of James's voice, she was glad for his interruption. She'd detected a bit of flirting on Rob's part. He seemed sweet, but she definitely wasn't interested. But for her fascination with the eaglet, she would've found a way to stay hidden in the background of the confrontation between

James and these wildlife people. Not to mention that as much as she appreciated the company of some men, there was never a time in her life when she had been attracted to one romantically.

After examining the eaglet, Rob secured the red band to its right leg.

"Is there significance to the color of the band and which leg you put it on?" Alex asked.

"Yes, red indicates that it's a bird banded by the State of Maine. For males, we put the band on the right leg and females, vice versa. That way when we see them in the distance sometime in the future, I hope, we'll know the sex of the bird and where it's from. There's a very good chance that unless this bird dies and we find the body, this is as close as we'll ever get to him again."

"It's a male, then."

"Yes, a healthy boy."

"I really appreciate that you let me help. It's amazing to be so close to something that's otherwise untouchable. I hope you see him for many years to come."

"Me too. As long as we can make sure he gets through the first couple of years of his life, there's a good chance he'll be around a while. Since your family owns this island, you'll be a key part in its survival. I hope we can work together."

"Excuse me," James said. "How much longer is this going to take?"

"Just about done, Mr. Bastone," Rob answered.

So many times in Alex's life, she had struggled to see past her anger at her parents to glimpse the things she still loved about them. "My father has always cared about protecting wildlife. I have no doubt he'll want to do what's right."

"That's really good news. These eaglets are going to need all the help they can get."

Alex tried to sear the image of the eaglet into her mind. There was a good chance she'd never be this close to something so wild again. It was a privilege she'd always be grateful for. "Would it be all right if I touch him before he goes back to the nest?" she asked.

"Sure. You'll find that his downy feathers are much softer than they look."

Alex placed the palm of her hand on the eaglet's feather-covered chest and pressed her fingers into the silky down. The eaglet breathed slowly in and out. Its life force vibrated through her hand, up her arm, and into her body. For a fleeting moment, she felt its wildness inside her. "Good luck, little one." She pulled her hand away and turned from Rob so he wouldn't see her emotion. "Thank you."

"You're more than welcome. Let's get this little guy back up into the tree with his parents." Rob placed the eaglet into the bag, swiftly removed the leather hood, and zipped the bag before the eaglet had a chance to protest. He placed the bag on a portable scale set up next to the toolbox, made some notes in a notebook, and clipped the bag containing the eaglet to a carabiner at the end of one of the hanging ropes. Removing a handheld radio from its holster on his belt, he said, "All set, Zoe. You can pull him up."

The radio crackled. "Will do. Is our company still down there?"

"Roger that. Mr. Bastone and Mr. Marcotte's daughter, Alex, are eager to talk with you."

"Tell Bastone not to get his knickers in a twist."

A laugh escaped Alex before she could contain it. No wonder James didn't like the woman in the tree. She obviously didn't buy into his phony charm.

"Is she always this disrespectful to tax-paying land owners?" James asked.

Alex gave him a look of disbelief. "I've never paid a penny in taxes on the camp, and I'm pretty sure you haven't either. The camp still belongs to my father."

Rob folded his arms across his chest. His gentle expression turned hard, and his posture suggested defensiveness. "I'll admit that Zoe doesn't always communicate with the softest touch, but she means well. She's also the best at what she does."

"What exactly does she do, anyway?" James asked. "Make certain that people can't use their land? By the way, Alex, I'm speaking as the camp manager. I get paid to speak for and protect your father's interests."

"I'll bet you do," Alex said.

Rob gave Alex an apologetic look. "I assure you that the department's motivation is to protect wildlife by working with land owners, not against them. You both have my word on that."

The remaining hanging rope started to sway. Alex looked up in time to see a fit, compact woman lowering herself down the rope from the top of the tree. Zoe Kimball, no doubt.

Holding onto the rope below and behind her with her right hand, Zoe used her left hand to grasp a large knot that allowed her to slide down the rope at a controlled rate. When she pulled down on the knot, she slid down the rope. She stopped by letting go of the knot, which appeared to be what held her in place along the rope's length. Her movements were quick and efficient.

When she reached the ground, she unclipped the harness from the rope and took off her helmet, revealing a mop of short, wavy, light-brown hair and piercing green eyes. Alex smiled at the sight. Zoe walked toward them with the same quick grace she'd used to come down out of the tree.

Alex decided that if a bolt of lightning came packaged in human form, this woman fit the bill. It was going to be interesting to watch James try to tangle with her.

Smart like a fox, he turned on the charm. "That was an incredible opportunity for us to see one of the town's newest additions. It's truly amazing to have these eagles here. I just wish we had known about it sooner, though, like I asked. If we hadn't been in the right place at the right time, we would've missed it."

"I'm glad it was your lucky day, then." Zoe stepped out of the climbing harness and undid the knots tied into the end of the rope. "Given your excitement, you'll be happy to know that Mr. Marcotte's island is host to two very healthy eaglets for the first time in our lifetimes that we know of." Her expression reminded Alex of the impenetrable hardness of the granite that held up the island. "I intend to keep it that way."

Alex saw James flinch.

Rob intervened. "Zoe, this is Mr. Marcotte's daughter, Alex. She was kind enough to give me a hand with the examination and banding of the eaglet."

Alex took Zoe's outstretched hand. At five feet ten inches, Alex stood almost a foot taller, but Zoe gave the impression of being someone larger than life. For such a small woman, her grip left no doubt as to her strength. Alex had to admit she'd pictured someone much more imposing based on James's description. Nevertheless, Zoe's presence was a force to be reckoned with. She had to admit, the woman was pretty adorable too. "It was a once in a lifetime experience. You're right, it was our lucky day. It's very nice to meet you."

James butted in. "Rob said that now you've banded the eaglets, you won't need to get close to them again. As the manager of the camp, I can assure you that you can count on us to keep an eye on things from here on out. We'll be your eyes and ears and the first to let you know if we see any problems. We have a large telescope set up in our main building, and I'm sure the kids would love to be able to watch the eagles from there."

Zoe let go of Alex's hand. "That's very benevolent of you, Mr. Bastone. It won't be necessary, though. While it's true that we won't likely need to access the nest again, I've been assigned to do a close study of this breeding pair. I'll be around all summer to monitor the eaglets through fledging. This is a bigger deal than you recognize, having these eagles here." She tipped her head in the direction of the opposite shore. "I'll be camping the next three months or so at the state park. My boss wants me close enough to study everything from what foods the eaglets are being fed to where their parents are hunting, and what, if anything, causes them disturbance. The study and findings will be published by the department later this year. So I'll be the eyes and ears of the eagles. You and me, we'll be neighbors."

James didn't respond immediately. "Then I insist that you stay with us at the camp," he said after a few moments. "You'll be far more comfortable. I could arrange for you to have a private room and shower in the staff quarters."

"Trying to keep your enemies close, Mr. Bastone?" Zoe asked.

Alex had to give Zoe credit. Not only could she see right through James—just like her—she didn't hesitate to say so. She enjoyed watching James being pushed off his game by this small, scrappy woman. Zoe seemed to be one step ahead of him.

"That hurts, Ms. Kimball. We're as concerned as you for the welfare of our resident eagles. Isn't that true, Alex?" James asked.

*Ah, trying to pull me into the game. I don't think so.* However, watching James be tortured daily by Zoe was worth putting her two cents in. "I'm sure my father will insist," Alex said. "It would be a great learning experience for all of us if you stayed. We'd love to know more about the eagles."

"Do you have a place where I could leave my kayak and gear?" Zoe asked. "I'll need it for my work."

"That should be easy enough to arrange," James said.

"All right. I'll take you up on the offer. I'm sure we can make it benefit both of us."

"Hmm." James grunted. "Very well. When should we expect you to arrive?"

"A little more than a week from now. How about Monday morning on June first, provided that's not too early?"

"That'll be fine. We'll have your room ready by then. Unfortunately, my schedule is quite busy for Monday. We're getting ready for our first influx of campers. Perhaps Alex could help get you settled?"

"I'd be happy to," Alex said.

"You sure?" Zoe asked. She glanced at James and back to Alex. "As much as I'm looking forward to being best friends with Mr. Bastone here, I don't want to impose on you if you have other things to do."

Alex got a kick out of Zoe's uncensored directness. She had a way of slicing James down to size piece by piece, leaving him speechless in the process. "It would be my pleasure and no imposition at all. Monday morning it is."

"Good, I'll see you then," Zoe said.

Alex noted that her difficult morning had just ended on a high note, thanks to Zoe and the eaglet. "I look forward to it."

# Chapter 5

In the staff room where Zoe would be staying, Alex pulled a cotton blanket from the chest at the foot of the bed. She laid it on top of the sheet and unfolded it.

Claire stood at the other side of the bed. She grabbed the end of the blanket and pulled it over. "I was wondering, since we're going to have a wildlife biologist staying with us this summer, whether we should ask Zoe if she'd be willing to do a presentation for the kids while she's here. With the eagles on the island, it would be a great addition to the education program."

Alex smoothed the blanket and tucked it in. "You should ask her."

Claire tucked in her end under the mattress. "I think I will after I run it by James and your dad."

"I thought you were the Education Director."

"I am. But the camp has been struggling in this economy. James has really tightened the purse strings. I wouldn't want to ask Zoe unless I knew what we could pay her."

Alex tossed a pillow with a clean pillowcase matching the sheets onto the bed and sat down. "That sounds so inconceivable to me."

"Why should it? Everything has been hit hard. Why should the camp be an exception?" Claire sat down next to her.

"It's not that." Alex leaned on her palms and let her head fall back, remembering the time from her childhood when things changed from bliss to torment at the hands of bullies. "I still can't wrap my head around the idea that James has anything at all to do with my family's camp."

Claire stared out the window for several long moments. "I never got the chance to tell you how much I missed your brother after he died."

"You didn't have to. I know how much you cared about him. Besides, I was too destroyed by what happened to hear anything that anyone said anyway." Alex remembered shutting down to everyone and everything. "There was also the little problem of my mother insisting that I be hospitalized after Jake died. How else could she hide the last of her dirty little secrets? Me staying around would only add to the destruction of her make-believe, perfect world." She looked at Claire. "How can you still not be angry at the people who tormented Jake, including James?"

"Sometimes I am. But I can't live carrying all of that anger around. I don't think Jake would want us to either. He was the sweetest person I've ever known." Claire smiled and tugged at a loose thread on the blanket. "Your brother was my first true love."

Alex took Claire's hand in her own. "He loved you too."

"Jake was the first boy I ever kissed. I used to follow him around like a puppy after that. But things were never the same again between him and me. He'd hardly look at me, let alone talk to me." Claire squeezed her hand. "After I found out he was gay, I would've settled for being just his friend."

The conversation reminded Alex that she wasn't the only victim left in the wake of his death. Jake had broken Claire's heart. She was an innocent bystander in the saga of her brother's tormented teenaged years. "He never meant to hurt you or anyone else. Jake did the best he could under the circumstances. It all turned out to be too big for him to handle. He shut us all out, even me."

"You might be surprised by something I've realized over the years I've missed him."

"What's that?"

"The thing that hurt the most wasn't that he couldn't love me the way I loved him. It was that he wouldn't at least trust me to be his friend while he was going through all those things at school. The bullying made him suspicious of everyone." Claire stared down at the scuffed hardwood floor. "One time when a group of boys pushed him up against the locker and called him awful names, I tried to break it up. They let him up and laughed even more. One of them made a snide comment about a girl having to come to his rescue. Jake didn't see that as friendship. He acted like I was the enemy too. Me trying to help only made it worse for him."

"It's not what you did," Alex said, "that made it worse. I'm the one to blame for making it unbearable for him. I talked him into telling our parents that we were both gay, remember? I'm also the one who insisted that he tell them the truth about how he was being bullied at school because of it."

She laughed sarcastically. "Tortured is a much better description. It turned into a complete disaster. I never dreamed my parents would react the way they did. I get that it was a shock to find out both your twins are gay, but they were still supposed to love us."

She stood and went to the window, opened it, and gazed out at the lake through the screen. The horizon shimmered in the heat. "It's why I don't want to see my mother. The things she said to him are unforgivable." She shook her head. "She may as well have been the one to kill Jake while my father sat back and let it happen."

"They didn't know how else to act. I wish you could understand that," Claire said. "They weren't perfect, but the whole thing turned out to be too big for them as well. I'm not making excuses for them. I'm only asking whether you can find a way to forgive them."

Alex turned back around to face her. Anger at the question simmered inside of her. "I was a kid and so was Jake. They were the adults. Our parents were supposed to protect us no matter what, yet all my mother could think about was how people would look at her. My father's only concern seemed to be the same as it's always been: placate my mother and protect the camp at all cost. They were worse than any of the kids at school. I'll never forgive them for that. Sometimes I don't feel anything at all for them other than anger and disappointment."

Claire rose to her feet. "They're your parents. You don't really mean that. I've known them my whole life. Your father is one of the most generous and kindhearted people I know. He's not perfect, though. None of us are. Not even our parents."

"I do mean it." Alex considered her father's reputation, not only in Glasgow, but in the entire state of Maine. People loved him. He was always the first to donate time and money to causes that helped the disenfranchised. The camp itself had become a beacon of hope for so many who had nothing but the inspiration it gave them to strive for a better life by respecting others and nature, staying in school, and working hard. The absurdity of the distinction between Daniel Marcotte the man versus Daniel Marcotte the father infuriated her. How dare he choose what the world thought of him over his son and daughter? "Those things don't matter to me anymore without Jake."

A knock at the door interrupted their conversation.

"Come in." Claire took a step toward the door.

Bob Kiln ambled into the room. "Ms. Claire, the supplies you ordered just arrived. Where do you want me to put them for now?" He spoke to Claire as if Alex weren't in the room.

Claire must've picked up on that too. "Alex is planning on helping me with putting together some of the education programs this summer. What do you think, Alex? Should we have them placed in the workshop for now until we can organize the classroom? It's a summer's worth of stuff. I'm sure there are lots of boxes to sort through."

"That makes sense." Alex looked at Bob, who averted his eyes.

"Sure." Bob backed out of the room.

Claire shut the door behind him. "I'm sorry about that. The man has no manners."

"I don't think it has anything to do with lack of manners. I expected people like him would still look at me as if I were from another planet. Or avoid me altogether. I'm still the remaining half of that scary pair of gay twins from Glasgow."

"I know it's hard to believe, but this town and the rest of Maine have come a really long way. It's definitely not as bad as it was."

"Unfortunately, that's not the only strike against me. They all think I'm crazy on top of it. For a lot of people that's even scarier."

"Did you ever stop to think that what you're doing is the same thing your mother did?"

"What on earth are you talking about?" Alex bristled at the notion that she was in any way like her mother.

"Sounds to me like you're spending an awful lot of time worrying about what other people think."

Alex grabbed a pillow and tossed it at Claire. "I'm glad you're a teacher."

"Yeah, why is that?"

"Because you are one of the smartest people I know."

Claire tossed the pillow back at her. "What else do we need to do to get this room ready for Zoe?"

Alex glanced around. "It's all set. Thanks for your help and for the company."

"You're welcome. It felt like old times. When will Zoe be here?"

"Tomorrow morning sometime."

"Good. Once she gets settled and I can get the go-ahead, I'll ask her about that presentation. I really do think it's a huge opportunity for us to have her here. I have a good feeling about it. I'm looking forward to meeting her."

"Should I give her a heads-up?" Alex asked.

"Yeah, that would be great." Claire embraced her. "I really am happy to see you again."

Emotions swam around inside Alex. She lingered in the circle of her old friend's arms and longed for the time before her world collapsed. It was as if she could see it but couldn't touch it through the wall of hurt and anger. "Thank you for still being such a good friend."

"I always will be," Claire said. "Nothing will ever change that. I know Jake can never be replaced. But maybe someday, you'll consider me more of a sister as well as a friend. I love you, Alex."

"I love you too. You're bossy, opinionated, and a good friend, the true makings of a sister." Alex returned the hug.

# Chapter 6

Zoe took off her sweatshirt and hung it over the back of the desk chair in the Wildlife and Fisheries' southwest field headquarters office in Lewiston. The first Monday in June had arrived, accompanied by an early summer heat wave. "You'd think it was July instead of the beginning of June," she said. "It's so freaking hot out already, and it's not even eight in the morning yet."

"Doesn't look like there's any letup in sight either," Rob said, "according to the long-term weather forecasts. We need some rain, and soon." He poured coffee into a cup with the department logo printed on it. "This is turning out to be a pretty sweet assignment for you this summer. You get to be in the field for three months straight and stay in some cushy digs while you're at it."

"I don't know how cushy it'll be. It's a summer camp for kids, remember?" Zoe put some pencils into the shoulder bag resting on her desk. "The place is going to be crawling with loud, wiggly kids. Not my cup of tea."

"Ah, but the lovely Alex Marcotte will be around."

"Yeah. So?" Zoe rifled through her desk drawer. "Do you have any extra field notebooks? I can't find any."

Rob pulled two unused notebooks from the top shelf above his desk. "I still can't believe Bastone offered to have you stay there."

"He has an ulterior motive, which is to keep an eye on me. What doesn't make sense, though, is that it's a zero sum game because I'll get to keep an eye on him at the same time."

"You'll have to pay attention for clues as to whether he has a more nefarious plan for keeping you around, then." Rob tapped the end of a pencil on his desk. "I have a favor to ask."

"Sure, what is it?"

"Since you're likely going to see Alex often, would you mind scoping her out for me? You know, things like whether she's got a boyfriend or a husband?"

Zoe stopped packing her shoulder bag and gave Rob a look. "I'm going to study the eagle pair, not find you a girlfriend. Besides, I think you're barking up the wrong tree."

"Why do you say that?"

"I got a vibe."

"You got a vibe. How come whenever a beautiful girl is in the picture, you get a vibe?"

Zoe slid the strap of the bag on her shoulder and hoisted it off the desk. "You wouldn't understand, and I don't have time to explain it. By the way, a more precise term is 'woman,' not girl. It's probably why you don't have one."

"You're just trying to throw me off the trail so you can have Alex all to yourself." He studied her a moment. "Are you taking the kitchen sink with you? Your bag is bulging at the seams."

"Now you're starting to annoy me. I don't have anything more than you'd carry. My bag just looks bigger on me than on anyone else. We have this conversation all the time." Zoe rolled her eyes. "As for Alex, I'm too busy chasing after wildlife to be chasing after women on either your or my behalf, for that matter. Not to mention, a beautiful woman like her, even if she is gay, would pay about as much attention to me as she would you."

"Did the always self-assured Zoe Kimball just show me her insecure side? Gasp." Rob put the back of his hand to his forehead.

Zoe playfully mimed punching him in the stomach. "I'm going to show you my cranky side if you don't get out of my way." She glanced at her watch. "I told Alex—I mean, Ms. Marcotte—I'd be there early this morning."

"Do you need any help getting your kayak secured to the top of your truck?"

"No, everything's ready to go once you stop pestering me."

The District Manager, Tom Holder, stuck his head out his office doorway. "Good, you two are still here. We have a problem with the Stetson Road nest over at Limerick Pond that can't wait. I know you're heading out to meet the Marcottes this morning, but it's an emergency."

"What's going on?" Zoe asked.

"A brush fire broke out last night that the local firefighting crew is having a tough time containing. It's already burned about eighteen acres and is headed straight for the nest. They've called for more help, but you might need to get the eaglet out of the tree until they can get the fire extinguished."

Rob grabbed his keys and department baseball cap from his desk. "We can take my truck, Zoe, since yours is loaded with your boat and equipment."

"Good, I'll meet you out front. I have to grab my climbing gear," Zoe said. "Tom, would you mind calling the camp and letting them know I'll be late? The number's on my desk there."

"No problem." Tom took a cell phone out of his vest pocket and picked up the sticky note with the number. "Listen, I don't want you up in that tree unless it's safe to climb. I'll trust your judgment, but I'm asking you to use it wisely." He dialed the number and put the phone to his ear. "Be careful, Zoe." He turned toward his office, saying into the phone, "Mr. Marcotte, please."

# Chapter 7

The drive took a little more than an hour. Although the site of the fire was only fifteen miles from field headquarters, once they turned off Route 121, Zoe and Rob traveled over a winding dirt road that meandered through hilly, forested property owned by a local logging company.

Zoe smelled the heavy smoke before she saw it. The smoke lodged in her nose and chest, making it hard to breathe, and they hadn't even reached the location of the fire.

Rob accelerated the truck up a steep section of road. At the top of the rise, the flames came into view. A wall of fire thirty-feet high and stretching across approximately a hundred feet roared toward them. Thick, black smoke spewed into the air and blew directly over the nest area. Cinders shot out randomly ahead of the fire, bolstering its spread.

If the fire wasn't stopped and the wind continued to blow in that direction, the tree that held the nest would soon be consumed. A small fire burned ahead of the larger one. Burning embers carried by the wind must have started it. "I have to get that eaglet out of the nest *now.*"

Rob pulled up alongside several other trucks that included two fire tanker trucks loaded with water. Men and a few women wearing firefighting gear scrambled around. They were shouting about a plan for digging a trench with a tractor currently being unloaded and setting a backfire in the hope of stopping the momentum of the main blaze.

"The fire's too close," Rob said. "We won't have time to set the ropes so you can get up and back down the tree before the fire reaches it. We're going to have to let the eaglet go and hope they can stop the fire before it burns the nest."

"The eaglet will suffocate first. I'm going up to get it, and I'm not going to use ropes. I'll use my climbing spurs instead."

"Are you out of your mind? Not only could you fall, but you might suffocate too."

"That's why you're going to go sweet talk one of those firefighters into letting me use an oxygen tank while I get my gear ready."

Rob twisted in the driver's seat to face her directly. "I hope you live long enough to get fired."

"I hope you'll stop talking and get me what I need so I can get that eaglet out of the tree."

He shoved his door open. On the way out, he asked, "Do you have any idea how bad an idea this is?"

"Do you have a better idea besides arguing with me while that bird dies?"

Zoe hopped out of the cab and climbed onto the back bumper to retrieve her gear bag. Smoke filled her lungs and made her cough. She unzipped the bag and rummaged for a bandana. When she found it, she tied it around her mouth to keep the smoke out. She zipped the bag closed and slipped the strap over her shoulder. Carrying the heavy bag, she jogged toward the tree with the nest. The little bit of exertion combined with the hot wind and difficulty breathing left her drenched in sweat.

When she got to the tree, she threw the bag down on the ground next to a large boulder and quickly unpacked her back saddle with harness, climbing spurs, leg straps, and an eight-foot-long steel core flipline. She hadn't used this gear in a while and didn't have a whole lot of time to inspect it.

She ran her bare hands along the length of the flipline feeling for nicks and checked the edges of the spikes. The flipline appeared to be in good shape, but the spikes could use sharpening. This was one time she felt fortunate to be small. If she were any heavier, it would make climbing on dull spikes that much more hazardous.

She glanced up into the tree's healthy looking branches and wished she didn't have to climb it with the spurs. She only used climbing spurs on trees that were already dead because of the damage they caused to bark, but if the fire couldn't be stopped, this tree would surely die anyway. At least she could try to save the eaglet.

Zoe pulled on the harness and cinched it tight. The hot wind from the fire bore down on her and reminded her that time was of the essence. With or without an air tank, she was going up into that tree. She sat down on the ground, attached the climbing spurs to her boots, and secured the leg straps. As she reached into her bag for her helmet,

Rob and a firefighter raced toward her. The firefighter carried a small oxygen tank and mask.

"I hope that's for me." She stood.

"Yep, but you'd better hurry," the firefighter said. "That fire's getting closer, and the blowing embers could start another blaze any place in front of it wherever the wind takes them. You don't want to be up there in that tree if it catches fire." He hoisted the tank onto Zoe's back.

It felt heavier than she'd expected. She turned to face Rob and the firefighter, adjusted her helmet, and placed the tank mask over her face. The firefighter tightened the tank's straps and turned the cylinder on.

Rob shook her by the shoulders. "Be careful."

"We'll be right here in case you need us," the firefighter said.

Zoe nodded and sucked in a big breath of oxygen. It made her feel a little light-headed.

"You okay?" Rob asked.

She gave him a thumbs-up.

"Keep your breathing slow and steady, so you don't get dizzy," the firefighter said. "Focus on the task at hand and get back down on the ground as quickly as possible."

"She's like a laser beam when it comes to focus," Rob said. "She borders on being one dimensional."

Zoe shook her head. Just like Rob to take advantage of her not being able to speak. She heard his laughter over the fire and the noise of the firefighters. She stepped in front of the tree and attached one end of the flipline to a carabiner on the left side of her harness. She tossed the other end around the back side of the tree and caught it with her right hand. She clipped that end onto a second carabiner hanging off of the right side of her harness and adjusted the length of the flipline to fit the tree.

*Damn it*. Her climbing gloves were still in the bag. There wasn't a second to spare to wait for Rob to get them for her. They didn't fit her well anyway. In a split second, she decided it was better to have good dexterity and get moving rather than wait for skin-saving gloves that might slow her down.

Zoe raised her arms to eye level and adjusted the flipline, letting it catch the back of the tree above her. She raised her right leg high and dug the spur attached to the inside of her boot hard into the bark. It went in deep. She lifted the other leg and did the same, sliding the flipline up as she went, essentially walking up the trunk.

The weight of the tank on her back helped keep her torso away from the tree so the flipline stayed tight. After several rounds of sliding the flipline and walking her way up the tree, the muscles in her thighs and shoulders burned.

Her breathing was heavy, in part due to the exertion, but also because of how unnatural it was to breathe with the tank and mask. She couldn't allow herself to pass out from the exertion or too much oxygen. "Slow down, Zoe," she muttered.

Looking down, she saw Rob and a small group of firefighters gathered below her. She looked up. She had another forty or so feet to climb with several branch whorls in the way.

As she reached each one, she climbed into it, undid the flipline to get past it, and reattached the line. Ignoring the pain in her legs and arms, she closed her eyes and concentrated on keeping her wits about her. Sweat in the palms of her hands and her tight grip on the flipline had already caused the beginnings of blisters.

She willed herself to keep moving one step at a time, and in a climb that seemed to take forever, at last made it to the base of the nest. She'd have to detach the flipline to get over the edge of the nest, and the only things stabilizing her would be her handhold on the nest and whatever purchase she could find with the spurs. Dwelling on that fact would only cause her to hesitate, which she couldn't afford to do. *Don't think about it. Just do it.*

She reached over the edge of the nest with her left hand, but she couldn't climb any higher with the spurs. If she did, she'd end up parallel to the ground with her belly against the bottom of the nest and nothing to keep her from falling. *Damn these short legs.* She stepped down a couple of feet. Her only option involved holding herself with one hand at the edge of the nest, keeping her spurs dug into the tree, and unclipping the flipline.

Her legs shook as she undid the flipline and reached up with her other hand. She took a deep breath and held on tight to the nest as she let her feet go. She had to lift not only her own weight into the nest but the weight of the tank as well.

"Those chin-ups are about to come in handy, Kimball," she said under her breath.

Using every ounce of strength she possessed, she pulled herself into the nest. Her heart sank at what she saw. The eaglet lay on its side, barely moving.

On her hands and knees in the nest, she scrambled for the canvas bag in the pouch of her harness and placed the limp eaglet into it. She zipped the bag closed and slung it over her back. Now she'd have it and the tank to contend with.

If she was going to fall, this would be the time. She scanned the branches that secured the nest, looking for good handholds. She needed to hold herself steady while she worked to dig her spurs into the trunk. The smoke made it difficult to see. The only good news was that the fire seemed to have slowed its forward momentum. It didn't reach nearly as high into the sky as it had when she and Rob arrived.

In the tangle of branches that held the nest, she spotted two thick branches close to each other. She lay on her belly, letting her feet dangle over the side near the two branches. Carefully, she scooted her body over the edge of the nest until only her arms held her. She kicked her feet, hoping to make contact with the tree, but the effort was futile with her short legs. Without hesitation, she gripped one branch and then the other, and hung by her arms a foot and a half below the nest. She raised her knees and slammed her feet hard into the tree. The spurs sank in deep.

She took a brief rest, holding steady by her feet to take some of the burden off her exhausted shoulders. The end of the flipline hung down at her left side. Her next crucial step would be to let go of one of the branches so she could attach the flipline.

Before she could make her move, the right branch gave way. Zoe instinctively tightened her grip on the left branch and felt a jolt of pain in her hand as a sharp piece of bark cut into her flesh. Her shoulder felt like it was being pulled from its socket by the weight of her body, the tank, and the eaglet strapped to her back. She reached across her chest for the end of the flipline attached to a carabiner. "Don't fucking drop this thing, Zoe."

On autopilot now, she unclipped the flipline, for once grateful that the department hadn't splurged on the more expensive locking carabiners that required two hands to open. With this one, all she had to do was unscrew it by pushing the locking mechanism with her thumb several times.

Once she had the carabiner undone, she held it tightly and clipped it onto the right side of her harness. Her shoulder burned and her legs ached. She grabbed the free end of the flipline and wrapped her arm as far around the trunk as she could reach.

She pressed her body against the tree, bounced slightly on the spurs to make sure they were still dug in, and let go of the branch. Her left hand tried to meet her right around the back of the tree, but the trunk's diameter was too great. Maintaining a bear hug grip on the tree with her right arm, she flung the flipline around with her free hand until she was able to grab it with her fingers. She pulled it down to the right side of her harness and clipped it into the carabiner, slid the flipline up the tree, and let it catch on the bark. Only then did she lean back into the harness saddle for a sweet moment of rest.

A long rest wasn't an option if she hoped to save the dying eaglet. Sweat drenched her clothing, and the inside of her hand burned. Blood streaked the flipline where she held onto it.

She moved so methodically down the tree, she didn't notice a television film crew had arrived on the scene until her feet touched the ground. Ignoring them, she unclipped from the flipline, dropped to her knees, and tried to catch her breath.

Rob knelt next to her. "You okay?"

Zoe threw off her helmet and the oxygen mask. "Open the bag, Rob," she said, panting.

Rob unclipped the bag from her back, laid it between them, and unzipped the top. Zoe reached into it to retrieve the bird. It wasn't breathing. Remembering a recent story about a veterinarian who had successfully performed artificial respiration on an adult eagle, she leaned over, covered the bird's beak with her mouth, and breathed several times. Finally, the eaglet moved slightly and squeaked in a breath of its own.

"Thank you." She fell back onto her butt. "We have to get it to the raptor rehab facility in Lewiston."

Rob took her hand and turned it over. The palm was covered in blood and dirt. "I'll take the eaglet. You stay here and have the paramedics look at your hand. You might need some stitches."

Zoe was too spent to argue. "How's the fire?"

"Better than when we got here. They're still working on it but finally making progress. You going to be all right?"

"Yeah, go. Don't make climbing that tree be in vain while you fret over me," Zoe said.

"You still have your smart mouth. Now I know you're fine." Rob wrapped the eaglet in a towel.

Zoe watched him whisk the eaglet away through the crowd of onlookers. Someone thrust a microphone in her face.

"That was an amazing thing you did," the person said. "I'm a reporter for the local news. Can you describe what it felt like to climb that tree with the fire heading toward you?"

"Hot," Zoe said, pushing the microphone away. "Please, I'm no mood to talk right now."

A paramedic knelt down next to her and placed a first-aid kit on the ground. "Do you mind if I have a look?"

The reporter interrupted. "People care about what you did to save something as precious as an eagle. It's our nation's symbol, after all."

Zoe held her injured hand out to the paramedic. "Seriously? From what I can tell, people only care if there's a dramatic story involved that doesn't harm their interests. It's hot news when a wildlife biologist climbs a burning tree to save an eagle. But I'm vilified when, in order to save an eagle, I prevent someone from building a parking lot."

"The public has a right to know about this story. Do I need to remind you that the tax-payers of this state pay your salary?"

Zoe bit back a response. What she wanted to say would surely get her into trouble with her boss. She'd love to remind the fickle public about its hypocrisies that were too many to count. Things like America being the land of the free and home of the brave, unless one was gay or lesbian, of course.

"Hmm," she said with a grunt.

The paramedic took a piece of gauze out of the first-aid kit. "She said she's not interested in talking. Why don't you give her some space?" He placed the gauze over the cuts in her palm.

"Man, that hurts," Zoe said.

"Yep, that's why we're taking you to the hospital to get it cleaned and stitched up." He taped the gauze in place and helped her to her feet.

The reporter stepped out of the way. "Can we catch you later for an interview?"

"We'll see." Zoe had no intention of talking to any reporters. "I have an appointment this morning that I'm already late for. Today is out of the question." She walked with the paramedic to a waiting ambulance.

# Chapter 8

The shower after her early morning run rejuvenated Alex. Running in the hour before sunrise had been particularly peaceful. Maine at dawn was breathtaking in its silence except for the sounds of birds waking to the day. The rising sun under the clouds painted the sky in fiery oranges. Normally, she would've run earlier, but she'd wanted to make sure she was available when Zoe arrived.

Now standing at the top of the stairs in the home she grew up in, just across the street from the camp, Alex looked at the pictures filling the space along the staircase's wall—photographs of the Marcottes who'd lived in the two-hundred-year-old saltbox through the years. She ran her palm along the length of the smooth balustrade as she made her way down the stairs. Years of polish and oil from human hands left the wood silky soft to the touch.

A framed photograph of her family hung near the bottom of the stairs, taken when her brother was still alive. Jake had always disliked getting his picture taken, but in this one, his head was thrown back in laughter. It always amazed her how much they looked alike. He was the male version of her with thick dark hair, brown eyes, and a long, lean frame.

Alex smiled and touched the glass that held the memory. Her mother had promised them both a stop at the local creamery for ice cream if they cooperated with the photographer. To ensure that her brother kept his end of the bargain, she had told him a joke that always made him laugh, timing it right before the photograph was taken. Tears threatened to replace her smile when she thought of the sound of her brother's voice. She finished making her way to the landing at the bottom of the staircase.

Her grandmother's prized possession, a colonial era mirror, held its place along the wall. Rather than her physical appearance, Alex's reflection in the milky, warped glass resembled what she felt on the inside: a ghost of the girl she used to be. She also had a resemblance to her mother that seemed to become more prominent as she aged.

Voices coming from the living room suggested that her father was up and watching the morning news program. For as long as she could remember, his day started before dawn, and he always took a morning break in his chair in front of the television with a cup of coffee as soon as the news came on.

She made her way toward the sound and stopped in the doorway of the living room. Sure enough, he was sitting in his chair, sipping coffee, and getting lost in the cares of the world broadcast by the local news network. She surveyed the room. The thirty-six-inch digital television set was the only modern piece of furniture in a house filled with antiques.

"Good morning, Dad," she said.

His eyes never left the TV screen. "How was your run?" he asked.

"Great. It's a beautiful morning. The fresh air in Maine is so much nicer than southern California."

He placed his coffee cup on the end table and turned to her. "We could've used your help this morning. I hope we'll be able to count on you at least some of the time while you're here."

"All you have to do is ask. I'm happy to adjust when I run, as long as I get one in."

Daniel gripped the armrests of his chair and hoisted himself up, taking several seconds to find his balance on unsteady legs. "I shouldn't have to ask."

Guilt and resentment toward him battled for prominence in Alex's heart. There was so much she wanted to say to him. The voice of the television news anchor intruded.

"We interrupt this broadcast for breaking news. As firefighters battle to control a brush fire in Castor, State Wildlife Biologist Zoe Kimball made a daring climb this morning up a sixty-foot-tall pine tree to save one of this year's eaglets from the encroaching flames."

An image of Zoe sitting on the ground, covered in soot and sweat, while a paramedic examined her hand flashed across the screen.

"She successfully performed artificial resuscitation on the bird after it was overcome by smoke. Kimball sustained a minor injury and has been taken to a local hospital for treatment. The eaglet is said to be doing well at the raptor rehabilitation facility in Lewiston. Stay tuned for updates on the news at noon."

"I was supposed to meet her later this morning," Alex said.

"Her supervisor called while you were out. One of Ms. Kimball's colleagues will be dropping off her truck and equipment later this afternoon. He said we should still expect her this morning. She's insisting on keeping her schedule. I admire her dedication. Please show a little by sticking around until she arrives." Daniel moved toward where she stood.

She didn't budge from her place in the doorway, effectively blocking his path. "Are we going to do this the whole time I'm here?"

"What's that?" he asked.

"Not talk to each other."

"That's what we're doing now, isn't it? If you'll excuse me, I have a busy day ahead of me. Our first group of campers is coming in tomorrow, and I have to help James get things ready."

"You know that's not what I mean by talking."

"I'll tell you what I know. You left me all alone to take care of this place and your mother. You never once looked back. It's as if your family never even existed. You've been here more than a week, and you've yet to consider going to see your mother. I don't expect we have all that much to talk about until you stop being so selfish."

It didn't matter that Alex was a successful thirty-year-old professor of history. In her father's presence, she struggled to be more than a twelve-year-old girl. The doorbell rang. She stepped aside.

As Daniel pushed past her, he asked, "Will you get that, please?"

Anything she might say remained tangled in a mess of competing emotions. Her aging father still loomed large. She despised herself for not being able to follow through with standing up to him. She went to the door and opened it, finding a tall, skinny, teenager.

"Sorry to interrupt," he said. "I'm Eric, one of this year's camp counselors. You must be Mr. Marcotte's daughter, Alex."

"Yes."

"It's good to meet you. James wanted me to let you know Zoe Kimball is here." Eric pointed over his shoulder toward the camp's main building. "Did you hear about what she did this morning to save the eaglet? That is so wicked cool. The kids are going to love getting the chance to meet her."

"I saw the news coverage this morning." Alex felt the need to protect Zoe after seeing what she'd gone through. "Before we turn the kids loose on her, we should make sure she's interested in talking with them first. She might be quite busy with her work. Please tell her I'll be right there."

"Sure."

Alex shut the door and scanned the metal rack on the wall next to it. Several protruding hooks held an assortment of keys to the camp's various locks and equipment, including her father's boats.

After the conversation with him, if it could even be called that, she craved going someplace quiet to be alone with her thoughts. She'd need a boat to get where she planned to find some solitude.

She found a key attached to a piece of Styrofoam with the number *2* written on it. It was her father's way of marking the boats for camp counselors and ensuring that if they dropped a key in the water, it would float instead of sink into the depths of the lake. Once she got Zoe settled, she planned to disappear for a while.

Alex called out to Daniel, "I'm going out on the lake after I see to Zoe."

He didn't answer. It was just as well. At least she couldn't be blamed for not letting him know she'd taken a boat.

She headed out the door and across the street to the camp's main building where she noticed Zoe leaning against the sugar maple dominating the small front lawn. The more-than-a-century-old tree had been there before the camp was built.

Zoe held a cell phone to her ear. Alex heard her say, "I really don't see why it's necessary for me to talk to the news people. Have Rob do it. He was there too." She shifted her weight from one foot to the other. "Yeah, it's fine." She held up her bandaged palm. "No, I didn't need any stitches. When can I expect my truck and boat to arrive? I want to get to work. The eaglets aren't going to wait for me while I take it easy." She rubbed her temple. "Fine, if I'm not going to see my stuff until later this afternoon, I guess I'll be forced to take a day off, won't I? I can hardly wait to spend a whole day trapped here at this camp waiting for a bazillion rug rats to show up."

Alex decided now would be a good time to make her presence known. Bad enough eavesdropping for as long as she had, but she wanted to spare Zoe any embarrassment of saying something she might regret if she knew someone was present who adored those "rug rats." She cleared her throat.

Zoe turned and stepped away from the tree. "I have to go." She pushed the call End button and slipped the phone into her pocket. "Hi, sorry I'm late."

"Looks like you have a good excuse." Alex smiled.

"Sorry for my appearance. The day started a little dirtier than I would've expected." Zoe brushed at the soot and dirt that covered her pant legs.

"I heard. You were the big news on television this morning. How's the eaglet?" Alex asked.

"It's going to be fine. Unfortunately, the firefighters couldn't save the tree after we got the eaglet out of it. Its home is destroyed, and who knows where its parents have flown off to."

"What will happen to it?"

"It'll have to cultivate its wildness from humans at the rehab facility if it intends to fly free someday," Zoe said.

"That sounds a little hard to fathom."

"Why do you say that?"

"Shouldn't it be the other way around? I can't imagine an eagle, of all things, learning to be wild from a human. I'm guessing that we're the tamest of all Mother Nature's creatures."

Zoe crossed her arms over her chest and grinned. "I can't argue with that. But trust me, we all have some wild in us. We lose sight of it in all the stuff we surround ourselves with like computers, televisions, and cell phones." Something caught her attention behind Alex. "Damn it, speaking of television, I can't believe they're already looking for me. I just got off the phone with them two minutes ago." She glanced up into the maple tree. "I wish there was somewhere I could hide for a while until the excitement over the eaglet dies down."

Alex turned to see a WKBZ television truck crawl by with a passenger craning his head in the direction of the camp. She sympathized with Zoe. She knew what it was like to be harassed by news people when she only wanted to be left alone. Reporters had hounded her family morning and night in the days after Jake's body was found.

She grabbed Zoe's hand and pulled her around the tree to hide her from view. She briefly brushed up against Zoe when she did. Despite the soot on Zoe's clothes, she could smell the outdoors on her skin. The peaceful sweetness of Maine's North Woods came to mind. She breathed in deep and took a step back, surprised by the little flutter that came from being so close to Zoe.

"You interested in escaping with me for a little while?" She held up the key with the Styrofoam key chain.

Zoe glanced in the direction of the bunkhouses lined behind the main office. A flurry of people wearing matching T-shirts with the camp's name across the back bustled around the buildings. "Kids are arriving today, right?"

"They'll start showing up around noon." Alex noticed Zoe's furrowed brow and suspected that being around so many kids might be a shock to her system. Part of her wanted to protect Zoe from it, the other part wanted to stay in her company. "Things get a little crazy in the hours after a group of kids shows up. It takes them a little time to get settled in before they calm down. If you go with me, maybe by the time we get back, it'll be a little less hectic. If you prefer, you could take a quick shower and I can find you a pair of shorts and a T-shirt to borrow. I overheard that your clothes and equipment won't be here until this afternoon."

Zoe put a hand on the maple tree's trunk. "Hmm. The shower and clean clothes are awfully tempting. As for escaping, I'd already put together a plan. A girl could get lost up there."

Alex followed Zoe's line of sight up into the tree's canopy of branches and new spring leaves. "You were thinking of climbing the maple?"

"Yeah, it would be perfect." Zoe pointed into the reaches of the tree. "All I'd have to do is throw a rope up over that main branch, and I'd be up in the cradle in no time. There's even plenty of room to tie in for a nap. No one would ever think to look for me there."

"Do you spend a lot of time up in trees?"

"Every chance I get, especially when I need a little peace and quiet." A group of giggling camp counselors came from the main building. "Which might be often while I'm here."

"Not into kids and camping?"

"Camping, yes. Kids, not so much, I'm afraid."

"I guess that means if you turn up missing, I'll know where to look."

"I hope you'll keep my secret."

The word *secret* conjured the restless skeletons inside Alex. They rippled through her, foretelling of the fright they could bring. The moment of reprieve Zoe had brought from the things that haunted her ended. She felt anxiety's hand at her throat.

She said, "I know what it means to need to have a place to hide. I wouldn't dream of giving yours up. I have a few of my own. Come on, I'll show you to your room before we go." Alex breathed in deep, trying to push back the anxiety that came for no good reason at all sometimes, and always when it damned well felt like it.

She hoped Zoe hadn't noticed the panic skittering over her like a sneaky spider.

# Chapter 9

Zoe stole another glance at Alex. Rob was right. This was turning out to be a sweet deal.

She'd been at the camp less than two hours, and she and the lovely Alex Marcotte were already escaping on a field trip together. And she was wearing Alex's clothes to boot. Her skin tingled with attraction beneath the borrowed T-shirt.

Yet something about Alex nagged at her. She seemed to carry a dark weight around her. Despite that observation, Zoe couldn't help being drawn to the glimmers of light that managed to find their way to the surface.

Alex stood at the wheel while she operated the motorboat across the wide expanse of the lake. Her profile revealed her slight nose, smooth skin, and feminine jawline. Thick lashes framed her dark eyes. The long braid of her black hair hung down between her slender shoulders.

Her last name suggested a French Canadian heritage, and she looked the part. She had a ruggedness about her that melted into a softness Zoe found compelling. This paradox about some women made them utterly attractive and reminded her of one of Maine's most gorgeous wildflowers, the lupine. It could withstand the harshest Maine winter, only to bloom into heart-stopping beauty by late spring.

Alex turned her head. Hoping not to be caught staring, Zoe pretended to watch a flock of ducks fishing near shore. "Where are you from?" Alex asked.

"Hmm?"

"You don't sound like you're from New England. I was wondering where you're from."

"I'm from the Midwest. I grew up in Iowa on a soybean farm."

"Really?" Alex shifted her gaze ahead. "How did you end up so far from home, climbing trees for Wildlife and Fisheries in Maine?" She slowed the boat as it paralleled a heavily wooded shoreline.

"Maine's always been and always will be my home," Zoe said. "Iowa just happens to be where I grew up."

"I've never known anyone who didn't consider the place where they grew up as home at some point in their life. What's your definition of home, then?" Alex turned the boat toward shore.

"I'm not sure I can give a definition. It's more a feeling or need to be in a certain place. Sort of like migrating birds. They just know where they're supposed to be. Some of the science suggests they can tell north from south by a magnetic attraction to the earth's poles. They're also masters at catching winds that will carry them where they need to go." Zoe gazed at the shoreline. "It's how I felt about Maine after the first time I came here. It pulled at me, drawing me into it like a magnet. I wouldn't have been able to stay put anyplace else but Maine."

"That's such a nice sentiment. I guess Maine's siren call got the better of you," Alex said. "When was the first time you came here?"

"We visited here when I was a kid. My family's soybean farm isn't too far from Dubuque, but the only thing between the farm and the city is miles of fields. You hardly ever see a tree. I guess I became obsessed with them because of their scarceness.

"When my oldest brother was getting ready to leave for basic training in the Army, my mom and dad brought all four of us kids to Acadia National Park for our first and only family vacation. I fell in love with everything about Maine that summer, including its trees. I made a vow that, one way or the other, once I graduated from high school I would find a way to go to college at the University of Maine."

"Since you're here, I'm assuming you were able to make that happen. How did you do it?"

"I lucked out and got a gymnastics scholarship. I guess I was meant to climb trees."

Alex looked Zoe up and down. "You look like a gymnast."

"Really, why do you say that?"

"You're compact and muscular." Alex grinned. "You're put together very nicely."

Zoe felt her face flush. "Thanks." She searched for something clever to say but her words were jumbled in a mess of nervous attraction. "After I graduated, I got a job at Wildlife and Fisheries, and I've worked there since."

"Do you ever miss Iowa?"

"I miss my family sometimes. But, like I said, Maine is home." Zoe raised her palms. "Here I am, and here I'll stay. When I'm an old lady, you'll find me enjoying the quiet of winter when snow covers the cedars, the sound of waves crashing on the rocky shore during a storm, a foggy morning, and fields of purple lupines. Oh, and as much lobster and crab as I can eat."

Alex laughed. "I'm not sure I've ever met anyone as passionate about Maine as you. Not even the most dyed-in-the-wool Mainer who's been here her whole life. I've visited a lot of places around the country, and Maine is still the most beautiful one to me. I can see why you love it as much as you do."

"What about you?" Zoe asked. "Where do you consider home to be?"

Sadness crept into Alex's expression. "No place, really," she answered and looked away. She steered the boat in the direction of a wooden dock, the only human-made structure in the vicinity of the shoreline. She slowed the engine to a crawl. "I'm going to pull up next to that dock. When I do, would you mind hopping out and grabbing the rope at the bow so we can tie off?"

"Sure, no problem," Zoe said as the boat glided next to the dock's weathered planks. Because she spent so much time with animals, she was well schooled in the art of reading body language. Alex's suggested that their conversation had entered into a place that made her uncomfortable.

She let Alex's answer about home drift untouched while she stepped out of the boat and onto the dock. "Ready." She caught the end of the rope that Alex tossed her and looped it snugly over the dock cleat.

Alex took the key out of the ignition and stepped across the deck toward the dock. When a wave rolled under the boat, she moved with the fluidity of a woman who had spent a good part of her life on the water, as though she and the boat were an extension of the lake. She took Zoe's outstretched hand and held it firmly as she stepped over the bow and onto the dock.

The difference in their heights mocked Zoe when Alex stood inches from her. She hesitated, held in place by a force similar to what she'd described as attracting her to Maine. She felt her cheeks flush. A world of difference existed between Maine and Alex: One she could have. The other, she could only dream of. Like she'd told Rob, women like Alex didn't recognize twerps like her.

"Thank you for the hand," Alex said.

"You're welcome." Zoe let go and stepped back while Alex finished securing the boat. Being in Alex's presence reminded Zoe of interacting with wildlife. In some ways, Alex was like them. She was graceful, beautiful, mysterious, and untouchable.

Alex reached under the boat's seat and retrieved a backpack. "I thought we might be out for a bit so I brought us some lunch." She slung the backpack over a shoulder and patted it. "I have lots of bug spray too. Since you've been here awhile, you already know the black flies in springtime will carry you off if you're not careful. Let me know if you need some. You're so tiny, I'd hate for them to fly away with you."

"You've thought of everything," Zoe said, disappointed that Alex had made a point of recognizing her small stature.

Alex hesitated. "I hope I didn't offend you by saying that."

"To be honest, I'm a little sensitive about my height."

"You shouldn't be." Alex tilted her head. "Just ask all those people who saw you on television this morning. You're a larger than life presence wrapped up in an adorable little package."

"No way."

"Yeah, you couldn't be cuter."

Zoe sighed. "Always resigned to cuteness. I suppose I should be grateful."

"What's wrong with being cute?" Alex asked.

"Every now and then, a girl wants to be something more than just cute."

"Really? Like what?"

"Oh, I don't know. Sexy, maybe." Zoe ran a hand through her unruly, light-brown mop of hair and thought about her usual attire. "Short legs, messy hair, and work clothes habitually covered in dirt and pine pitch don't make for sexy, I suppose."

"I don't know about that." Alex laughed. "Come on, there's something special I want to show you." She turned and headed toward a break in the trees.

Zoe followed Alex along the narrow path through the woods, wondering why she could talk to Alex as if they'd known each other for years rather than minutes. Not to mention that Alex's comments undid her in a good way, like looking down from the dizzying heights of Maine's tallest pine trees. "Tell me what you want to show me."

"No, I want to see your expression when you first lay eyes on it. If I tell you now, it might take away some of the surprise." Those glimmers of light inside Alex shined a little brighter as she picked up the pace.

"I'm curious. You don't even know me, and yet you're pretty sure I'll be happy with whatever it is you plan to show me. Why is that?" Zoe asked.

The path rounded a row of birches that bordered a meadow filled with lupines not yet in bloom. When the path opened up into the meadow, it became immediately clear what special thing Alex meant to show her.

Zoe stood dumbfounded. "Un-freaking-believable!"

Alex grinned. "I thought you might appreciate it. I wasn't wrong. Was I?" She gestured toward a giant tree standing alone, surrounded by grasses and budding wildflowers.

Zoe jogged toward the massive, rare, American chestnut. "No. It's magnificent."

Without any self-consciousness, she wrapped her arms around the chestnut to feel its energy vibrate against her. She pressed her chest to the tree and could swear she felt its life force thrum. How could she not? This enormous and exceptional tree was very much alive. "Do you have any idea how rare this is? This tree has to be at least two hundred years old."

"It's one of only a handful left in New England. My family owns this woodlot. My father has always liked to keep this tree's existence a secret. He says it's too valuable for others to know about."

"He's right about that." Zoe put her hands on her hips and marveled. "Wow, I cannot believe I'm actually standing in the presence of a mature American chestnut. I knew there were still a few around. I never guessed I'd get the chance to see one so old and so perfect."

"My grandfather used to tell me that when his parents were kids, chestnuts were everywhere. But then the blight started killing them off in the early 1900s. I've always wondered how these few managed to live through something that pretty much killed off their kind." Alex laid a hand on the trunk. "What was it that made this tree so indestructible?"

Zoe shook her head. "I don't know. Maybe a little bit of the right kind of genes and a whole lot of will to live." She gazed up into the tree's broad, rounded crown of branches covered in long pointy leaves. Its catkins were on the verge of flowering in the early warmth. She imagined the intoxicating fragrance that would waft into the air when it was finally in full bloom.

"They still do grow in New England, but the blight kills them before they mature. Not this mother tree, though. She is amazing." Zoe felt Alex's energy mingle with the chestnut's when she stood next to her. She had to force a breath into her lungs. "It was so nice of you to share with me."

"I'm glad it made you as happy as I'd hoped it would. You deserve it after what you went through this morning to save that eaglet." Alex slid the backpack off her shoulder and took out a blanket. She spread the blanket on the ground at the base of the tree, sat down, and smoothed the wrinkles. "The bugs aren't bad at all. It's probably been too dry for them to get going. We could sit awhile until they find us."

Zoe sat down next to her under the expansive canopy. "Do you think your father would mind if I climbed this tree? It would be a once-in-a-lifetime opportunity."

"I could ask him," Alex said. "You really do love trees."

"Have you ever climbed one?"

"Sure, but only when I was a kid."

"I'm assuming not too high, then," Zoe said. "If you're willing, I'd love to teach you how to climb at least"—she pointed at a branch hanging overhead about eighty feet off the ground—"as high as that branch. Then you'll understand why I love trees so much. There's nothing like being cradled in a treetop away from all the troubles people make on the ground."

"That's a tempting thought." Alex glanced away from the treetop and out at the meadow. "But I don't think I could do it. It's probably best for me to keep my feet on the ground." She pulled a couple of plastic containers from the pack.

"Not into climbing trees?"

"I don't like being afraid. If you got me up as high as that branch and I froze, you'd be stuck staying up there with me." Alex handed Zoe one of the containers. "I hope you like peanut butter and homemade blackberry jam. My father always has a supply of it on hand. For as long as I can remember, he's picked the wild blackberries that grow at the edge of the camp and made jam."

"Being stuck up there with you wouldn't be so bad, as long as we had these sandwiches. I love blackberry jam." Zoe accepted the container. "I know you said that no place is home, but if you don't mind my asking, where do you live? Sounds like you've been away awhile. You don't have much of a Maine accent either."

"Southern California. As for my accent, I made an effort to lose it when I went away to college."

"Why?" Zoe asked.

"It made me stand out more than I wanted. I prefer to blend into the background and go unnoticed."

Zoe wanted to tell Alex that she was too beautiful to be overlooked. "What's in southern California?"

"I teach history at Southern Cal." Alex took a bite of her sandwich.

"It must be kind of hard to blend into the background in front of a room full of students."

Alex finished chewing and swallowed. "Not really. When I'm in the classroom, I have my professor's hat on. That's all they see. They can't see the real me underneath."

"Ah, the incognito professor. Do you at least like teaching while you're hiding out?"

Alex crossed her legs and leaned against the chestnut tree. "Not really." She took another bite of sandwich.

"So why do you do it?"

Alex swallowed. "History's my passion. Teaching just comes with the territory for a lot of historians. I'd love to be able to get by on research and writing alone. But I do need to pay the bills. Maybe I should say instead that I choose to pay the bills over doing exactly what I want."

"That's a healthy way of looking at things. Life is all about choices, even when we think we don't have any."

"Sometimes our choices aren't all that palatable." Alex smiled. "I hope I'm not giving you the impression that I'm a total downer."

"Honesty isn't a bad thing. Why don't you tell me a truth about something that makes you happy?" Zoe elbowed Alex. "Even a Debbie Downer like you must have something."

Alex made a funny face. "All right, I'm really enjoying my morning with you. It's the best one I've had since I got here."

Zoe's brain and tongue abandoned her at Alex's compliment. Fortunately, she was able to rally a response. "Do you usually come back to Maine during the summers to work with your father?" *I can't believe you just changed the subject. What is the matter with you?*

"No. The truth is, this is my first summer home since I left for college. My mother's dying and my father needed help." Alex slapped at the top of her thigh. "Geez, I think the black flies are on to us."

"I'm so sorry about your mom." Zoe weighed the wisdom of putting her arm around Alex and decided against it. Notwithstanding their ease with each other, Alex was still a stranger in the big picture. Even though Alex's vibe suggested she was gay, Zoe wasn't completely sure.

Alex wiped her hands on a napkin and put it in the empty plastic container. "Don't be. I don't deserve it."

"Why would you say such a thing?"

"My mother's already gone in my heart. I said good-bye to her years ago. My father despises me for it. Our family doesn't deserve the sympathy." Alex seemed to hold back a heavy wall of emotion. The pain etched on her face betrayed the weight of it. "I'm the one who should be sorry for laying this on you." She swatted another black fly. "We should head back. My father will get cranky if I'm gone much longer with one of his boats. Besides, these flies are becoming relentless." Alex's hard shell, which Zoe had noticed when they first met, returned to cover her like protective armor.

Zoe stood and reached out a hand. "Sure. You're probably right. Besides, my gear should be arriving soon. I need to get to work looking after the eaglets on your father's island."

Alex took the offered hand and rose to her feet. "Any chance I could go with you sometime? I'd love to learn more about them." She gripped a bit tighter before letting go. "I haven't been able to stop thinking about the one that your colleague, Rob, let me help band."

"They do get under your skin, don't they?" Zoe pressed the palm of her hand—the one that had been held by Alex—against her hip to still its vibration. Alex had managed to get under her skin too. "Thank you for bringing me to see the chestnut tree."

"Thanks for coming. I didn't expect to make a friend while I was home this summer," Alex said.

"I didn't either. I'd love to you have your company sometime when I'm out observing the eagles." Zoe considered the irony of wanting to spend time with Alex when her usual mode of operation was to escape people whenever she could. But Alex wasn't just any person. She was different from anyone else she'd ever met.

# Chapter 10

Alex placed the heel of her foot on the long pine board that formed the picnic table's seat and leaned over to stretch her hamstring. The early morning sun beat down on her bare shoulders with an intensity more like August. She should've brought extra tank tops for running, but she'd never expected Maine to be this warm in early June.

A shadow passed over her, similar to the one she'd noticed on her first morning back in Glasgow. She looked up in time to see an eagle with widespread wings gliding toward the nest on the island. Something lifeless dangled from its talons. On cue, the eaglets chirped wildly as their parent came near.

The eagle flapped its wings a couple of times, picking up speed as it swung around to the back of the island to approach the nest at a spot with fewer branches. When it touched down, the eaglets went silent. Alex assumed they were filling their bellies.

"Hi. I didn't think anyone else got up this early in the morning." Zoe came down the hill toward her, carrying a small dry-bag, lifejacket, and kayak paddle. "They're amazing birds, aren't they?"

"Yes. I can't help watching them whenever I see them fly." Alex put her foot down on the ground and leaned back a little to stretch her back. "Speaking of birds, I'm not surprised that you're an early one too. You must be heading out on the water by the time I go for my morning run. I'm not sure how we've managed to miss each other the last couple of days."

Zoe smirked. "I don't know. Maybe the seventy-five wiggly ten-to twelve-year-olds have something to do with it. You seem to disappear into that group whenever they're set free from their bunkhouses in the morning." She placed her dry-bag on the picnic table and set about adjusting the direction of her paddle's blades.

"Do you ever have the occasion to spend time with little kids?"

"Only during the holidays when I go back to Iowa. The trouble is my nieces and nephews are usually hopped up on sugar and whatever ideas they have about what Santa will bring them. I'm afraid they've tainted my perspective." Zoe shook her head. "I do love them, but it's never a relaxing scene at Christmas time."

Alex rolled her head from side to side, stretching her neck. "We don't let the campers eat much sugar when they're here, and they get plenty of exercise. Kids are actually quite charming when they aren't under the influence of bad food and all the stuff they think they need to have. For some of them, coming here is the only time in their lives when they get to experience nature. I love watching them be transformed by it. Some of them are ecstatic that the eagles are here. They can't wait to watch the eaglets learn to fly."

"I have to be honest about something." Zoe picked up her dry-bag from the picnic table. "It's nice to see kids out playing the whole day. When I came here, I thought it would be a battle between me and the camp over protecting the eagles. I'm glad they're as interested in them as you are. Having the camp's support in protecting them is a big deal."

A car door slammed shut. Alex glanced toward the parking lot and saw James carrying a leather briefcase. He was dressed like someone who should be headed to the boardroom of a large company instead of the camp's main office. "I can't say for sure whether that'll always be the case."

"I don't understand," Zoe said.

"I care, but James doesn't, and he has my father in his back pocket." The look of disappointment and concern on Zoe's face bothered Alex, but she had to adjust Zoe's expectations. "I haven't been involved in the camp for years. I can't even say that I'll be here the entire summer, let alone have any kind of influence over my father and the camp. I don't belong here anymore."

"It surprises me that you'd say that. I mean, obviously I don't know you all that well, but as an outsider looking in, I'd say this place fits you like a glove."

The truth was, being with the kids and seeing them flourish felt to Alex like crawling back into a comfortable skin. But the terror she ran from lived there too. There wasn't room in her head for both. "Things aren't always as they seem."

"Hello and good morning!" Alex turned her attention up the hill toward the back of the main office building as Sally stepped through the sliding screen door and closed it. The woman practically bounced down the hill.

"I don't think we've met." She put out a hand to Zoe. "I'm Sally Higgins and you must be the wildlife biologist."

"That's me." Zoe shook Sally's hand.

Alex smiled. "Sally is the town librarian, but I'd call her the town gem."

"How are the eagles doing?" Sally asked.

"They're doing very well so far. In fact, I was just on my way to go spend some time observing them. I was hoping I could talk Alex into joining me."

The muscles in Alex's legs ached to be tested, and her body craved the morning jolt of endorphins that came from running. The idea of spending time with Zoe jousted with her body's need for exercise. "I'm sorry. I'd love to," she said. "But I'm fairly inflexible when it comes to making sure I get a run in every day. It helps keep me sane around all those kids."

"You're going to need that sanity today, my darling," Sally said

"Oh, no." Alex shook her head. "What do you have up your sleeve this time, Sally?"

"Puppies." Sally waved at the office. One of the camp counselors slid the door open, and seven tiny dogs barreled out. Buddy moseyed after them, barking whenever a puppy tried to veer off course. A gaggle of floppy ears, wagging tails, and determined canine faces— the epitome of happiness—roared toward them as Sally clapped her hands. "Come, my dears."

Alex and Zoe dropped to their knees and let the puppies crawl all over them. Their laughter blended with the playful puppy yelps.

One of the puppies lunged into Zoe hard enough to push her off balance. Alex instinctively caught Zoe in her lap. Instead of releasing her, she wrapped her in a tight embrace. The sounds of the puppies and Zoe's and Sally's laughter filled her with a lightness she hadn't felt in years.

It didn't take long, though, for the feeling to drop out beneath her. She found herself in a dark tunnel devoid of anything but Zoe. Her heart begged her to hang on. Her brain chided her not to taint Zoe with her darkness. She let go, but not before letting herself feel the softness of Zoe's hands on hers. She stood, smoothed her tank top, and put her hands behind her back to hide the slight shaking.

"I thought we could get the kids started on making those fashion collars today," Sally said. The concern on her face suggested she had seen Alex disappear inside herself.

"Yeah, sure." Alex patted a puppy that licked her knee. "They'll adore these guys." She waited for Zoe to stand. "I'd love to go out and see the eagles with you sometime, but I have to leave now. It was good to run into you this morning."

Sally looked from Alex to Zoe and back. "Maybe Zoe would want to join us helping the kids." To Zoe, she said, "You seem to enjoy puppies."

"Who doesn't?" Zoe asked. "I'm not that good with kids, but I do love animals. I'd be happy to help. Just let me know."

"No, we shouldn't bother you," Alex said. "I know you're busy. Besides, if you think sugar makes kids gonzo, wait until you see them around puppies. I'll just catch you some other time." She glanced at her watch and said to Sally, "I'll be back in an hour or so. We can get started then."

Alex turned to do the thing she did best. Run away.

# Chapter 11

Gentle swells rolled rhythmically under Zoe's kayak near the wooded side of the island facing the camp. It had been several days since she last saw Alex. Of course, Alex was more than busy with the kids and the camp, but Zoe let self-doubt creep in and wondered whether Alex might be intentionally avoiding her. She chastised herself for enjoying being in Alex's arms—literally falling into Alex's arms—way more than she should. Maybe Alex had picked up on her feelings and been uncomfortable. *What were you thinking, Kimball?*

Zoe raised a pair of binoculars and watched the eaglets. They chirped relentlessly, hungry for their mid-morning snack. She lowered the binoculars and jotted her observations in her field notebook. She scanned the other trees on the island for one or both parents. Given the young age of the eaglets, at least one parent would always be near while the other hunted for food.

She pulled the visor of her Wildlife and Fisheries hat low to shade her eyes from the morning sun. "There you are."

A pure-white feathered head contrasted against the green needles of a tall pine not far from the nest tree. One of the parents sat perched on a branch two-thirds of the way up the tree. From what Zoe could observe from below, both eaglets appeared to be thriving despite the obvious difference in their sizes. The dutiful parents shared the responsibility of guarding and feeding their babies. They appeared to be doing a good job. If she stayed long enough, the other parent would soon arrive with something to offer the eaglets' hungry mouths.

Sounds of a slowing motorboat and loud voices came from the back side of the island. Zoe guessed where the boat and its people might be landing based on the proximity of their clatter to the place where she floated in her kayak. When she heard the engine cut off, she tucked her field notebook into the dry-bag stowed at her feet and paddled toward the sounds.

Two men struggled to drag a boat high up onto the narrow sliver of sand nestled between the rocks that circled the island. The two women with them carried a cooler. One of them had a blanket tucked under her arm.

Zoe landed her kayak next to the boat. She rolled her eyes when she read the name on the boat's stern, *Looking for Trouble.*

"Sorry, lady, but we got here first," the skinnier of the two men said. He must have noticed the logo on her hat. "Don't worry. We have the required number of life jackets on board. I'll show them to you if you'd like."

"That's not necessary." Zoe unfolded her petite body from her kayak and stood as straight as possible to her full height. She suspected she'd need every inch with this crowd. "The hat says Wildlife and Fisheries, not Warden Service. I'm a biologist, not a warden. I am going to ask you to leave, though."

The other man, whose belly hung over the waistband of his shorts, cocked his head. A thick clump of dark hair covered his chest. "I don't see any No Trespassing signs, and the last I knew, this is a private island managed by a good friend of mine, James Bastone. We've been coming here for years. Who are you to tell us we have to leave?"

What Zoe really wanted to say was that he ought to consider not walking around with his bare, mountainous midsection hanging out for the world to see. It really wasn't a pretty sight. "I didn't say I was telling you, but I'm asking you."

The big-bellied man glowered at her. "Why? Is there some rare weed growing in the bush that you're trying to save? Tell us where it is, and we'll be sure not to step on it."

Zoe was reluctant to give up the location of the nest, but she didn't have a choice if she wanted to make her case. She pointed to the top of the tree that held it. "I don't know what's worse, ignoring your presence, or telling you there are two eaglets born less than a month ago in that tree."

The women set the cooler down and gawked up at the nest. One of them said, "That's so cool."

At least she appeared to have the sense that this was a good thing. Maybe she would see the light and convince her friends to leave. Zoe said to her, "They're easily disturbed and that's why I'm asking you to go. I know the parents must be around waiting to feed them, but us being here hinders that. They're probably close by right now, waiting for some privacy to feel secure."

The big-bellied man snorted. "You sound like a damned tree hugger. I don't buy that. If they were so sensitive in the first place, why would they choose to nest on an island that people use all the time? Huh?"

*A tree hugger?* Granted, there was some truth to that, but he didn't have to say it like it was a bad thing. She didn't have a problem with humans coexisting with wildlife. Cutting every tree in sight and paving the entire planet was her problem.

"Were you here in late February when they chose the island to build their nest?" Zoe asked.

"That's a ridiculous question. Of course not. Who camps in Maine in February?"

"Definitely not someone as soft as you."

The man folded his arms across his chest, resting them on the shelf of his wide girth. He flexed his biceps when he did. "Humph. You do-gooders think the rest of us are stupid. I watch the news. George W. took the eagle off the endangered species list when he was president. Why would he do that if they weren't doing fine?"

Zoe zipped her lips against answering any kind of question about the former president. No good would come from that, she was sure. She'd already started to dig a hole for herself with the "soft" comment. "They're still protected by the Bald and Golden Eagle Protection Act. It's my opinion that your presence may disturb them, and that's still against the law."

The skinny man interrupted. "You're going to have to prove it, then. Good luck with that. You didn't find us standing over the carcass of an eagle with a smoking gun. You and I both know that unless you did, the best you get is a civil claim against us and I doubt the feds are interested in the hassle given that you can't prove we've done anything wrong. The eagles are still up in the tree, and this island isn't posted as to their presence or that trespassing isn't allowed." He cocked his head. "I happen to be an attorney. I'll give you my card. You can call me on Monday. But for now, we have a day to enjoy." He motioned to his companions. "Let's get our picnic set up."

One of the women looked horrified. "What if she has us arrested?"

"She doesn't have the authority. She knows it. And I know it." He snickered at Zoe. "Take your best shot, little lady." He craned his neck down in her direction with more drama than necessary. "Unless you can show me that you're the eagle police, I'm asking *you* to leave. Better yet, perhaps I'll give Mr. Bastone a call and you can deal with him."

"Fine, since you're an attorney, I don't have to remind you that there are some pretty hefty civil fines for disturbing nesting eagles. You'll be taking your chances on that."

One thing that pushed Zoe's buttons faster than anything was a man who thought he could use his size to intimidate her. God, she despised bullies. She'd have to resort to her best weapon, her intellect. Given her size, people often underestimated her. Adversaries often let their guard down at just the right moment, which meant that if she were patient and strategic, she could slay him in one fell swoop. Getting into a tiff with him now was not going to play in her favor. For the moment, he had the upper hand and she certainly didn't want Bastone complicating things.

One way or the other, she needed to prevent people from picnicking on the island in the future. She couldn't order this group to leave. The only law that had enough teeth to come close to stopping them wasn't even one that the state had any jurisdiction to enforce. The man was right. There would have to be proof that their activities were causing a disturbance, and even with evidence, the federal agency with the authority would have to be convinced to make the effort to enforce it. The best and most immediate alternative would be to convince Mr. Marcotte to close the island to any human activity altogether. Given that James would be a huge obstacle, she'd need to convince Alex to persuade her father.

"I wish you'd do the right thing and leave," she said.

"Seems to me that if leaving was the right thing, you could make me."

Zoe bit her lip. *Patience, Kimball.* She pushed her kayak off the sand into the shallow water and slid into it. Despite the dire necessity to find Alex to enlist her help, she was glad for the excuse. She ignored the voice in her head that suggested she might be getting her personal feelings mixed up with her job.

"I thought so," the big-bellied man said.

She ignored him. He'd find out soon enough that some of the smallest creatures on the planet could also be the most dangerous.

# Chapter 12

Alex ascended the dimly lit, narrow staircase leading to the library attic. The narrow space comforted her. Unlike many who suffered from anxiety, she didn't mind being in tight places. Many offered the opportunity to vanish amid the clutter of them.

The only peace and quiet she'd been able to find since arriving back in Maine had been during her morning runs and under the chestnut tree with Zoe. She'd never taken anyone to that secret place before. To her surprise, having Zoe's company had been more pleasant than being alone. Holding Zoe in her arms that brief moment with the puppies had the same effect. Guilt and desire told her she shouldn't try to avoid Zoe indefinitely. Or was it that she couldn't? With Friday on the horizon and a few days to get hold of herself, she hoped to cross paths with Zoe over the weekend.

Sally called up to her from downstairs, "The light switch is on the wall to the right at the top of the stairs. All the archived newspapers are in boxes arranged by year."

The musty smell of old books and papers hit Alex in the face when she landed on the top step at the attic's entry. She ran a hand along the wall and found the light switch. "Got it, thanks."

She flipped on the light and scanned the neatly stacked boxes and plastic containers. They held a treasure trove of the town of Glasgow's history waiting to be discovered. She reveled in the process of uncovering old truths, a way to escape her own. "I might be up here awhile," she called to Sally.

"Not too long, I hope. The air isn't healthy up there."

Alex felt the tickle of mold and dust as it settled in her nose and lungs. She put a hand to her mouth and coughed. "I see what you mean."

The single lightbulb that hung from the center of the low ceiling cast a muted yellow glow on the rows of shelves lining the walls. Thin rays of sunlight coming through the slats of the attic eaves added some illumination, but not enough. Alex turned on the flashlight she carried and aimed it at the neat handwriting on the boxes, written with a thick black marker. Nearest to her were more recent collections ranging from years 2005 to 2010.

She closed her eyes and forced in a deep, slow breath. The voice in her head warned her to avoid the year 1998, but the contents of that box seemed to rattle too loudly to be ignored. She'd come to realize that, sometimes, the only way to silence the recollections of her brother so she could sleep was to let them consume her.

Fighting was futile. One way or the other, the memories always had their way with her no matter how hard she fought them. They'd come in the night like the monster under the bed. Sometimes she'd struggle against them. Mostly, though, she was too tired and would simply give in so it could be over. But it never really was over. Her mind remained her tormenter.

Alex reached for the box and moved it closer to the edge of the shelf so she could open it. Her hands shook as she fumbled with the flaps. A newspaper lay on top of the contents inside. She put a hand to her mouth to stifle a cry. The headline read, "The Body of Jacob Marcotte, Son of Daniel and Carolyn Marcotte, Pulled from Sebago Lake in the Early Morning Hours. His Sister, Alexandra, Questioned by Police."

She spun around at the sound of footsteps at the top of the attic stairs.

Sally stood in the doorway. Her gaze settled on the box. "I should've moved that one out of your sight. I'm sorry I didn't think of it earlier."

"It wouldn't have mattered. I would've looked for it anyway." An edge of panic framed Alex's voice.

"You look as though you've seen a ghost." Sally stepped toward her. "How about a break?"

Alex closed the box and slid it back into place. "No, I'm okay. Sometimes letting myself remember is the only way I can feel close to Jake again. Besides, I'm a historian. I'm used to spending time with ghosts."

"Ghosts are one thing, demons quite another. Sorry to disturb you. Zoe Kimball is here to see you."

Alex wiped dust from her hands. "Did she say what she wanted?"

"No. Do you want me to ask her to come back later?"

"I'd really like to see her."

"What was that I just saw?"

"What?" Alex glanced around the attic.

"You went from revisiting the worst day of your life to a gleam in your eye at the mention of the delightful woman downstairs. Is there something you want to tell me?" Sally poked her in the ribs. "Come to think of it, she wore the same expression when she asked for you. I saw it the other day too, when the two of you were in that tangle of puppies. If I had a nickel for each of the young women who've had crushes on you since you were a teenager, I'd have enough money to save every stray dog and cat in the state of Maine."

"I hardly know her," Alex said, amused that the only straight person in Glasgow with any kind of open acceptance for gay and lesbian people happened to be an eighty-something-year-old woman who had never missed a day of church in her life. "How is it that you came to be the most tolerant person in this town?"

Sally pointed at the box Alex had been looking at. "I saw what closed-mindedness did to your brother. It still infuriates me after all these years." She caressed Alex's shoulder. "All kidding about Zoe aside, I only want you to be happy. Are you going to be okay?"

"I don't know. It's so much harder to come home than I thought it would be. I knew it would be difficult, but my father's barely speaking to me. And the only one whose feelings seem to matter to him is still my mother. My parents act as if Jake's death only happened to them. They weren't there to see what those other kids did to him. I was." Alex stared down at the old wooden planks in the attic floor. "I'm sorry. I shouldn't have opened that box. I hate myself for doing it, just like I hate myself for letting my parents treat me the way they do."

"Oh, honey, please find a way to stop hating yourself. You always have been and always will be such a lovely soul." Sally pursed her lips together and sighed. "I love your parents, but for the life of me, I can't understand why they've done the things they've done to you, especially after Jake died. You've been protecting them by making yourself scarce around here and by taking the blame for too long for something that was never your fault."

"I'm not protecting them." Alex's voice quivered. "You give me too much credit. The only thing I feel for either of them is anger."

"Take it from me, darling, anger is a cover for what you really feel. You came home for more complicated reasons. I hope you figure them out while you're here." Sally put her arms around Alex and squeezed her tight. "I'm glad you're home." She patted her on the back. "And Zoe is awfully cute."

The warmth of Sally's embrace did wonders to ease the cutting pain that always came with thoughts of the day her brother died.

Knowing that Zoe was downstairs waiting for her felt good too. "I don't even know if she's gay."

Sally put her hands on her hips. "I may be as straight as they come, but I'm older than dirt and have been around long enough to know when a lady's playing for the other team. And so have you."

Alex smiled at Sally's intuition. She was a rare soul who could dismantle a person's façade in an instant to see their reality. "Tell her I'll be right down. I need a minute to get my head on straight, so to speak. Okay?"

"Sure thing." Sally gave a little snort and disappeared down the stairs.

Alex sat down on the dusty floor and wrapped her arms around her knees. She focused on her breathing. Slowly in and slowly out. Her heart rate slowed with each successive, deliberate breath. She didn't want to let Zoe see her fragility. When she felt more in control, she rose to her feet and took her time down the stairs, gathering her composure.

Engrossed in a book, Zoe and Sally stood with their backs to her. Alex studied Zoe, whose hands were in the pockets of her heavy canvas work shorts. She wore a dark-green T-shirt and hiking boots. Her short, shaggy hair suited her easy, confident demeanor. Her backside was sure to turn the heads of men and women. Zoe had a distinctly athletic, yet feminine and very attractive build, but it was Zoe's heart that really drew her.

"Let me guess, you're looking at a book titled *American Angels,*" Alex said.

Zoe closed the book, turned, and read from the cover. "The story about everyday people who do extraordinary things to protect companion animals."

"Did Sally show you chapter twelve?"

Zoe grinned. "You didn't tell me such a huge celebrity lived in town." She winked at Sally. "Chapter Twelve: Sally Higgins, the Angel of Glasgow, Maine."

Alex caught the glimmer in Sally's eyes. Sally had always loved the attention that came with the success of saving so many unwanted or neglected animals. Attention she unequivocally deserved. "She's not the only celebrity. From her digging around in the dump to rescue abandoned kittens to you climbing a burning tree to save an eaglet, I'm in rare company."

Zoe's cheeks turned pink. "Sorry to interrupt your work. Sally told me you were doing research for a book you're writing. I love books. You'll have to let me know when it's published, and I'll get a copy. Maybe I can talk you into autographing it."

"I'd be happy to."

"What's it about?"

"The forest fires that happened here in 1947. It was terrible. Entire towns across Maine burned."

"It's a timely subject," Sally said. "When you had to climb that tree the other day, you saw how similar this year is to the summer that preceded those fires. Fires like that in springtime are a bad sign here in Maine. I was seventeen the October that the fires broke out here in Glasgow and around the state. We hardly had any snow that winter and no rain to speak of in spring or summer. The whole place was a tinderbox waiting to go up in flames. Just like now."

"How much of the town was damaged?" Zoe asked.

"Every building in town burned except for the camp owned by Alex's family," Sally answered. "I was working there as a counselor that summer. We didn't have the kinds of things available to us to fight fires like they have today. All we had were shovels, small tank trucks for water, and buckets."

"My grandfather used to love to tell me the story of how the camp was saved," Alex said. "Do you remember, Sally?"

"I sure do. Everyone in town knew we only had enough resources to try to save one or two buildings. We all agreed that the camp and your family's house were the most important. The camp was the heart of this town and did an awful lot of good. We had to give it a shot. Our army assembled at the top of Thistle Hill. That fire was not going to get past the hill if we had anything to do about it. Everyone played a role in keeping the fire at bay. The men fought it at its line, and we ladies made sure they had plenty to eat and drink while they were at it," Sally said.

"The fire was no match for a group of people working together, hell-bent on saving the soul of this town. It's funny how all the politics and squabbles between the people disappeared when their backs were against a wall. Too bad we had to have our collective butts in a sling before we could come together as a town for a good cause. But we managed."

"Until the fire flared up again after hiding underground for a while," Alex added.

"I've never heard of such a thing. How can a fire hide in the ground?" Zoe asked.

"One reason the fires were so difficult to fight in '47 was that they sometimes smoldered undetected beneath the surface of the ground in the crevices between boulders and tree roots. There are lots of leaves and brush to provide fuel. The firefighters thought the fires were out, but then they would roar back to life in the least expected places." Alex considered the parallel between the fires and her anxiety. It too liked to smolder beneath the surface, only to flare up uncontrolled.

Sally leaned against the library's reception desk. "They say it could never happen again with modern fire-detecting equipment. Something about infrared heat detectors or some kind of contraption like that."

"Thinking about the fires out west," Zoe said, "and detecting equipment, it's not enough to know the location of the fire. You still have to be able to put it out. I imagine putting out a fire burning underground is a whole different ball game even if you know where it is."

Sally slapped the desk. "I like this girl. Finally, someone from the government who has some good sense, don't you think, Alex?"

"Yes, I like her too," Alex answered. "Very much."

Zoe put her hands in her pockets and fidgeted. "I'm glad you like me because I have a huge favor to ask you. It has to do with the camp."

"I can't make any promises, but I'll do what I can," Alex said. "What is it?"

"I need you to help me convince your father to close the island to protect the eagles. When I was out today studying them, a group of people showed up to camp. Human activity on the island is too close to the eagles. It's too much of a disturbance, especially for a new pair nesting on the island. In fact, it would be best if we could set buoys as well so boats don't go within two hundred feet of it."

"I'm sorry, Zoe. James will never agree, and he has all the influence over my father. I don't have any. Isn't there anything the government can require?"

"Yes, but unfortunately, it would take a lot of time to put everything in place. Without notice being posted, people just going onto the island very likely wouldn't be considered a crime unless they got caught doing something egregiously harmful to the eagles. Any harm would otherwise be a civil violation, and since the bald eagle is no longer on the state's rare species protection list, the state doesn't have any jurisdiction. By the time I could convince our federal counterparts who have jurisdiction to do anything about it, it might be too late."

Zoe pulled a photograph out of her pocket and handed it to Alex. "I took this of the eaglets a couple of days ago. You could show it to your father, and maybe he can see the importance of protecting them."

Alex studied the photo of the two eaglet siblings in the nest. It hurt to think of something so precious suffering because of human selfishness. Why anyone would want to use the island with them there was beyond her comprehension. "They look darker than when I saw them last." She handed the photo back to Zoe. "They're beautiful."

"Yes, they're starting to replace their gray down with feathers that are more conducive to flying. Please, we at least have to try," Zoe said.

"James will refuse. I have no doubt about that, especially if I'm the one asking. Alumni of the camp who donate lots of money use the island every year. It's never been closed."

"I'm not asking you to get James's permission. Go over his head and get your father's. It's his camp."

"I'm the last person my father will listen to."

"Now, wait a minute." Sally raised her voice. "Daniel may be difficult in a lot of ways, but I've never known him to be cold-hearted toward wildlife. Why don't you at least try to talk to him? It might do you both some good for you to ask something of him for a change."

"We'll ask him together," Zoe said. "Maybe between the two of us, he won't be able to refuse."

"No." Alex wasn't able to keep her urgency in check. "That's okay. I'll talk to him myself. It might be better." She didn't want to have to suffer the embarrassment of Zoe witnessing Daniel's typical treatment of her. "I'll try."

"Good girl," Sally said. "My advice would be to catch him when he's in a good mood."

"Today's probably as good as any for him to be in better spirits," Alex said. "There's a dance tonight for the campers, and he said something about doing some work in his shop this afternoon. Music and woodworking are two of his favorite things, and all in the same day." She breathed in deep, thinking about asking him for anything, but it was for Zoe and the eaglets. How could she not?

"I really appreciate it." Zoe smiled. "Thank you."

"You're welcome. I want to help the eagles too." It was more than that. She wanted to make Zoe happy. "If you're interested, the dances are always great fun. You should join us if you're free."

"Oh, what a wonderful idea," Sally said. "You haven't had a good time until you've danced to Alex playing the ukulele."

Alex shrugged. "I don't know about that. I haven't played in years, and I'm not planning on it anytime soon."

"I'll go if you promise to play," Zoe said.

"Just like I can't promise to have success with my father agreeing to close the island, I can't promise I'll play. I'd certainly enjoy your company, though."

"That's enough for me. What time?" Zoe asked.

"Stop by around seven. We'll be gathered at the campfire outside the main building."

"See you then. Will you be there too, Sally?"

"You bet, honey. I never pass up a party."

Alex laughed. "A party isn't a party without you."

"I'll see you both tonight." Zoe held up the book she and Sally had been enjoying. "Do you mind if I check this out?"

Sally beamed. "I love this girl. Of course not."

# Chapter 13

The high-pitched buzz of a table saw coming from the barn confirmed for Alex that her father was busy. Working with wood meant to him what running meant to her. It was how he relaxed. Growing up, she'd always been able to find him in his shop if he'd had a bad day or simply needed to be alone to decompress from the hustle and bustle of the camp.

She reached for the barn door. The smell of freshly cut hardwood wafted out as she opened it. The scent brought her back to happier times when Jake was still alive. They'd cook up all kinds of adventures after school, playing in the barn while their father puttered in his wood shop. Like clockwork every evening, her mother would interrupt them for dinner and grouse about how they left a trail of sawdust all over the kitchen floor.

Serving warm and healthy meals with a loving smile, her mother, Carolyn, never made anything she or Jake genuinely disliked. If they cleaned their plates, they could always count on Mom for a freshly baked dessert. Laughter and sharing stories from their respective days around the dinner table remained the happiest times of her life. In hindsight, those moments were nothing more than an illusion built on lies about the meaning of family.

Daniel looked up as he was about to slide a piece of reddish brown wood into the saw's blade. Cut pieces were stacked on the bench behind him. He switched off the saw and removed his earplugs, connected by a strand of rubber around his neck. The whir of the blade slowed and went silent.

"That's very nice cherry." Alex stepped closer.

"Yes, it is. I'm glad you still remember the different types of wood." He picked up the piece he'd been about to cut and handed it to her. "I don't think I've ever seen a nicer board. The grain is remarkable. Got it over at Bilkes's Lumber."

Alex closed her eyes for a moment and lifted the piece of wood to her nose. Each type of wood had its own distinctive smell, and cherry's was sweet and pleasant. "Mmm." She opened her eyes and saw her father watching her with an almost wistful expression. She averted her gaze, ran her hand over the smoothly planed surface, and admired the undulating dark and light lines. "How is Mr. Bilkes?"

"He's had better days. He had to give up managing the lumberyard. The damned arthritis got to be too much." He crossed his arms over his chest and leaned back against the bench. "He's lucky, though. You remember Reed, his oldest son?"

"Yes, he was two grades below me in school."

"The boy took over the business for his dad. Reed's doing right by his father and is managing things like a pro. He's a son any father could be proud of."

Alex was not about to be baited into a discussion about her failings as a daughter or be compared to Reed Bilkes. She didn't have anything against him, but how could it be fair to compare her to Reed? In school, all he'd ever talked about was working for his father when he graduated. He followed his dream. She still didn't know what hers was.

She changed the subject. "What are you making?"

"Humph." He shook his head and reached for the piece of wood he'd handed her. "A jewelry box for your mother's birthday. I wanted to do something extra special for her. I hate seeing her so sad, trapped in a bed she's never going to leave." He turned his back on her, set the piece of wood on the stack of the others, and fiddled with a tool on his bench. He wiped his face with his shirtsleeve.

"She'll love it," Alex said.

"She's too out of it to even notice." His voice quivered. He picked up a hand planer and turned around to face her. "I'm certain she'd know you, though. She asked about you the last time I visited her. She's aware that you're home."

Daniel might as well have shaken her violently by the shoulders. Alex's insides jangled as nervousness crept up the back of her neck. "I'm sorry. I'm not ready to see her."

He studied her as if contemplating whether to argue. "I'm really busy. What do you need?"

"I want to talk with you about the eagles on the island."

"What about them?"

"Zoe says that people using the island are disturbing them. The state can't require that we close the island, but she thinks it would be the best thing in order to give the eaglets a fighting chance of making it."

"Why didn't she come ask me? Since when do you care about matters involving the camp anyway?" His tone hardened.

"I wanted to ask you myself."

"Why?"

"Because I care about this. It matters to me. If you could see the eaglets, you'd understand. I've never been more moved by anything so beautiful. They need our help to at least get them through this summer."

"What specifically does Zoe want us to do?"

"Put up No Trespassing signs and set buoys around the island so boats can't get too close."

"Do you have any idea what kind of stir that would cause?"

"Yes, but I think it would be even worse if we did nothing and the camp was blamed for the eagles dying. Instead, we could set an example for the community about being good stewards of the eagles. That's always been the camp's goal, right? To teach kids about doing the right thing. This could actually be a huge positive for us."

James came into the barn. "Or a crazy debacle." He stood next to Daniel. "I'm sorry, Alex. I shouldn't have used such insensitive language. Sometimes I forget that you spent time in the hospital for a mental illness. I shouldn't have said that. I'm sorry."

Alex stared in disbelief at James's gall, trying to use her breakdown when she was a teenager to create a wedge between her and her father. "Don't be. It was a long time ago." Anger at his blatant disrespect masked her vulnerability.

"Good. I can be blunt then. Closing the island would be a disaster in the making. The only reason we're able to give scholarships to five percent of our campers who come from low-income families is because of the generosity of alumni. They ask nothing of us in return other than to use the island every summer as they always have." He made eye contact with Daniel. "There's a reason the island is affectionately known as Alumni Island."

"Are you kidding me? If you didn't waste so much of the camp's money on expensive boats and that obnoxious P.A. system, you wouldn't have to sell the eaglets out for donations." Alex tried to keep her voice calm. "We used to give scholarships to a lot more kids than five percent. Where's all the money gone?"

James pointed at her. "With all due respect, this camp is among the top ten in Maine. I must be doing something right with the way I'm managing things. You've been missing in action for years. Don't think you can waltz in here and automatically hold sway over how I run the place. Your father hired me to do a job, and I intend to do it.

The economy is a whole lot different now than when we were kids. We certainly can't give the camp away like we used to. Every dollar of donations is needed."

Alex looked to Daniel to say something. James was taking credit for what their family had built. Instead, he sat silently by. "This camp's always been special," she said, "even before you came along. And it will be when you're finally gone."

The unedited comment caught her by surprise. The men too, judging from their reactions. Daniel stood straighter and James glared at her.

James shifted so that his back was to her. He said, "Daniel, I know it must be tough for Alex to come home after all these years. I value her opinion. She is a Marcotte. However—"

"Don't talk about me," Alex shouted, "as if I'm no longer in the room. How dare you?"

"Please calm down." James turned to her and said, barely above a whisper, "Obviously you're still suffering from your anxiety, even after all this time."

"Enough." Daniel put up his hands. "James, you have a right to speak about any facet of how this camp is managed. You don't, however, have a right to discuss my daughter's personal affairs. Now, I'd like to speak with Alex alone, please."

"Of course. I apologize for stepping over the line." James swallowed hard. He looked as if Daniel had slapped him with one of the boards lying on the workbench. "Let me know when you're available. I'd like to get your input on some things having to do with the dance tonight for the campers." He nodded to Alex on his way out. "I'm sorry, Alex."

Alex waited for him to be out of earshot. "Thank you for standing up for me."

"That's not what I was doing. My family isn't anyone's business but my own. I was merely standing up for the Marcotte name," Daniel said.

She shivered at the coldness of his words and channeled for calm. "Then in the name of our family and the history of the camp, I'm asking you to recognize that protecting the eagles is important. Setting a good example for the community is what our camp has always been about. This is a rare opportunity for us to make a difference and teach the kids about the importance of sharing their space with wildlife."

He rubbed his chin. "Is your use of the word 'us' indicating a change in mindset about staying and helping me with the camp?"

"Are you giving me an ultimatum?" Alex asked.

"I'm sorry. We aren't going to close the island." He laid the hand planer he'd been holding down on the bench. "James has been a godsend ever since you left. He's been like a son to me. He was there when your mother and I needed him." His tone was stern. "He has good business sense. I'm going to listen to him on this one. I can't afford to lose the camp right now. Not with your mother so sick. If people on the island are such a problem, then let the government tell me I need to close it. Until then, it'll remain open."

He slipped on his earplugs and powered up the saw. He placed the wood he'd been working with on the table and moved it toward the blade as if Alex were no longer in the room. His hands trembled.

She thought about flipping the switch that powered the saw and smashing the tool with the sledgehammer resting in the corner of the barn—anything to finally get his attention. She and Daniel existed on the same planet, yet she couldn't reach him. Maybe it was time to accept once and for all that he would never be able to see or hear her. She was nothing more than a ghost from the past to him. He was as lost to her as Jake.

# Chapter 14

Wearing only a bra and cargo shorts, Zoe held a wrinkled, gray T-shirt up against her front. "I can't go to the dance wearing this. I'll look like I just rolled out of bed," she said to herself.

She tossed the shirt aside and contemplated the remaining three shirts laid out on the dresser in her room. The orange one might not match her shorts, but it was one of her favorites. She put it on and tucked it in. "Oh, come on, a freaking pumpkin with green shorts for a stem?" She took the shirt off, wadded it into a ball, and threw it on the bed. She let out a big sigh. "Since when do you care about how your T-shirt looks?"

She scratched her head to think and remembered something Rob had said once. He'd told her she should wear blue more often because it brought out the color of her green eyes. *I can't believe I'm about to take Rob's advice.*

She grabbed the blue T-shirt. "This one will have to do," she muttered. *It's not like Alex will notice anyway*. She pulled the shirt over her head, smoothed it out, and purposely didn't look again at her ensemble before hurrying out of her quarters.

A fire glowed in the fire pit at the water's edge as Zoe made her way down the hill. A crowd milled around a two-foot-high ring of stones that surrounded the blaze and kept it contained. Four brown-brick benches were placed across from each other, separated by, and a safe distance from, the flames. The benches were lined with kids roasting marshmallows on sticks. Zoe shuddered to think about the effect of that much sugar on a group of kids this late in the day, especially since Alex had said the camp generally limited their sugar intake.

Camp counselors, campers, and what appeared to be locals mingled together, deep in their respective conversations. She looked for Alex. She saw her and the education director, Claire Durand, whom she'd met a few days earlier, sitting in lawn chairs along with a couple of counselors fiddling with guitars. Alex glanced up and waved.

Zoe's heart skipped a beat. Alex wore a sleeveless lavender sundress. Her thick, dark hair, freed from the ponytail or braid she usually wore it in, framed her slender shoulders. The campfire's flickering glow illuminated her flawless, milky skin. "Goddess" was the only word suited to describe her.

Zoe didn't think she'd ever seen a more stunning woman. Her knees threatened to buckle. She mustered a wave in return and headed in Alex's direction. Unfortunately, at that moment, a group of kids started dancing around to the song the guitar-playing counselors began to strum. Except for her desire to find out how things had gone with Daniel Marcotte and wanting to be near Alex in that sundress, she would've high-tailed it out of there, away from all those energetic kids.

A little boy took Alex's hand in both of his, leaned back, and tugged with all his might. Alex grinned at him and got to her feet. She held up a finger to Zoe and mouthed, "Give me a second."

Zoe nodded and smiled. Clearly, she and Rob weren't the only ones who had a crush on Alex.

The boy giggled and did his best to twirl Alex around, although he was only half her height. For the first time since they'd met, Zoe saw Alex truly relax and appear to have a good time. She was even more beautiful without the mask of sadness she usually wore.

Zoe sat down in a lawn chair as the number of people dancing multiplied. The two guitar players strummed a peppy tune that made it difficult to sit still. Claire picked up the ukulele resting near the empty guitar cases and joined in.

A ruddy-faced camp counselor moved between her and her view of Alex dancing. He extended a hand. "I'm Roger. May I have this dance?"

"Ah, no, thank you." Zoe answered.

"Don't be like that. Everybody else is dancing and having a good time. You can't sit here all by yourself. Be a sport. Dance with me?"

"I don't dance." She didn't want him to think she was a weird, reclusive biologist, even though she was. "I'd love to, but I'm terrible at it. I wouldn't want to embarrass you, or me."

He shuffled his feet in a clumsy sort of jig. "You can't be as bad as me."

"After that thing you just did, you might be right," she said. "But I'm still not going to dance with you."

"Maybe not with me." He pointed and covered his finger with the palm of his other hand so no one but her could see. "Mr. Marcotte over there, he absolutely loves to dance. I guarantee that if he sees you sitting all alone over here, he's going to ask you. I grew up spending my summers at this camp. Mr. Marcotte doesn't like to see anyone, particularly a pretty lady, not having a good time." Roger made a funny face. "I am a lot younger. I mean, he's a good-looking guy for his age, but..." He put his palms up. "Guess it depends on what your preferences are."

*Did he just call me a pretty lady*? Zoe shook her head. "Pretty" and "lady" weren't adjectives anyone had ever used to describe her. Cute, tough, and short were common, but never pretty or lady. She wondered what this kid had smoked before he showed up at the dance.

"Don't you have a girlfriend you could pester instead of me?" she asked in an amused tone. She considered her options, assuming it might be true that Mr. Marcotte would ask her to dance if he caught her sitting alone. She suspected that young Roger was full of a lot of bull given that he just complimented her.

"I do have a girlfriend. Unfortunately, she's back in Boston." He grinned. "I'm only asking you to dance, not marry me."

She decided to call his bluff. Although she'd much prefer to embarrass herself in front of Roger than Daniel Marcotte, she was betting that Roger might be scamming her. "I'm going to have to take my chances with Mr. Marcotte. You're a bit young for me."

"What about me?" Alex's voice came from behind her, sounding like a spoonful of honey tasted.

Zoe turned slightly at the waist to see Alex. "Uh... you're definitely not too young. Not at all." She squeezed her eyes momentarily shut. Her biologist brain kicked in. It routinely asked questions or made observations at strange moments. Instead of answering the question, she pondered why people instinctively closed their eyes when embarrassed. Was it to think more clearly or to disappear? Either would do right now. *Kimball, get a grip.* "What I'm trying to say is that I don't know how to dance."

Alex came around from behind the chair and took one of her hands. "Everyone can dance, even you. Come on, I'll show you."

Zoe remained rooted where she sat while Alex tugged her arm. What could be worse, looking like a goof in front of Alex, or having to dance with Daniel Marcotte or ruddy-faced Roger?

Alex leaned down and whispered in her ear, "The music is fast, no one will think we're gay. At least not you, anyway. They already know I am. Besides, girls dance with girls all the time at the camp."

*What*? Alex smelled intoxicating. Her warm breath on Zoe's neck melted her into a puddle. Did she just admit to being gay? Zoe peeled herself out of the chair. Was this what having a yin-yang moment felt like? On the one hand, being asked by Alex to dance was the equivalent of an invitation to heaven. On the other, the idea was sheer terror. "Promise you won't laugh."

"I would never," Alex said. "Laugh, that is. I'm good at keeping a promise."

"I might, though," Roger said. "Have fun. Once Alex proves to you that everyone has moves, maybe I can catch you for a dance later."

"Don't count on it, young Roger. But thanks for asking." Zoe felt a little like she might throw up from nerves as she followed Alex to a spot in the crowd where they could move.

Alex took her hands. "All you have to do is hold on to me and move your feet to the music."

*Until I pass out from being so perfectly close to you.* "You make it sound so easy."

"That's because it is. Just move, that's all you have to do." Alex squeezed Zoe's hands tighter.

The respectable distance that separated their bodies didn't stifle the heat radiating off Zoe's body. Unfortunately, her body also had a mind of its own with Alex so near. She wished her palms weren't suddenly sweaty. She tried to swallow the apparent hairball stuck in her throat.

The music stopped and the crowd groaned. As much as Zoe loathed the idea of dancing in public, a pang of disappointment poked at her. She took a step farther away from Alex.

"You're not off the hook." Alex lowered her hands but continued to keep Zoe's fingers entwined with hers. "Claire's going to play us a song on the ukulele that's fitting. Think of the kind of music your grandparents listened to, and I'll bet you know this one." She bobbed her head as Claire began to strum a little ditty.

The song sounded familiar. Zoe followed Alex's lead and nodded a little. She tapped one toe and then the other. Not too much. She didn't want things to get out of hand and have her end up looking like a complete goober.

"Do you know the song?" Alex asked.

"I know I've heard it before, but I can't remember the words."

"It's 'Has Anybody Seen My Gal?' Talks about a girl who's five foot two with eyes of blue." Alex sang the words as she spun Zoe around. She caught Zoe by the waist when she stumbled. "Sorry." Alex held her gaze.

Zoe's heart raced. She didn't think she'd stumbled enough to warrant the tight grip Alex had on her. She certainly wasn't going to complain, though. The sundress Alex wore had a low neckline. Her cheek rested on the bare skin of Alex's chest above it. The difference in their heights worked in her favor in this regard.

She regained her footing and reluctantly moved back a step. If their bodies remained pressed together a second more, there was no telling what she would do. *God, how nice it would be to put my lips to the softness of her neck.* Given that they were surrounded by tons of people, including Alex's father and a bunch of kids, she needed to keep her desires in check.

"Look at you two having such a nice time." Sally came to stand next to Zoe and Alex as Claire finished playing. She held a small leather instrument case in her arms.

Zoe let Alex go. "Hi, Sally." Her voice cracked. She hoped she didn't look like she felt, which was like a kid caught with her hand in the cookie jar.

"Hello to you, my dears. It's good to see Alex playing like old times. Speaking of, I was hoping you'd play something on your old ukulele for us." Sally held the case out to Alex. "You do still play, right?"

Alex's expression changed to the damned sad mask Zoe loathed. "Sometimes."

"For old time's sake." Claire joined the conversation.

Alex took the case and ran a hand over its length. The leather was frayed along the seams stitching it together. "I haven't opened this since Jake died." The corners of her eyes moistened.

Zoe wondered whether this Jake was the source of Alex's grief. He must have been someone she loved deeply. The depth of her affection and sadness was written all over her face at his mention.

Alex crouched down and laid the case on the ground. She undid the silver metal clasps and opened it. A finely polished, honey-colored ukulele lay inside. She took out the instrument, cradled it, and lightly brushed the strings with her thumb.

"What do you say?" Sally asked.

By now, the people from town who obviously knew Alex and her history had gathered around. They shushed the kids. A story was written in the lines of their faces, a sad story that gripped them all, Zoe thought.

Alex didn't make eye contact with anyone. Even though her body was present, her mind appeared to be someplace else. "Okay," she said, her voice heavy with emotion. She stood and seemed to notice the kids, who remained obviously untouched by whatever history the adults were reliving. They smiled and giggled in anticipation of more music. She warmed and sounded more upbeat when she asked the kids, "Anybody ever heard of 'Hey, Soul Sister'?"

Zoe suspected Alex was trying to shake off what had pulled her down. She didn't dance much, but she still loved music. Train's hit song was one of her favorites. "I've heard of it," she said. "If I know that song, you kids must too. Right?"

"Yeah!" a group of children bellowed in unison.

One of them yelled, "That's my favorite video on TV!"

Zoe caught the subtle smile that flashed across Alex's face. The same feeling that came from being in the treetops washed over her. In that moment, a thread of something she couldn't articulate connected her to Alex. She found herself wanting to share the treetops with her and protect her like she protected innocent wildlife from the harm done by human destructiveness.

Alex tuned the ukulele and started to play.

The kids danced around and Zoe joined them, uninhibited, without caring what anyone thought. Not a single person stood still. The kids giggled when they sang the words to the song.

Zoe didn't care anymore if she moved like a goof. Alex was making music, and she couldn't keep herself from moving to the sound of it. She watched Alex play. Alex had slipped seamlessly into a different place while she strummed the ukulele. She wondered where and whether it was a place Alex used to be happy in.

When Alex finished, she sat down on a log near the fire and stared into the flames.

None of the adults spoke. It seemed that ghosts lingered among them, ghosts from an earlier time only they could see.

Sally put a hand on Alex's shoulder and asked, "Are you all right, my darling?"

Alex put her hand over Sally's. "I need to play a certain song for Jake."

"What's that?" Sally asked.

"'I'll See You in My Dreams.'"

Sally caressed Alex's cheek. "He'll always be in all of our dreams." She lowered her head.

Before she did, Zoe saw her lips quiver. The pain of loss didn't belong only to Alex. People around them stood still like stone. Something terrible had happened to this town, and the awful wound had yet to heal. When Alex started to strum, not a person moved.

Zoe studied Alex. Pain and love played across her face as the song came from her heart through her fingertips, manifested into the sound of the ukulele. She yearned to know the story behind this song, if only to be closer to Alex and share the burden she carried.

A man's deep, rich voice blended with Alex's melody. The crowd loosened its ranks as Daniel Marcotte moved forward. The same pain etched on Alex's face was etched on his. A tear ran down Alex's cheek when he sang the words to the song. He cried too. Something heavy weighed on each of them. Their bodies sagged under its bulk.

Alex's fingers stopped moving when a sob escaped her throat. She rose to her feet and handed the ukulele to her father. "I died that day too. Why can't you see that?" she asked in a voice racked with anguish.

Daniel took the ukulele in one hand and reached for her with the other. Alex bolted from him toward the beach.

Zoe's feet moved before her brain realized it. She gained on Alex. "Wait."

Alex stopped. "I'm sorry."

"For what?" Zoe asked.

"I'm a disaster." Alex covered her face with her hands.

Zoe pulled the hands away. "What on earth are you talking about? Why say such a thing?"

Alex's face was streaked with tears. "I don't know how to be normal anymore."

"Do you want to talk about it?"

"I can't."

Zoe put her arms around the suffering woman. She'd give anything to be able to think of something comforting to say. Instead, she did the only thing that felt right. She held Alex tightly. "I'll walk with you away from here to wherever you want to go."

Alex collapsed into Zoe's embrace. She tried to say something, but the words tangled in tears.

Zoe held her tighter. "Can I ask who Jake was?"

Several moments passed. Alex stepped back and wiped her eyes. "My twin brother. He drowned in the lake when we were only fifteen."

"Oh, Alex." Zoe let out a breath. "I'm so sorry."

"All I want to do is disappear." Alex started to walk away.

Zoe caught up and grabbed an elbow. "Please don't." She wasn't usually an affectionate person. She kept a respectable distance from most people. Alex made things different. She couldn't help wanting to touch her, to keep her safe, and not let her be sad anymore.

Alex turned to face her, wiping the tears welling in her eyes. "Will you walk with me?"

"Wherever you want to go."

Alex led the way down the beach until they came to a path that turned back onto the dirt road that paralleled the lake. They walked in silence for miles along the road until coming to Bates Road, which hooked around in the direction of the Marcotte house.

Zoe didn't mind the silence. What mattered was whether she could, in some way, carry part of Alex's burden for her even if it meant doing so without words.

When they approached the well-kept, two-story saltbox house several hours later, the only light came from the porch. It angered Zoe that Daniel obviously hadn't found it important enough to wait up for his daughter. On the top step of the porch was a stack of No Trespassing signs.

Alex reached for the sticky note attached to them and read it. "I can't believe this." She handed the note to Zoe.

Zoe read the single sentence on the note that said simply, "You may close the island."

Alex sat down and patted the top step. "He's decided to protect the eagles after all."

"I'm so relieved. This is going to go a long way toward helping the eaglets be okay." Zoe joined her, close enough for their shoulders to touch. When Alex leaned into her in response, she took one of Alex's hands in her own. "What about you, though? You sure you don't want to talk about your brother or what upset you tonight?"

"I wouldn't know where to start. Besides, it hurts too much to think about it." Alex stared at the ground. "Sometimes, it feels like what happened to Jake has me by the ankles and is pulling me under. I'm trying so hard to keep my head above water."

"I'll give you a hand to help, if you'll let me."

Alex turned her hand palm up and laced her fingers with Zoe's. "You're the sweetest person I've ever met." With her free hand, she reached over and caressed Zoe's cheek." Trust me, though, it's too heavy. I don't want to burden you with it."

Concern flooded Zoe. "I care about you." Her heart felt like it was going to beat out of her chest, and her stomach churned as she argued with herself over whether to kiss Alex or not. The act of considering the matter set the ball in motion. Inertia moved her against her better judgment. She turned her body to face Alex and put a hand to the side of Alex's face.

Alex complied with Zoe's gentle pressure to turn her head so they faced each other.

Zoe swallowed back nervousness and touched her lips to Alex's, letting it happen before she could stop herself.

Alex put a hand to the back of Zoe's head and parted her lips so that their tongues came together in a long, slow kiss.

Heat flared through Zoe's body, and her limbs tingled. She rubbed Alex's back and ached to caress every inch of her body. She savored the feel and taste of her.

Alex pulled back and gazed at her with an unreadable expression.

"I hope you don't mind that I kissed you," Zoe said.

"I wanted you to kiss me the second I saw you tonight." Alex sighed when she filled her fingers with Zoe's hair. "You make me feel safe."

Zoe leaned into Alex and embraced her. The sound of heavy footsteps coming down the stairs on the other side of the front door tore them apart.

The door swung open. Daniel stood in the doorway. "I see that you've found the No Trespassing signs, Alex." He gave Zoe a nasty look. "There are buoys in the barn as well. You'll need them if you plan to cordon off the island. You should set them in the morning before I change my mind about the whole thing. Now that I know you're home, I'm going to bed." He turned and slammed the door behind him.

Zoe jumped at the bang. A thick, impenetrable wall shot up between her and Alex when the door shut. She could feel the barrier as surely as the wooden step beneath her backside.

Alex stood. "Thank you for walking me home tonight. I'll be happy to help with the signs and buoys tomorrow, but only after my run in the morning. If that's too late, I can get one of the camp's maintenance men to help instead."

"No. I'd rather spend the time with you," Zoe said when she stood.

"Okay, but we'll have to work fast. I have lots of things to do with Claire tomorrow for the camp. I'll meet you in the morning down by the beach, around seven." Alex took several steps to the door, stopped at the landing, and turned. "Good night, Zoe. Again, thank you for walking with me." She disappeared inside the house.

Zoe felt her heart go with her. *Good night.*

# Chapter 15

Early the next morning, Zoe laid her kayak paddle across the cockpit of her boat. As she floated near shore waiting for Alex, she leaned against the backrest, lifted her face to the warm sun, and searched the blue sky for any sign of the eagles.

Fatigue from lack of sleep made her limbs heavy. She'd been up all night worrying about Alex and remembering the feel of her lips on Alex's when she'd kissed her. She never expected she'd fall for someone so quickly. *It was only a kiss, Kimball.*

The sweetness that came from feeling something for another person was tempered by the fact that Alex's heart was surrounded by a tangled thicket almost impossible to penetrate. Almost. Zoe didn't give up easily.

Not a hint of breeze wafted over the lake to cool her skin. The early summer heat wave that had settled over Maine became more brutal each day. She hoped the eaglets were staying cool.

Terry and Dac had grown considerably over the past several weeks. They were already venturing out onto the edge of the nest to spread their wings, which was why she was so relieved that Mr. Marcotte had agreed to close the island.

She surveyed the lake's glassy surface. A handful of fishing boats sat as motionless as statues on the shimmering horizon. The calm could be deceiving. A stiff wind blowing east off Mount Washington could kick up the water into a choppy tizzy with two- to four-foot waves in no time. The weather forecast for the day predicted continued dry, hot weather with the possibility of blustery winds coming in by afternoon. For now, tranquility reigned.

A few of the camp's early morning risers bustled around the picnic tables. Miniature humans with sleepy faces stumbled around like little zombies, probably in search of breakfast.

A young girl sat alone in the sand on the shore not far from where Zoe floated. The girl's blonde mop of hair stuck out in different directions. The clothes she wore hung off of her body and appeared to have seen better days. The girl folded her arms on her knees and rested her chin on them. A frown covered her face. It looked like she'd been crying.

Zoe picked up her paddle and took a couple of quick, efficient strokes toward shore. She landed her boat on the sand, got out, and sat down next to the little girl. "Hi, I'm Zoe. What's your name?" No response came, so she leaned forward to peer at the girl's face. "You okay?"

Tears spilled down the girl's cheeks at the question. She buried her head in her folded arms.

"Do you miss home, or is something else wrong?" Zoe asked.

"I hate it here."

"Isn't there a lot of fun stuff to do here?" Zoe asked. "I bet if you played with the other kids, the time would fly by and you'd be home before you know it. I'll bet you'd even like it here if you did."

"They won't play with me because they hate me," the little girl mumbled into her arms.

"Why do you think that?"

"They laughed at my clothes and shoes." The girl stretched out a leg and pointed at her tiny foot. She wore a pair of old sandals at least a size too big. The tops of her little toes were hidden beneath the strap that was supposed to cover the top of her foot just below them. "My mom spent all our extra money so I could come here. We went to the thrift shop to get me some clothes. This is all they had. The other kids said my shoes are stupid. I'm sick of everyone making fun of me. I wish I was either like them or invisible so they would leave me alone."

*Jerky brats.* This was why Zoe preferred the company of wildlife to people. Mean kids often grew up to be cruel adults. There were way too many abusive people in the world who made it a sport to prey on the weak. She thought about giving the kids gathered at the picnic table a piece of her mind, but having an adult stick up for her would probably make things worse for the little girl.

"You haven't told me your name yet," she said.

"I'm Michelle."

Zoe placed her palms on the sand slightly behind her butt and leaned on her arms. "I know it's hard, but be glad you're different. Being different means you're special. It sounds like you have an awesome mom who loves you very much." She stretched out her legs in front of her and crossed them at the ankles. "I don't fit in, either, and I actually like it that way. There are lots of things about me that people don't understand."

"Like what?" Michelle asked.

"Look how short my legs are." Zoe jutted her chin in the direction of her feet. "I'm shorter than every grown-up I know. When I was your age, bigger kids liked to beat me up just because I was smaller than them. I always got picked on and laughed at for being little."

"What did you do to stop them?"

"I have a question before I tell you."

"Okay."

"Do you like Kool-Aid?"

"Yeah."

"Do you ever get to make it yourself?"

"My mom lets me sometimes."

"I'll bet when she does, you add a lot less water than you're supposed to."

"How did you know?" Michelle asked.

"That's what I used to do too," Zoe said. "It tastes so much better that way. Do you know why?"

"It's sweeter because it's more concen... concentrated? We learned about that in science class."

Zoe laughed. "That's exactly right, and it's also the way it is with me. When those kids started to make fun of me, I told them I wasn't short, I was concentrated, so they'd better watch out. They stopped after that because they weren't smart like you. They didn't know what concentrated meant, so it scared them and they left me alone."

"Really?"

"Yeah. I could climb trees much better than other kids. They were too big and heavy to drag themselves up into the branches. But I could do it easily. I'll bet there are lots of things you can do that they can't. You're a smart kid. I can tell." Zoe heard someone walking toward them in the sand behind her. She didn't have to guess who it was. She felt Alex near. She looked over her shoulder and smiled. Time and her early morning run must've taken the edge off of last night. Alex seemed more relaxed.

"Good morning." Alex sat down next to Michelle. "Kool-Aid?" She chuckled.

Zoe sat up straight and brushed the sand from her hands. "You caught that?"

Alex grinned. "I did, and I couldn't agree more. Concentrated is a perfect way to describe you." She squeezed Michelle's shoulder. "Do you remember the story we told you kids about the wildlife biologist who climbed the tree to save the baby eagle from the fire?" she asked.

"Yeah, that was so cool."

Alex looked at Zoe and raised an eyebrow. "Do you mind?"

Zoe winked at Alex. She reached out to shake Michelle's hand. "That was me. And I wouldn't have been able to do it without these short legs of mine."

"No way!" Michelle's eyes widened in excitement. "You were like Spider-Man that day. They showed you on the news. I saw the whole thing."

"I prefer to think of myself more as Spider-Woman than Spider-Man," Zoe said. "Since I think you're really special, Michelle, I want this to be our secret, okay?"

Michelle nodded. "Cool! Can I tell my mom, though? She'd be amazed that I got to meet a real life Spider-Woman who saved a baby eagle."

"Sure, but only your mom. Remember, superheroes don't like their real identities to be known. Nobody was ever supposed to know Clark Kent was Superman."

Alex stood up and ruffled Michelle's hair. "Why don't you go get some breakfast now, kiddo? Zoe and I have some work to do out on the lake."

Michelle jumped to her feet and threw her arms around Zoe's shoulders. "Nice to meet you, Spider-Woman. I promise not to tell anyone it's you." She skipped away toward breakfast, a kid on top of the world.

Alex watched her go and turned to Zoe. "One of the camp's few low-income kids. She'll eat better in the next couple of weeks than she probably will the rest of the year. It's a crime that any kid in this country goes hungry, and it's a little unfortunate for us."

"What is?" Zoe got to her feet and brushed the sand from her bottom.

"James says if we close the island, there will be less money to bring low-income kids here on scholarships. As much as I want the eagles to survive, I hope it's not true."

"I work for the government. Trust me. People like to make excuses all the time about why wildlife should suffer in order to save this or that. If you ask me, it's possible to do both if we didn't spend money on so much nonsense. Maybe the camp needs a more creative manager who has both interests at heart."

Alex seemed to contemplate Zoe's words. She glanced away and back to her. "Yeah, maybe it does." She gave her a long look. "You have a way with kids for someone who doesn't think she likes them. Thanks for taking the time to help make Michelle feel better."

Zoe smiled. "She and I are kindred spirits. I remember what it felt like to be bullied as a child."

"You and I must be kindred spirits too."

"Why is that?" Zoe asked.

Alex stared out at the lake. "I can't stand bullies. They thrive on making us afraid." She turned to her. "But last night, you made me feel safe for the first time in so long. Thank you for that."

"Anytime you need company or someone to talk to, I hope you know you can ask me."

"You really are sort of like a superhero," Alex teased.

Zoe felt her cheeks flush. Her sunglasses hung around her neck. She slid them over her eyes to hide her expression. "And you're going to be my trusty sidekick today like the Girl Wonder. Together, we'll shut Eagle Island down to all those evildoers."

Alex chuckled. "Can I wear black spandex?"

"Oh, my God." Zoe shook her head and laughed. *I'd love to see that.* "You can wear anything you like."

"You're going to be an easy superhero boss to work for."

Zoe hadn't noticed the breeze starting to kick up until that moment. Little ripples crawled across the lake's surface. "My first order is going to be that we get out there quick to get these signs posted. The wind is going to get progressively stronger. We should get your kayak in the water now."

"If you don't mind, I thought we'd take one of my father's boats instead to set the buoys. That's why I grabbed the keys. I thought it would be faster. Besides, if we're going to set buoys, we'll need cinderblocks. I assumed you'd want to do that, so I had a couple of counselors help me load them into the boat. And I stenciled the buoys with a warning this morning before my run. We're ready to go."

"You've thought of everything, Girl Wonder." Zoe pulled her kayak farther up onto shore and secured her paddle inside the cockpit.

"If you get to be Spider-Woman, I want to be Batwoman." Alex pouted.

"You know she's gay, don't you? By the way, just to be clear, my version of Spider-Woman isn't the same as the Spider-Woman in the Marvel comic strip. I have no desire to exude pheromones that attract men."

Alex laughed. "Well, I get that. The reason I chose Batwoman is because she's gay." She turned and headed toward the boat.

*A gorgeous lesbian superhero with a broken heart.* "You can be anyone you want to be." Zoe unlashed her life jacket from the bow of her kayak and called after Alex, "Feel free to wear spandex too." The sound of Alex's laughter reminded Zoe of the melodies sung by songbirds in springtime. She could listen to it forever and never grow tired of it.

# Chapter 16

Alex gave the four-foot-long stake a final pound into the ground with her hammer. She wiggled the stake to make sure it was secure and twisted it slightly so the No Trespassing sign attached to it was clearly visible to anyone who might consider landing on the beach. "That's the last of the signs. Do you want to set the buoys now?"

"Look at this first." Zoe held up a long white feather.

"An eagle's tail feather?" Alex asked.

"Yeah." Zoe handed her the feather. "Beautiful, isn't it?"

Alex brushed her fingers along its length. "I still can't believe eagles are nesting on this island. It's incredible."

Zoe put her hand out. "I'd better put that back where I found it."

"You're not going to let me keep it?"

"It's illegal to have eagle feathers without a permit. I can't let you keep it."

"You're such a good Eagle Scout. I like that about you." Alex swept her hand once more along the feather's wispy edges. "I wouldn't want either of us to get into trouble. Thanks for at least showing it to me." She returned the feather to Zoe. "This may sound hokey, but the other day when I helped band the eaglet, I made eye contact with it, and I felt like it could see right through me. Like it knew exactly what I was thinking."

Zoe tucked the feather out of sight under a thicket of sweet fern bushes. "That's not hokey at all. Animals absolutely communicate. They just don't use words like we do. If we paid more attention to them, we'd understand just how much they have to say."

As if on cue, the eaglets started to chirp.

Zoe pointed toward the nest. "What they're saying now is that their bellies are empty. They're calling the parents to bring them some food. We should probably get off the island and set the buoys so we don't prevent Mom and Dad from bringing their breakfast."

Alex raised her eyes to the nest. A dark gray head peeked over the edge and squeaked at her. "Hello, my little friend," she whispered.

She placed the hammer she'd used to secure the signs back into the toolbox. "Let's get those buoys into the water."

She and Zoe pushed the boat off the sand and climbed in over the bow. Alex turned the key and the engine came to life. She slowly backed the boat away from the island and headed toward the front side where boaters would have the best view of the nest and, therefore, be most likely to want to get close. The wind kicked what had been ripples on the lake into whitecaps. The boat bobbed over and down into the troughs of the building waves.

Alex pointed at one of the buoys tied to a cinderblock. "Decide where you want the buoy to float. Toss the cinderblock in at that point, and I'll motor away from it so the line doesn't tangle."

"Got it." Zoe pointed to a spot on the lake. "There."

She hoisted the block over the side of the boat. It sank quickly as the line attached to it followed. When it came to rest on the bottom, the red buoy floated above it about two hundred feet from shore. The words painted in black read, "Keep Out, Wildlife Protection Area."

Zoe reached for a second cinderblock as Alex continued to navigate the boat along a track in line with the first buoy. She tossed the block over the side. "That's perfect, Alex. One more to go."

Alex glanced up as Zoe heaved the last block over the side and into the water. One of the eagle parents soared toward the nest. A large fish wriggled in the death grip of its talons. The eagle flapped its wings a couple of times, spread them wide, and glided into the nest. Two dark heads bobbled above the rim as the eagle tore into the fish. The eaglets clamored and shoved against each other for the food in their parent's beak. "Their bellies should be full after that," she said.

"Hopefully, both of their bellies," Zoe remarked.

"Why wouldn't they be? That's an enormous fish."

"True, but the thing about eaglets is that they can be brutal to each other while their parents turn a blind eye. It's survival of the fittest in the harshest form. Eagle parents go to great lengths to protect their babies from predators, but they don't lift a talon, so to speak, to protect them from each other. The larger eaglets tend to peck at and horde food from the smaller ones. Sometimes they even manage to push a sibling out of the nest. The little guys have to be strong-willed if they want to survive."

Two siblings struggling against each other to live conjured the ghost of Alex's brother. She tried to blink away the memory of his face. Her brother's death surged forward from the depths of her hidden recollections. His eyes were wide and his mouth contorted in a scream muted by the water. A silent scream only she could hear. It wailed inside the walls of her mind with a deafening echo. The switch to her anxiety had been flipped.

The boat slammed into the trough of a huge wave as it rolled underneath them and jostled Alex away from the controls. She regained her footing and tightened her grip on the steering wheel to catch her balance. "Damn it."

Her pulse raced and the palms of her hands went wet—not from water splashed into the boat, but from fear. Sweat rolled from her temples down the sides of her neck. Goosebumps broke out over her body. She wrapped her arms around herself and sank to the floor of the boat. Like her brother, she was suffocating. The rational part of her brain spoke calmly, reminding her that this was an anxiety attack and she had the power to control it if she could only catch her breath. The other part of her brain drove her toward chaos, pulling her into a place where she couldn't think, a state of emotional anarchy that terrified and consumed her.

A voice called her name. She closed her eyes and gulped for air. Her body trembled. The unfamiliar voice called her name again. She glanced around for a means of escape.

"Alex... what's the matter?" A hand shook her by the shoulder.

Alex realized the voice belonged to Zoe. She fought to escape from the darkness inside herself, but it pulled at her.

Zoe's voice cut through again. "Talk to me. What's happening, Alex?"

Alex felt Zoe's grip tighten on her shoulders. The physical connection created a lifeline she could grab. She concentrated on taking slow, regular breaths. Embarrassment moved in to replace the paralyzing terror. At least it meant she was coming back into the present.

She got to her feet and moved away from Zoe as the wind dragged the boat too fast toward the rocks around the island. She put her hands to her face and rubbed her eyes. "I'm so sorry," she whispered. She reached for the throttle and threw the boat into reverse.

Zoe gripped her elbow. "Tell me what just happened."

Alex pulled away. "Let it go."

"I don't want to let it go."

"Why does it matter to you? The island is closed to trespassers, and I'm taking you back to shore. There was no harm done. That's all you should be concerned with." The customary anger that always followed an anxiety attack bubbled and frothed in Alex's belly. It was wrong to be angry at Zoe, but she couldn't help feeling furious at everyone and everything. Anger was the means by which she could cap her fear and gain control over it.

"It matters because I care about you," Zoe said.

"Don't."

"Why are you so angry?"

Alex ignored her and drove the boat faster toward the camp. The speed caused the boat to bounce hard in the troughs of the waves. She couldn't restrain her bad behavior even though she recognized it as clear as day. She purposely let the boat glide up on shore too quickly. The boat jerked to a stop on the sandy beach in front of the camp.

"I prefer anger to fear," Alex said.

"Why do you have to feel either?" Zoe paused. "They're both toxic."

Alex clenched her jaw. "That's all I've known since my brother died." She stepped over the bow. The realization that she could've possibly gotten them both into trouble out on the water while she had a panic attack sobered her. "I shouldn't have put you in harm's way. I promise it won't happen again." She grabbed her backpack and slid the boat key into the pocket of her shorts. "I have things to do. I'll see you later."

Zoe followed her out of the boat and stepped into her path. "You checked out while operating a boat in some pretty deep water. The depth on the back side of that island drops off to over two hundred feet."

"You think I don't know that?"

"It wasn't me I was worried about." Zoe put her hands on her hips. "I can swim fine. I was never in any danger. But you—"

"Stop." Alex's growing need to have someone close nearly broke her resolve, and not just someone at that, but Zoe. "Please, don't say anything. I don't know what to do with whatever it is you might say. I can't handle anymore."

She stormed away, propelled by something other than fear that she couldn't quite articulate. Whatever she felt had its genesis in Zoe.

# Chapter 17

A sharp pain sliced into Alex's side beneath her ribs. Her legs burned. The steeper the hill became, the harder she pushed her body. The fact that it took longer and more effort than usual to wash away her anxiety suggested only one option. If she wanted to keep her sanity, she needed to get as far from Maine as possible, sooner rather than later. The panic attack she'd had the day before in the boat with Zoe was all the evidence she needed to know that coming back to Maine had been a huge mistake. She was running on fumes.

Instead of continuing toward the camp, she turned right onto Old Town Road. A little farther and she saw Hiccup parked in front of the library on the right-hand side.

The Town Hall's parking lot next door was filled with cars and trucks with out-of-town license plates. Most likely they were the many seasonal residents coming to pick up their transfer station stickers and fishing licenses. The Town of Glasgow had always been the summer place of escape for city people who worked too hard during the week and craved its easy peace and quiet on the weekends and vacations. Ironically, in so many fleeting moments since she'd been back, Alex had felt that way too, only to have her peace crushed by the awful memories haunting her.

She slowed to a walk to catch her breath. A rotund, orange tabby cat guarded the library entrance. It mewed at her when she scratched the back of its ear. "Hello, Sweet Pea," she said. "Where can I find Sally?" The cat purred and rubbed against her leg.

Sally was pouring a cup of coffee when Alex entered the library. Buddy was sleeping on his bed in a corner of the room while seven puppies played in the entryway, jumping over each other. One rolled in dirt from a potted plant tipped over on the floor, and another gnawed on a book.

Alex couldn't help laughing at the puppies, who seemed content in Sally's care. "I sure hope that isn't a book that gets checked out regularly."

"Hello, darling. A little spilled dirt, some puppy slobber, and frayed edges won't hurt a thing." Sally grinned as she replaced the pot in the coffeemaker.

Alex bent down and scratched the puppies that were eager for attention. "They all have such big feet. I guess they'll be big dogs when they grow up."

Sally joined in the scratching and patting of the puppies. "They're such irresistible darlings. Doc Parsons thinks they're part German Shepherd and Lab, so they'll certainly fill a lap and then some once they're grown." She straightened and smoothed her cotton dress with its big yellow sunflowers. "To what do I owe this lovely surprise? I hope you've come to talk about what happened at the dance the other night. You've been scarce since then."

Alex stepped over the puppies and into the room. "If you have a minute, I need to talk to you."

"Sure, honey. What's on your mind?"

"I'm going back to California in the next couple of days, as soon as I'm able to book a flight."

Sally's expression became serious. "I think we're going to need more than a minute. Let me pour you a cup of coffee too. We'll go sit out on the bench where it's comfortable to chat." She took a cup from the rack next to the coffeemaker and filled it. "A little cream and sugar?"

"Just cream, thanks. I gave up sugar when I came to the realization that I'd inherited my mother's anxiety. It's the one thing she and I have in common. Sugar only makes it worse."

Sally tipped some cream into the cup and handed it to her. "Come, let's go sit in the sun. Let's go, darlings," she said to the puppies, clapping her hands. The puppies dutifully lined up behind her. Buddy briefly lifted his head, but made no move to join them.

Sally laughed. "I suppose Buddy could use a few minutes of peace and quiet." She retrieved the cup of coffee she had poured for herself.

Alex followed Sally and her canine crew out into the perennial garden behind the library. A rustic stone walkway snaked through lupines in full bloom to a mahogany bench nestled among the flowers. "Your garden is as beautiful as always."

"I can't take any of the credit. Betty Raines still volunteers to do all the gardening here." Sally sipped her coffee. "You'd never know it's been so hot and dry outside. Betty has the greenest thumb in Maine. Her lupines are the loveliest you'll find south of the Androscoggin River."

"She must be in her nineties now, right?" Alex asked.

"The old girl turned ninety-three this past January."

"It's great that she's still getting out and volunteering."

"Her great-great grandson brings her over every few days to weed and water. He sticks around and does the heavy lifting for her. He's a good boy. Keeping busy is what helps Betty stay on her feet after all these years. She lives for her gardens in summer." Sally patted Alex's knee. "Now, you didn't come here to talk about flowers. What's this business about leaving so soon?"

Alex set her coffee cup on the wicker table next to the bench. She fiddled with the bottom hem of her shorts. "I had a bad anxiety attack yesterday. I lost it out on the lake while I was in a boat. The wind kicked up near the island." She breathed in deeply. "It brought back the night that Jake died. I couldn't help thinking about him going under. His face was all I could see."

"Instead of rushing off, is there someone you've been seeing back in California who you could call? I remember that you used to be able to call Dr. Kestler while you were away at school whenever you needed to talk things through."

"I was seeing a therapist for a while. But I've been so much better the last year or so that I stopped going. Exercise, diet, and distance from Maine have done wonders to keep the anxiety at bay. But being here is throwing it all right back in my face, and I can't handle it. That's why I need to get out."

"We haven't spent much time talking about my recollections of the day those fires burned this town almost to the ground all those years ago. A lot of people lost everything in the blaze. They rebuilt and went on with their lives, but for some the memories got too heavy to carry around after a while. Their hearts gave out under the weight, and they were forced to deal with what happened, one way or the other."

Sally looked at her. "Alex, darlin', Jake's death was even bigger than that fire. One of these days, you're going to have to stop running long enough to sort it through once and for all. Maybe you could call over to the Portland Hospital where you were hospitalized after your breakdown and find out if Dr. Kestler is available to talk to. I'm sure she'd be happy to see you after all this time."

"I'm not sure I want to talk about it again, even with Dr. Kestler. It's like being turned inside out, having to rehash things. I don't think I have it in me. All I want to do is leave so I don't have to."

"I know, honey. That was an awful time. Do me a favor, though. Why don't you take a few days to think about it and let things calm down first? Then decide whether to go back to California now, or at the end of the summer. Make sure it's the right thing to do."

"Zoe was with me in the boat the other day. I almost let us crash into rocks. It's one thing if I get hurt, but what if something bad happened to Zoe because of me?" Alex slumped against the back of the bench. "I completely lost it. I'd never forgive myself if I hurt her."

"You care about her, don't you? I could see that at the dance."

"I do, which is another reason I have to leave. I don't want to be a source of hurt for her. I know myself. It'll happen, and I won't be able to stop it. The best place for me is alone where my dysfunction can't hurt anyone else, especially Zoe."

"You want to go back to your cave where no one knows your history." Sally hesitated. "I'm not sure running away to California is going to solve anything. Your father told me you still haven't gone to see your mother yet, and here you are, planning to leave."

"Even if I did stay, I'm still not sure I'd go see her."

"Why is that?"

"Because I don't feel anything for her anymore. The mother I knew died when Jake died. The woman in that hospital room isn't someone I even care to know. So why bother?"

Sally was quiet for several moments before answering. "At my age, I know a lot about what it's like when people in your life die. When they go, feelings you can't imagine emerge from someplace deep down, even when it's a person you didn't think you had any feelings for. Your mother is going to die soon. That much is certain. You may not think so now, but you will feel something when that happens. My advice is to deal with her now while you still have a chance to tell her how you feel. It may end up being the most important thing you need to do to resolve things so you can go on with your life. You have to finally deal with this, Alex."

"I've been dealing with it my entire adult life. I'm just so exhausted."

"I know, sweetheart," Sally said. "Maybe that's why it's time to try something different so you can put it away for good. Think about my library attic. It's filled with the history of this town, all neatly tucked away in boxes. Every now and then, the boxes rattle at me and I find myself opening them and going through their contents. I get rid of the stuff that has no value and keep the rest neatly organized. That's how it is with life. If you don't get rid of stuff that's no good, you end up carrying it around unnecessarily. All it gets you is weighed down."

"I don't know if I'm even able to be in the same room with my mother, let alone resolve things. Please try to understand."

"Here's what I see. You were so young when your brother died. It was tragic and it never should've happened. You haven't let him go because you haven't found a way to forgive your parents. In particular, your mother."

A poisonous rage boiled in the pit of Alex's stomach at the thought. "She doesn't deserve my forgiveness." She balled her hands into fists. "I've tried so hard to feel something for her other than... I can't even say the word."

"Maybe you can't because deep down, you don't really feel that way." Sally put an arm around her. "Keep in mind, forgiveness isn't about the people who've caused the harm. Sometimes, we have to find a way to forgive the unforgivable in order to free ourselves. Sweetheart, no child should ever have to endure what you did. Unfortunately, parents are flawed human beings too and sometimes they do stupid, awful things. Stay home awhile. Take the time to sort it all out so you can finally leave what happened behind."

Alex rested her head on Sally's shoulder. "I wish I could go home, but I don't know where that is anymore. Glasgow was always home. Before Jake died, I never imagined that I'd ever leave. I loved it here." She sighed. "I wanted to feel that way again, especially being here in summer. The sweetest times of my life were spent here, playing on the lake in the sun." She closed her eyes. "Sometimes, I'm so lonely. All I can think to do is run."

"The trouble with running is that one of these days, you won't be able to run fast enough. The stuff that rattles around inside of us grows relentless. It'll consume you eventually if you let it. I wonder if you haven't given yourself the time to mourn your loss."

The statement didn't make sense. "I've mourned Jake's loss every day since he died."

"I'm not talking about Jake, honey." Sally pointed a finger at her heart. "You haven't mourned the hurt and betrayed little girl inside you. Find her, and let her go."

Alex didn't want to find her. She feared being reacquainted with that carefree, hopeful child and reliving the pain of seeing her crushed by those she loved most. The memory would be too unbearable. Better to leave her buried beneath the rubble.

Anxiety-inducing hormones she'd inherited from her mother, combined with being a person so lost, covered her in a blanket of concrete. She could barely move, let alone breathe. *I should've gone down with Jake that night.* The words hammered at her soul. Words she would never say aloud to anyone.

# Chapter 18

Later that afternoon, Alex sat at the desk in her father's study with the wireless phone to her ear. It would've been easier to make airline reservations online, but she hoped that if she spoke to someone in person, they might be able to find her a cheaper flight.

"No, I understand that the prices are a lot higher since I'm trying to fly out tomorrow morning. Yes, I'd like to go ahead and book it. Please use the same credit card you have on file." She scribbled down the flight information in a notebook. "Sure, two hours before. Thank you for trying to help with the price of the ticket. Good-bye." She pushed the Off button and set the phone in its cradle.

Daniel cleared his throat.

Alex jumped. "Hi, Dad."

He stood in the doorway. "The other night, you played the ukulele beautifully at the dance. I wish you hadn't run off like you did. We were all having such a good time. The dance pretty much came to an end after that."

It was typical of her father to ignore her pain only to focus on the camp instead. "I couldn't help it. I miss Jake so much, especially being here. That song was for him."

"You and Zoe did a good job of setting the buoys and No Trespassing signs. I had Chuck go over to make sure the buoys are still secure."

"Why do you always change the subject when it comes to Jake?"

"Why do you have to make everything about him? Why can't you move on? Get on with life already."

Alex considered trying to explain to him how she felt, but it would be futile. He didn't want to think, let alone talk, about Jake. What would be the point? "Thank you for letting us close the island. I really want the eaglets to make it, both of them."

He stared out the window behind her for several long moments. "I heard you on the phone. Are you going somewhere?"

She hadn't had time to figure out how she was going to tell him she was leaving. Unfortunately, he had her cornered, and she had no choice but to just do it. "Yes, home... to California." Alex let out a breath. "Tomorrow morning."

His hands trembled, and he shoved them into his pockets. "How can you do this to me and your mother? She's going to die. You'll never see her again." His disappointment bored into her. "This is your home." His jaw clenched.

"No, it isn't."

"We always told you kids you'd have a home to come to. Why can't you see that?"

Alex's mouth dropped open in disbelief. "Are you kidding me? Don't you remember the stipulations Mom placed on me and Jake so we could stay in this so-called home?"

"Your mother was worried about both of you. She was only trying to protect you." His voice filled with anger. "She did the best she could for you and Jake."

"No, she did the best she could for herself." Alex sighed in disgust and let the clean, untainted part of her soul be covered by the poison in her heart. Since she couldn't slam her fists against her father's chest, she'd let her words do it for her. "You want to know what Mom did? I'll tell you. It's because of her that Jake died. In fact, she might as well have been the one who killed him with the things she said. And you stood by and let it happen."

Alex stood and shoved her chair away from the desk. Her mother's hurtful rage reflected inside herself, and it made her feel sick. Her hands trembled. She held them up and considered them. These were her mother's hands. She hated herself as much as she was sure her mother hated her. An icy wind blew into her soul and froze any last remnants of warmth she may have felt for her parents. Now that she said these things to her father, one more piece of her was dead along with Jake.

Daniel stood as stunned as if she'd slapped him across the face. He seemed to wither around the edges. "We did everything for you kids." He spoke quietly and deliberately. A mucky quagmire of emotions played across his face. His eyes welled with tears, and his words didn't match his expression. "Jake turned out to be a coward, and you're nothing but selfish. You're right. This isn't your home anymore. I don't want you sleeping in this house tonight. You're welcome to stay in the staff quarters. But then I want you out for good."

His Adam's apple slid along his frail, skinny neck after the hurtful words left his mouth. It had the effect of dotting the i's and crossing the t's of what he'd said. He left the room without saying more.

Alex hung her head and fought for slow, deep breaths. The day she'd been waiting for had finally arrived. She'd expected that if she ever got the nerve to speak the truth to her father, she'd be free from the pain. It only hurt worse, though. He had it coming, but the inside of her mouth tasted vile.

Cold resolve settled over her. She sat back down to write Zoe a letter. The better part of her wanted to go find Zoe to say good-bye in person. She deserved that much. Unfortunately, her better self was silenced by the mean, cowardly person hell-bent on running away. Besides, if her leaving bruised Zoe, she didn't want to witness it.

Under her breath, she said, "I wish things could be different."

Thinking about Zoe made her ache. In such a short time, her heart had begun to feel things for her. Did Zoe feel the same? She tapped the pen on the paper and finally set it down on the desk. She'd write the letter later this afternoon. Even though she couldn't say good-bye to Zoe in person, she did want to see her one last time to apologize for the way she'd acted on the boat.

After she went upstairs and packed her belongings, she dropped them off in the staff quarters. There was an available room a couple of doors down from Zoe's. She left her things, locked the door behind her, and knocked on Zoe's door. Of course, she wasn't there. It was late afternoon, and she was probably out on the lake studying the eagles.

Alex went to the boathouse and launched her kayak. As she neared the island, the tip of a green kayak edged out from behind it.

Zoe waved. "Hey. I'm glad to see you. I've been worried sick since I last saw you." She picked up the pace of her strokes and slid her boat next to Alex's. "You okay?"

Alex thawed at the sight of Zoe, who wore the outdoors in her fresh, smiling face. Her green eyes were the color of the ocean. Her short, wavy hair fell free like a wild river, not messy, but not contained either. Zoe reminded her of everything she loved about the woods, rivers, mountains, and lakes of Maine. "I'm fine. I'm really sorry for melting down like that. I shouldn't have taken it out on you. It's a good thing you were there."

"I'm glad I was too. Please, stop being sorry, though. I don't know what's behind all that's happened to you, and if you don't want to tell me, that's fine. But I wish you wouldn't push me away. I'd like to help if I can," Zoe paused. "I… I want you to know that I care about you. I'm glad we're getting to be friends."

Alex wanted nothing more than to let "Spider-Woman" save her from this *thing* she was too tired to battle anymore, but only she could save herself. The only way to do that was to flee. She refused to hurt Zoe any further by letting her get closer.

"I'm glad we got to be friends too." She tore her gaze from Zoe's and turned it toward the nest in the tree. Two dark birds stood at the edge. The smaller of the two peeped. "Hello, little one. They're getting so big." One of the parents swooped in from a nearby tree perch and landed in the nest. "One of the eaglets is bigger than his mom. And the other isn't too far away. How can that be? They're still babies."

"They're not really bigger," Zoe said. "They just look that way because their feathers are different from their parents'. They've been losing their down feathers, which are replaced by the dark ones. They'll need those to learn how to fly. Down isn't too aerodynamic."

"When will their tail and head feathers turn white?"

"Not until they're around five years old." Zoe slipped her notebook into the dry-bag clipped to the bow of her kayak. "I'm finishing up here. You interested in getting some dinner with me?"

"I'm sorry. I have some things to do this evening." Alex felt like a jerk. The next thing Zoe would get from her would be a good-bye letter. She hoped this would be the best way to hurt her least. Every second they spent together brought them closer, so this had to be the last time they saw each other. "Thank you for everything. I'm really happy I met you. I hope you know how special you are." She took a couple of strokes away before Zoe saw the tears welling in her eyes.

"Wait," Zoe said. "Is everything all right?"

"Yes. I only wanted you to know that. I'd better go." Alex continued to paddle away before her feelings for Zoe made her change her mind about leaving.

# Chapter 19

Zoe tossed and turned in and out of sleep, still angry over the letter that Alex had left under her door. Her brain kept rewinding a particular passage.

"Even though we'll probably never see each other again, meeting you is something I'll always treasure. You're more special to me than you know."

*Really?* Zoe was furious and hurt that Alex would leave without saying good-bye in person. They'd seen each other only hours ago. She punched her pillow and willed herself to stay asleep.

She sensed she was on the edge of sleep in a dream. She kept her eyes closed, squeezed the pillow, and laid her head on the massive American chestnut tree as she leaned against it. It was an ally that kept her standing upright, a partner in crime stealing the same glance at the exquisite woman who emerged naked from the lake. The woman sauntered onto the sand of the beach and moved toward her, coming to a stop within a foot of her.

The full moon's glow illuminated her milky skin. A soft summer night breeze transported the sweet scent of wildflowers growing in the meadow behind her. The fragrance moved on the wind, wafting to Zoe's brain and making her dizzy with pleasure.

A loon called to its mate across the lake. Zoe wanted to call the same song to the woman, but she couldn't muster a sound. The vision of the woman, the feel of the warm night on her skin, and the perfume of the flowers stirred Zoe's senses. Until this moment, she'd never believed she'd ever see anything else quite as beautiful as a sunrise atop a mountain.

The woman's thick, dark hair fell across her shoulders, framing her lovely breasts. Drops of water slid along her skin. She moved to within inches of Zoe.

Tears fell from the eyes of the heartbreakingly sad woman. Zoe desperately wanted to wipe them away, but her arms stayed rigid at her sides and refused to budge.

The woman closed her eyes and leaned in to kiss her. Zoe smelled lavender and felt the woman's breath. She'd have given anything for her kiss to ease the woman's grief. She wondered if she'd died in her sleep and gone to heaven and been given this chance at somehow making the woman happy.

The piercing sound of a gunshot cut through the night when their lips touched. The woman backed away and covered her ears with her hands. Terror lived in her eyes. Zoe reached for her, but a second shot caused the woman to disappear before she could touch her. An eagle screeched.

Zoe's eyes flew open. It was dark. She felt her surroundings with her hands. She wasn't in the meadow with the chestnut tree and the woman; she was in her bed at the camp. "Only a dream," she whispered, disappointed. Eagles screeched somewhere out on the lake. She blinked away sleep to focus on reality. "That wasn't part of a dream."

She scrambled out of bed and went to the window. Firecrackers and some other types of fireworks blasted away in the dark night. The eagles continued to cry and call to each other. The sounds they made left no doubt that something was terribly wrong. She listened more carefully. Two parents and one eaglet cried for each other. She listened for the second eaglet, but nothing came.

"Damn it." Zoe struggled into a pair of shorts, sports bra, and a T-shirt, and stuffed a dry-bag with some extra clothes, a blanket, and her cell phone. She stumbled out of her room into the darkened hallway, crashing into a soft body when she turned the corner. The scent of lavender clued her in as to whose embrace kept her from falling. *Alex was the woman in the dream.* "What the hell are you doing here? I thought you left." She was glad for the low light, worried that Alex would see the remnants of her flushed skin caused by the dream.

"My flight leaves this morning," Alex replied. "I had a fight with my father about it, so I slept here in the staff quarters."

Between the dream, the screeching eagles, and Alex standing with her arms around her, Zoe's patience shattered. "What the hell, Alex? You say good-bye to me in a letter, yet you're sleeping down the hall. You didn't have the courtesy to stop by while I was here?" A loud boom rattled the windows. She pushed out of Alex's embrace. "What the hell is that?"

"Someone must have potent fireworks on the island."

"That has to be illegal."

"It is. Unfortunately, the authorities look the other way as long as people fire them away from houses. That's why a lot of people do it from the island."

"Yeah, but this time it's posted against trespassing." Zoe's anger rose. "Jackasses!"

Every time a boom went off, she got angrier at whoever was on the island and at Alex's cowardly written good-bye. She couldn't do anything about Alex, but she could protect the eagles. "I'm going out there in my kayak. I'm afraid something's happened to one of the eaglets. I only hear one of them calling to the parents." She rushed past Alex.

Alex grabbed hold of her sleeve. "Why don't we call the warden's office instead? It's dark and the water's too choppy." Her strangled voice went an octave higher.

"You call. I'm not waiting around for them to get to the island. If one of the eaglets fell from the nest, it may be injured, or worse, injured and in the water."

Alex tugged harder on her sleeve. Her voice rose. "You can't take a kayak out there now."

"Well, I'm not going to swim." Zoe yanked her arm free. "I'm wasting time. Call the warden, okay? Tell them to meet me out there."

"I'm going with you," Alex said. "We'll take one of the camp's boats. It'll be faster, and they're equipped with lights. My father keeps a set of spare keys to all the boats hidden in the boathouse. We can go now."

"You're not going anywhere with me, not after what happened in the boat the other day when it was daylight out." Zoe felt the fear vibrating off Alex's body. "I can't run the risk of having to worry about you while I'm trying to take care of a frightened or injured eaglet in the dark."

"And I can't stand the thought of you out there all alone near the deepest part of the lake in a kayak with no lights."

"Why on earth would you want to go out there under these conditions? I don't understand what frightened you out on the lake. How can I be sure it won't happen again? The lake is still choppy, and it's pitch-black to boot."

"We can't get into this right now. You said we're wasting time. Trust me. I have to go with you. Worrying about you and not being able to help would be much worse." Alex took a deep breath and let it out slowly. "Please. Let me go with you."

Too much time was being wasted arguing. Zoe could use the help anyway and taking the powerboat would be a lot faster. Saying "no" to people had always come easily to her until meeting Alex. Even though her brain told her it was a bad idea to let Alex go with her, she couldn't help wanting to be with her in the little time remaining before she left Maine. "Fine, but I insist you wear a life jacket. You make zero sense to me." She took Alex's hand.

Together, they raced out of the bunkhouse and down toward the boat they'd taken out the previous day. Alex disappeared into the boathouse and returned several seconds later with a set of keys. She pulled a life jacket from where it was stowed in the aft bench seat, put it on, and pushed the boat off the sand into the water. Zoe climbed in over the bow.

Zoe fished her cell phone out of the dry-bag to call the warden's office and Rob while Alex navigated the boat toward the island. If Zoe's instincts were right and one of the eaglets had fallen from the nest, and they were lucky enough to find it still alive, they would have to get it to a veterinarian at the raptor rehab facility right away.

Alex stood rigid and gripped the steering wheel as the boat cut through the choppy waves. Whoever was on the island with the fireworks must have noticed them coming. A boat engine roared to life behind the island. Within seconds, its lights receded into the inky darkness as it raced away, causing even more chop.

"Cowardly bastards," Zoe said. "Can't they read? They probably can, but they don't give a damn about anything but themselves."

Alex didn't respond. She remained focused on keeping the boat steady.

What was racing through Alex's mind? Zoe put a hand on one of Alex's. It felt cold despite the warm night. "Slow down here. I want to check the water." She flipped on the spotlight and shined it over the upset, frothy surface of the lake. The boat bobbed and dipped in the rises and troughs of the waves while the eagles continued to cry into the night for their lost offspring.

"Zoe, I saw something. Over there near the rocks." Alex pointed.

Zoe shined the light in that direction. "This is bad." The eaglet was in the water, thrashing near the rocks. Waves pushed it under as it struggled to reach shore. "We can't get the boat near enough for me to grab it." She bent down to undo her sandal straps.

"What are you doing?" Alex asked.

"I'm going in after it. There's no other way. If I don't, it'll drown."

Alex looked from her to the struggling eaglet, flapping its wings in vain. She put her hands to her face. "You'll be smashed against the rocks by the waves."

Zoe grabbed Alex's wrists and moved her hands away from her face to look her in the eyes. "You said you'd be all right. Now you have to be. I need you to keep this boat steady so I can get that eaglet and bring it back on board." She kicked off her sandals and let go of Alex.

"Okay." Alex breathed in deep and let out her breath slowly.

"Keep your head. I need you, and so does that eaglet." Zoe pulled off her T-shirt. Clad in only shorts and a sports bra, she dove into the dark water.

The water was chilly at first, but because of so many recent hot days, the lake was fairly warm. The current around the island from the chopping waves pulled at her. She took in a lungful of air, dove underneath the waves, and swam hard in the eaglet's direction.

She wasn't sure what was more dangerous, climbing a burning tree or diving into a wild and deep lake in pitch-blackness with the only person who could help her on the verge of an anxiety attack.

When she surfaced, she looked toward the boat. It bobbed up and down in the waves, but it held a steady position with the bow pointed in her direction. She squinted into the sudden brightness of the spotlight. Alex was managing to keep the boat in position while illuminating the area with the light.

Zoe lifted a hand and gave her a thumbs-up. "Good girl, Alex," she said under her breath.

Between waves, Zoe scanned the water near the rocks. She finally saw the eaglet in the trough of a wave that must have pushed it under. The young bird had lost most of its fight. It floated, gasping for breath, its feathers splayed at odd angles.

She swam to it. When she reached it, a wave slammed her into the rocks. The skin of her right shoulder scraped against rough granite. The burn of the water against raw flesh was instantaneous. She had to get away from these rocks soon, or she'd put herself and Alex in harm's way. She suspected that despite Alex's fear, she'd try to save her.

Zoe reached for the eaglet and secured its wings against its body to keep it from struggling. She tucked the eaglet under an arm and rolled over onto her back. She kicked and pulled with her free arm toward the boat, using every ounce of energy she had against the waves.

Alex's hands trembled. Her knuckles went white with the death grip she kept on the boat's controls. *Breathe.* She closed her eyes, and forced them open just as quickly. *Don't lose sight of her.*

Zoe made slow progress. Alex had to stay focused on the position of the boat. She had to keep her breathing even. She needed to illuminate Zoe's path. These actions kept her mind occupied. She couldn't allow any room for fear. Not for a second. She was not going to let her anxiety hurt Zoe. She'd give into it after Zoe was safe. Eventually, it would wear her down. It always did. But not yet.

Waves continued to wash over Zoe and the eaglet. Her struggle against the unrelenting water slowed.

"Come on, Zoe." Alex squeezed the wheel tighter. Irrational thoughts tried to force their way into her thinking. *You could jump in after her.* "That would be stupid."

A tall, rolling wave pushed the boat sideways. Alex gave the throttle some gas. She maneuvered the boat so Zoe would reach the stern first. The small ladder would be easier to use. She fought to aim the floodlight at Zoe the entire time. Seeing her coming closer and closer helped Alex hang on to her fragile rationality.

When Zoe was only a couple of feet from the boat, Alex cut the engine. She left the wheel to shine the light on the ladder. "Hurry, Zoe," she shouted.

Without power, the back end of the boat started to drift around. Alex leaned over the side as far as she could to reach Zoe's outstretched hand. Finally, their fingers made contact.

Zoe yelled something. A wave splashed over her. Its force pulled her away from the boat. Alex nearly lost her.

"No." Alex leaned farther out, and her weight shifted too far over the side. With one hand grasping the boat's gunwale, she lunged. The fingers of her other hand closed around Zoe's wrist. She yanked her hard toward the boat. Adrenaline coursed through her veins. She had spent most of her adult life doped up on the stuff. At least now it might be useful.

"Put your feet on the ladder. I'll pull you up!" Alex yelled. She took a quick peek over her shoulder at the direction of the boat's drift. They were headed toward the rocks. "Now!"

Zoe coughed and breathed hard. "Pull me in. I'm ready." She adjusted her grip on the eaglet.

Using both hands, Alex easily hoisted Zoe up the steps and over the edge of the boat. Although Zoe was small, her body was pure muscle and bone. She had expected that getting her into the boat would take more effort. Adrenaline really did give a person super strength.

"Geez, Alex." Zoe panted as she caught her breath. "You nearly... ripped my arm... out of the socket." She stumbled onto the passenger seat with both arms wrapped around the eaglet. Now that the eaglet was out of the water, it struggled against her. Despite being waterlogged, it looked enormous in Zoe's arms.

"Are you all right?" Alex's voice cracked with emotion. She grabbed the wheel, turned the key in the ignition, and threw the throttle into reverse. The boat jerked and bounced in the waves. She lost her footing but held onto the wheel.

She felt it. Anxiety. Her heart pounded against her chest. No longer kept at bay, the monster slithered from her ankles up around her whole body. All the moisture in her mouth left. She couldn't swallow. She felt faint. Looking over her shoulder, she saw Zoe struggling with the eaglet.

Zoe raised her voice over the noise from the engine and the waves. "We have to head across the lake to Windham. Not back to the camp. I'll have Rob meet us at the big marina over there."

Fear squeezed Alex's throat closed. It had been all she could do not to melt down with Zoe in the water. She stared ahead and tried to see through the black, moonless curtain of night. Just on the other side of the island was the deepest and most dangerous part of the lake. The thought of plowing through the waves to the other side petrified her. A parade of horrible "what ifs" cemented her limbs. She could barely move, let alone breathe.

"No," she said, "it's too dangerous."

"We don't have a choice if we're going to save this eaglet. There isn't enough time to drive around the lake. We have to go to Windham and have Rob meet us there. It'll take half the time. He can drive the eaglet the rest of the way to the rehab facility. It's our best shot." Zoe stood with the eaglet in her arms. It craned its head and made a strangled sound. "Grab the blanket out of my dry-bag. One way or the other, I'm taking the boat across the lake. I'm not going to let this bird die, and I need your help."

"I can't."

"Yes, you can. Look what we've already accomplished. It's only one more step."

"Please, Zoe."

"Listen to the facts, not what you're afraid of. The boat has lights, and it's built for a wild lake like Sebago. On top of that, you know its nooks and crannies like the back of your hand. Going across it doesn't have to be a big deal. We'll do it together. I promise we'll be fine. It's the eaglet I'm worried about."

That noxious, menacing voice in Alex's head, the voice that turned even the most benign scenario into a traumatic event, rattled in her ears. It mocked her that this was where her brother had died. Where she could die. Where Zoe could die. She took a deep breath and squeezed her eyes shut. The chances of that happening were slim to none. She despised the mocking voice. She turned the boat toward the darkest part of the lake and throttled forward. Her hands began to shake uncontrollably, and she felt nauseous.

Zoe stood next to her, the eaglet clutched to her chest. "Look at me."

Alex took a deep breath and let herself be connected to Zoe and the eaglet. Their presence pushed against her fear. Zoe's steady determination brought her a measure of comfort.

"We can do this. I'm going to drive," Zoe said. "You're going to keep the eaglet warm while you tell me how to get from here to Johnson's Cove Marina in Windham. Okay?"

"Okay," Alex whispered.

"There's a blanket in my dry-bag."

Alex fumbled for the blanket.

Zoe throttled down to slow the boat. She grabbed the wheel with her free hand while she held the eaglet tight against her body. "When you find the blanket, sit down and hold the ends of it out so we can wrap the eaglet in it."

Alex sat down on the seat next to Zoe. She unfolded the blanket and held it open.

Zoe let go of the wheel and placed the eaglet into the blanket against Alex's chest. She wrapped the ends of the blanket around the eaglet, covering its head and body.

Alex closed her arms around the bird.

"Hold tight, no matter what. We have to keep the eaglet warm and prevent it from moving around too much in case it's broken a wing or leg." Zoe retrieved her T-shirt, pulled it on, and gripped the wheel. "We'll be okay, I promise." She slowly maneuvered the boat against the choppy waves and farther into the murky darkness covering Sebago Lake.

The eaglet struggled against Alex. An instinct similar to what she imagined a mother might feel for a child crowded out the fear that dominated her chest. She wanted the eaglet to live as much as she didn't want to let Zoe down. She focused on her breathing, hoping to find calm for herself and the bird while Zoe took them across the lake. A soothing sensation settled over her. The eaglet had gone still in her embrace, its heartbeat an indication it was still very much alive.

Zoe yanked a cell phone out of the dry-bag and dialed a number with her thumb as the boat plowed through the waves. "Rob, it's me,

Zoe. I need you to meet me at Johnson's Cove Marina over in Windham in about a half hour. One of the eaglets ended up in the water, and we need to get it to the rehab facility as soon as possible." She glanced at Alex and the eaglet. "I'll be in one of the camp's boats. If you hurry, we should arrive around the same time. I'll explain all the details of what happened later, just meet me there." She pushed the Off button with her thumb and tossed the phone onto the seat beside her. "You okay?"

"I am." Alex imagined being somewhere safe. Any place other than on the water in the dark. *Breathe.* She did her best to ignore the jarring of the boat as it climbed and fell into the trough of each wave. With the eaglet pressed against her, she realized it was her embrace that protected it from its vulnerability and her own. Her intuition told her the eaglet would be okay.

If only her mother could have wrapped her brother in the same kind of maternal embrace. Maybe he'd still be alive.

# Chapter 20

Zoe helped Rob hoist the extra-large pet carrier containing the eaglet onto the bench seat on the passenger side of his pickup truck. "Is Dr. Marks on her way to the rehab facility?"

"Yeah, she's probably getting there right about now. I should go so I don't keep her waiting." Rob shut the passenger door. "We did wake her up in the middle of the night."

"I'm sure she doesn't mind. She'll be relieved that we were able to pull the eaglet out of the water in the dark. Besides, it needs to get checked right away. I'm worried that a leg or wing may be broken. If it is, the sooner the limb is set, the better. Who knows what other injuries it might have? Thank goodness it didn't land on the rocks." Zoe crossed her arms and leaned against the side of the truck. For the first time, she realized how physically and emotionally tired she felt.

She turned her attention to Alex, who was sitting on the end of the dock huddled in a blanket with her back to them. "I'm worried about her too."

"She doesn't look very good." Rob wiped a bead of sweat from the side of his face. "You sure you don't want to put the eaglet in the back of the truck? I think it would be fine in the carrier. If we did, there'd be enough room for you two to ride with me. We could drop it off at the rehab center together. I'd give you a lift back to the camp afterward."

"What about the boat?"

"It should be fine here. You could keep it moored and come back and get it in the morning once the lake settles down."

"If it settles down," Zoe said. "The forecast is for these winds to last another several days. It's really weird how hot and dry it is this time of year. And wicked windy."

"No wonder we've already had several brush fires," Rob said. "They seem to be popping up all over."

Zoe studied Alex, who had her arms wrapped around her knees, shivering more than someone should on such a warm night. She seemed a million miles away in someplace icy cold. Zoe wondered what old injuries had left Alex in such a state. Rob's offer was tempting. She'd already pushed Alex to the breaking point coming across the lake in the dark. But…

"No," she said. "It's too risky for the eaglet to ride in back. The wind and noise would be too much for it. The best thing is to keep it warm and calm. Do you happen to have a dry sweatshirt or something in your truck for Alex? I brought dry clothes for myself, but I hadn't planned on having her with me."

"Yeah, I always keep a spare on hand." Rob flipped open the heavy plastic storage box in the back of his truck and took out a dark-green fleece Wildlife and Fisheries pullover. "You could wait here for me, and I'll take you back after I drop the eaglet off." He handed her the pullover.

Rob was only trying to help, but his insistence pressed on her last nerve. Maybe it was the stress of the night. More likely, it had to do with his crush on Alex. Zoe had little to no patience with him. She had her own feelings for Alex to deal with, a task made more difficult by the fact that Alex was leaving this morning. "No, I'll take us back in the boat. But thanks. You should really go now."

A gust of wind rocked Rob's truck. "Well, at least wait until the sun starts to come up so you can see more clearly. Call me if you change your mind." He went around to the driver's side of his truck, opened the door, and hopped inside.

Zoe walked around the truck too.

Rob shut the door and said through the open window, "Be careful. And good luck, Zoe. You know where to find me."

"Thanks, Rob. I'll call you in a few hours."

"I'll take care of the eaglet. You take care of yourself." He turned the key in the ignition and put the truck in gear.

Zoe waved him off. As soon as he drove away, she sat next to Alex on the dock and held out the pullover. "Why don't you put this on?"

"Thank you." Alex removed the blanket from her shoulders and laid it next to her. She slipped the fleece on, pulled her knees to her chest, and wrapped her arms around them. "Do you think the eaglet will be all right?"

Zoe scooted closer to Alex until their bodies touched, partly to keep herself warm, but mostly to savor the last opportunity to be close. "There's a good chance. It had a lot of spunk when we put it into the carrier. That's a decent sign it still has the will to survive."

"Only fifty percent of eaglets make it past a year. That's what you said before. So the odds are against it. Aren't they?"

"Yes. Except that we found him before it was too late. If we hadn't pulled him out of the water, he would've drowned or starved to death. Now neither is going to happen."

Alex rested her chin on the tops of her knees. "What are the odds he'll be able to fly someday after this?"

Under the circumstances, the odds of that happening weren't great. "It depends on the extent of his injuries and how much time he has to be away before we can put him back with his parents. Being back with them will go a long way toward him learning to fly."

"He has to make it."

Zoe stretched her legs out in front of her and rested her hands in her lap. "If he does, he'll have you to thank. I know you were afraid and didn't want to go across the lake, but you did. Not to mention, I couldn't have gotten the eaglet out of the water without you. It would've been impossible to do it from a kayak in the dark with the water as wild as it was. You're braver than you give yourself credit for."

"Trust me. I'm not brave at all."

"What is it that makes you so afraid?" Zoe asked.

"I'm not sure. Maybe everything."

Zoe took one of Alex's hands and held it in her lap. Fear was an emotion she rarely experienced, but she recognized it now in the pit of her stomach. That nauseous feeling that came from not knowing what to do or which way to turn when it seemed like something bad was about to happen. Like the time she'd climbed the tree in the forest fire to save the eaglet. That had worked out because she was able to slow her thinking down and find a rational path out of the danger. The source of her current fear was Alex and her feelings for her. She had no idea what path to take. Alex was such a fragile mystery.

"You never told me what happened to your brother," she said. "How did he drown in the lake?"

Alex turned her hand palm up and laced her fingers with Zoe's. "He killed himself," she said, barely above a whisper. "Sometimes, I wish I had thought of doing it first."

The statement slammed into Zoe, knocking her off balance. She rummaged in her mind for something to say. Nothing came. She squeezed Alex's hand even tighter, as if to reach past her skin and into her heart. The fear that came from swimming in a wild, angry lake in the pitch-black darkness of night or climbing a tree with fire all around paled in comparison to the fear generated by Alex's words. Somehow, she had to convince Alex to stay and get help.

"I don't want to think about a world without you," she said.

"Don't worry, Zoe. I'm too much of a coward for even that."

If only she could find a way to throw herself in front of Alex to protect her from such despair, she'd do it in a second, Zoe thought. Unfortunately, the despair inside of Alex was hidden behind an impenetrable wall. Zoe had to find a way around it. "Why did he do it?"

Alex sat quietly for several moments. "Some days, I think I understand why. I'll have an epiphany and it all makes sense. But just as quickly, a million other reasons come to mind and I don't know again. Was it something that was always in him, or was he driven to it?"

"Why would he be driven to do such a thing?"

Alex stared stone faced at the lake. "Jake and I were fraternal twins. We couldn't have been closer. He was my best friend, and I was his. We were as alike as two people could be, including figuring out that we were both gay when we were in high school."

She took a deep breath and spoke quiet, measured words. "There was one big difference, though. I could hide it so much easier than he could. By the time we reached the tenth grade, the other kids started to suspect Jake. The boys, especially, brutalized him for it. Every day that he went to school was a nightmare."

"What did they do to him?"

"You name it." Alex's voice filled with sadness. "The worst was when they locked him in the boys' locker room closet at school. They took up a collection to pay a girl willing to be locked in with him to try to get him to turn 'normal,' as they put it. Jake would never hurt anyone. He wasn't ever going to hit that girl while she molested and humiliated him, egged on by the kids outside the closet. When they finally let him out, they took him behind the school and beat him up. They knew he'd never tell. How could he?" A tear slid down her cheek. She wiped it away with her free hand. "What they didn't count on, though, was that I would. That's why he's dead, because I told my parents."

Zoe put her arm around Alex. "You had to tell someone. I would've done the same thing."

"Except that my mother's reaction was worse than anything those kids did to him. She flipped out worse than she ever had before."

"What do you mean?" Zoe asked.

"My mother suffered from anxiety and depression for as long as I can remember. Instead of getting help, she let us take the brunt of it. Finding out that my brother and I were gay pushed her over the edge. She couldn't handle the thought, especially if it meant that people in town might look down on her and the camp. Her image has always been more important than our happiness or her own health."

Zoe thought about Alex's father. Daniel Marcotte struck her as a decent man who, if push came to shove, would protect his family. He was, after all, willing to anger users of the island to protect the eaglets, in part because Alex wanted him to. Surely he'd do the same for his family. "What did your father do?"

Alex grunted. "What he does best. He stuck his head in the sand and hoped that when he pulled it out, everything would be better. He sat back and watched while my mother dismantled the last of my brother's self-esteem. She left Jake with no option except to find the only escape he could."

Zoe observed an emotion other than fear taking over Alex. Rage. Not surprising, given that anger was what many animals, including humans, used to mask their fears. She tightened her arm around Alex to protect her as best she could.

Alex leaned into her. "I'll never forget the night Jake died. We all had dinner together in the silence that had come after my admission to our parents. Both Jake and I had been grounded indefinitely. We'd go to school, come home, and sit in utter silence with our parents, who had become blind and mute to us. My mother said it was to protect Jake from the kids at school, but the truth was, she did it to keep us from the world. She wanted to lock us up so no one could see what she saw, imperfection and ugliness. Maybe if people didn't see us, they would go back to thinking we were the perfect family. After we ate, I escaped to the barn to read. When I went to my room after dark, I found a note from Jake on my bed. He said he couldn't live with my parents' disappointment. That he wanted to stay forever in a place that he last remembered being happy."

"Oh, sweetheart," Zoe whispered.

Alex made a sound that suggested she was choking back tears. "This time, I didn't tell my parents. If I had, we might have been able to get to him in time. My father would've taken one of the powerboats to find him." Tears tumbled from her eyes. "Instead, I went alone in the kayak. Jake had gone out in a canoe to the deepest part of the lake on the other side of the island. He took a bottle of my mother's sleeping pills with him. They found it empty in the canoe.

He probably waited until grogginess made it impossible for him to change his mind and then slipped over the edge of the canoe into the water. By the time I got there, all I could see was the empty canoe floating away. I jumped in the water to find him, but I couldn't in the dark. They didn't find his body until the next morning." She spoke distantly, as if she were outside her body.

Zoe had always considered it cruel that eagle parents could sit back and watch their offspring kill each other over food. She had to remind herself that it was an example of survival of the fittest in the animal world. Their indifference had everything to do with teaching their offspring to be survivors in a harsh world.

This was different. Alex's parents had acted out of hateful, selfish pettiness at the expense of their children. "None of it was your fault."

"Really, Zoe? Even the police took me in for questioning. They thought it was suspicious that I didn't tell anyone about the letter. They thought Jake and I had cooked up some twisted revenge scheme against my parents that had gone wrong. I guess the only thing that saved me was that I had a meltdown of my own afterward. I wasn't guilty, but crazy. I suppose I can thank my mother for the anxiety and depression genes and her pulling the switch to activate them. I spent the last year of high school in and out of the hospital while doctors tried to cure me of my sadness and fear. Running away to college all the way across the country in California may have kept my anxiety and depression at bay, but it's always there, lurking in the shadows."

Zoe felt she understood why Alex had decided to leave without a good-bye. She needed to escape before her past got the better of her again. "But why did you decide to come back this summer?"

"I told you, Mother is dying. What I haven't admitted to anyone until now is that I hoped if I could find the courage to see her one last time, she might apologize." Alex shook her head. "I despise her so much, yet some days the only thing I think could help me is a hug from her. Just one real hug, and maybe I could finally forgive her and let go of it."

"What if she never apologizes?"

The sun had begun to rise. Its rays mixed with clouds on the horizon. To Zoe, they looked like dark orange-red ribbons painted on the edge of the sky.

Alex stood and pulled her to her feet. "She won't. That's why I'm leaving Maine. If we head back now, I'll still have time to catch my flight."

Zoe placed a hand on either side of Alex's face. "Please don't go. Not yet."

Alex put her hands on Zoe's wrists. She smiled sadly. "You remind me of summer." She leaned in, put her lips briefly on Zoe's, and pulled her into a tight embrace. "Thank you, for that. And thank you for listening." She let go and stepped away from her.

Just like after the dance and in Zoe's dream, Alex leaned close enough to touch, only to slip from her grasp. That kiss was all she needed to know for sure that she had to do everything in her power not to let Alex go. Alex was in desperate need of help. The people in her life who were supposed to love her had let her go without a fight.

Well, she had enough fight inside for both of them. That would only go so far, though. Like the eaglet, Alex needed to find a reason to hang on if there was any hope that she'd really live again and be happy someday. Zoe felt she needed to help Alex find that reason, even if it meant following her all the way back to California if she couldn't convince her to stay in Maine.

# Chapter 21

A crowd had formed on shore as Alex maneuvered the boat through the still choppy water back toward the camp. She wondered whether the strangeness of the weather was a metaphor for why she never should've come home.

Her heart felt barren in a place so normally lush. She stole a glance at Zoe. Ever since they left the dock on the other side of the lake, Zoe had repeatedly asked her to stay. She was tempted to agree. But if she didn't leave Glasgow, she would only end up pulling Zoe into the same abyss. Anxiety and depression were already tugging her in over the edge of madness. All she had to do was keep her grip through the rest of the morning, long enough to get away.

"Please, try to understand why I have to leave," she said.

"I do," Zoe replied. "I just wish you wouldn't."

"Unfortunately, if I don't leave, the terrible memories will never let go of me."

Zoe grabbed the back of Alex's fleece pullover and scrunched it in her fists. "Maybe it's not about it letting go of you, but of you letting go of it. If you stay, people who care about you can help." She looked toward shore. "People like Sally and me. Please, stay and get help."

Alex cut the engine as the boat approached the beach. Sally, her father, James, Claire, and Chuck and the other guys stood waiting for them. Staying was an impossible option. Facing down what had happened was too daunting. "I can't. Besides, it'll be my fault if I stay and hurt you. I don't ever want to do that. I won't taint you with this." The boat slid to a stop in the sand. She already missed Zoe desperately, but leaving was the only thing to do.

"You don't have a right to decide for me," Zoe said as Alex pulled from her grasp.

The crowd swooped on them. Chuck put out a hand to her. She took it and stepped over the side of the boat. At the same time she let go of his hand, Sally threw her arms around her and said, "Honey, we were so worried."

"I'm okay," Alex answered.

The eyes in the crowd bored through her. She felt like she was fifteen again. She heard the people in the crowd saying something but couldn't make out the words. The sense of déjà vu solidified her desire to leave. This would be the only time Zoe would be put through this kind of scene because of her.

She lowered her eyes and let Sally embrace her until the first waves of despair began to fracture the dam that held back her tears. She could feel them threatening to cascade over the edge of her restraint. Her father's voice stifled them.

Daniel grabbed her elbow and spun her around to face him. His expression was an incongruous mix of emotion. "Damn it, Alex. What is your problem? Going off like that in the night without a word. Just like bef—" The last word came out garbled as a sob lodged in his throat. He wrapped his arms around her, trapping her against his chest.

Something snapped. His arms, his accusation, and his fantasy of concern acted like a wick that drew the many feelings hidden beneath the surface of her heart toward the light of day. She lifted her palms to his chest and pushed out of his embrace as a geyser of emotions spurted out of her.

"My problem? You want to know my problem?" Her voice grew louder with each answer. "The fact that you have to ask is my problem. You are my problem." She gestured to the other people on shore. "This fucking homophobic town is my problem. Make up your mind about what it is you want from me. You didn't seem to care all that much when you threw me out of the house hours ago. What difference does it make now whether I drown in the lake like Jake? Maybe it would finally put you out of your misery."

Everyone stood rigid in her wake.

James had the gall to speak. "Your father was worried about you, and rightly so. We all were."

In her mind's eye, she looked over her shoulder and saw the years of pent-up emotions and memories bearing down on her like a raging torrent. There was no escape. She pointed her finger at James. "People like you killed my brother." To her surprise, standing her ground and letting the memories and emotions overtake her brought a calm to her words she wouldn't have predicted.

She turned to her father. "You didn't lift a finger to stop the bullying, and now the bully is running the camp. A place Jake and I loved." She watched as a tear slid down Daniel's cheek. "Don't pretend that you care now. It's too late. You were either impotent to protect us, or you never loved us." Maybe she wasn't entirely insane yet. If she'd lost her mind completely, would she feel so much guilt and still be so calm?

Daniel stood like stone at the accusation, an impervious, rock of a man. His mouth moved slightly, but nothing came out.

Alex made an effort not to look Zoe in the eyes before she turned to walk away. She couldn't endure letting her see the vacant shell that remained after the flood of pain had washed out of her and over her father and James. She was lost and could never be found again, not even by Zoe.

Zoe studied the faces of the people left behind by Alex. Their expressions reminded her of the moments before a violent storm. No one spoke. Each seemed to retreat from the darkness and worry that had settled over them, helpless to do anything other than be still and wait it out. She suspected that in each of their own ways, the people standing on this beach were still living the death of Jake Marcotte. Their paralysis was the problem. Someone needed to keep Alex from leaving. She was the key to all of them finally moving on.

Zoe was about to run after her when Sally shot her a look that stopped her in her tracks.

"Leave her be, honey." Sally may have only been slightly taller than Zoe, but she towered over everyone present with a sternness that left no doubt as to her authority. "What are you waiting for, Daniel? Go after her this time before she's gone forever."

"What am I supposed to say to her anymore?" Daniel clenched his fists. "She accused me of killing my own son. She refuses to go see her mother before she dies. Alex wrote us all off a long time ago. What do I do with that?"

"You start by telling her that you love her. And for once, listen to what she's saying. Did you ever stop to think that maybe she keeps you at arm's length because she's afraid of being hurt by you again?" Sally gripped his elbow. "You've already lost Jake, and your Carolyn doesn't have much time left for this world. Don't lose Alex too. Follow her to the ends of the earth if you have to. Whatever you do, keep her from getting on that plane." Her voice quieted. "Nothing that was ever said or done in the past matters now. Deal with the present, and finally put all that awfulness away. It's killing your family one day at a time while you let it."

"What if I can't stop her?" He broke down and cried.

"You don't have a choice," Sally answered. "Alex needs a father now, not a broken man trapped in his own heartbreak. Go after your daughter."

Without another word, Daniel took off in Alex's direction. Claire made a move to follow.

Sally blocked her path. "I know you mean well, but stay out of it. This is between Daniel and Alex, as it should be."

Claire nodded and said to Chuck, "Maybe I should help you and the other fellows get the boat back into the boathouse. The water's too rough to leave it on shore."

Chuck motioned to Bob and Martin. "Good idea."

Martin remained rooted to the spot. In the time that Zoe had been at the camp, she remembered him only ever saying maybe three words at most. He was a follower who pretty much kept his mouth shut and did what he was told. Not this time. He kicked at the ground and batted a pebble around with the toe of his boot. "You know those two kids were never right after they came up with that garbage about being gay," he said. "Maybe what happened was God telling them that there's no Adam and Steve. God created man to be with woman."

Zoe jumped when the usually mild-mannered Chuck slammed his fist on a nearby picnic table and glared at Martin. "And I suppose you believe that God created heaven and earth in seven days too. Maybe you should've stayed in school and spent more time working on your math, because the math just doesn't add up. If you think about it, that whole seven days thing doesn't make sense, what with fossils being found that are millions of years old." He scowled. "God made those two kids perfect, as sure as He made me and you. You'd better say your prayers tonight and ask forgiveness for being so hateful. Go on home for the day. Bob and I will take care of things here. I don't want you in my business right now."

"Fossils are just a bunch of hogwash," Martin blurted. "My church says they don't prove anything except that evolution didn't happen."

"I'm done listening to so-called church men who can't be trusted to tell me the truth." Chuck pointed to his own chest. "My heart tells me that what this town did to Alex and her brother was wrong. I love those kids, and I always will. I only want Alex to be happy, just like she was when she was a little girl before hatefulness hiding under the name of God took Jake."

James intervened. "Maybe I have some things for Martin to do. The last I recall, I'm the manager here with the only authority to send people home."

Chuck smirked. "Authority you haven't earned. I've been working at this camp before you were even a glimmer in your daddy's eyes. Don't you ever try to assert authority over me until you gain my respect."

"How dare you speak to me like that? Maybe I should fire you."

Chuck took a step closer to James. "You and I both know that what Alex said was true. Fire me if you want, but I don't intend to stay quiet anymore. I'll never forgive myself for not speaking up for Jake and trying to protect him when I had the chance." He glanced around at everyone else standing with them. "None of us did. And look what happened. You don't need to fire me. I'll quit. I suggest you think long and hard about that, though. You may get away with an awful lot around here where Daniel is concerned. Firing me, or allowing me to quit, won't be one of them."

James put up his hands. "I don't want you to quit." His jaw clenched and he seemed to be weighing his words. "For Daniel's sake, let's calm down. There's too much going on here at the camp for anyone to quit." He turned to Martin. "Take the afternoon off as Chuck suggests."

"Are you serious?" Martin asked.

"Yes," James answered. "Apologize while you're at it." He glared at Chuck. "We have a camp full of kids to run. I can't let Daniel down. No one is quitting or getting fired."

Martin mumbled to Chuck, "I'm sorry I said what I did. I spoke out of line. I'll leave now. Can I come back in the morning?" he asked James.

"Of course."

"Be here at the usual time," Chuck said. "And be sure to show up a better man than you were today. If you can't do that, then at least keep your trap shut about things you don't understand."

"Yes, sir." Martin headed in the direction of his truck.

Chuck nodded at Sally. "Please keep me in the loop about Alex. Let me know if there's anything at all I can do to help."

"I will." Sally said. She pointed a finger at James. "As for you, maybe you should go home with Martin and think about the role you played in all this mess instead of acting like the king around here. Once a bully, always a bully, but guess what? It stops here, right now, with me. Just like Chuck, I'm done with this kind of nonsense in this town too."

Zoe hadn't thought it was possible, but did she see a flicker of shame on James's face?

"We were just kids," James said. "We never meant for things to happen the way they did. Besides, you know that depression runs deep in that family. That's what took Jake." He glanced up the hill. "Unlike Alex, some of us stayed here in town to help her parents hold this camp together. There are lots of other places I could go where I'd make a ton more money than I do here. Maybe she ought to finally take some responsibility."

A smile spread across Sally's face. "You know, that doesn't sound like a bad idea at all. I could envision you taking leave of this town for good, and Alex coming back to stay. I'd love to see that happen. No one could run this place better than a Marcotte, most especially Alex. She actually cares about the kids and what this camp means to them as opposed to her own ego."

"Humph," James said and grunted. "This place wouldn't last a year with Alex running it. If you'll excuse me, I have work to do." He spun around on his heel and stormed off toward the main building.

Zoe felt bony fingers close around her forearm just as she was about to add her opinion.

"Don't waste your breath. He's an ass," Sally said. "You must be hungry."

The statement took Zoe by surprise. "I am, but food is the last thing on my mind. We can't let Alex leave. Someone has to stop her."

"I know. And that someone should be her father. I suppose she told you about her brother?"

"Yes, she did. She's in trouble. Alex is going to drown herself just like he did if she can't get free of her sadness. I can't stand the thought."

"You have feelings for her, don't you?" Sally asked. "I wasn't born yesterday. Those feelings you have are more than as a friend."

"Yes, and I'll do anything to get her to stay," Zoe said.

Sally patted her cheek. "Good girl. Because when she comes back with her father, she's going to need all of us."

"How can you be so sure she'll come back?"

"I saw her hit rock bottom with what she said to him. Underneath all her emotional problems, Alex is a strong woman. She'll recognize it's time to stop running and fight to get well. I have every confidence in her. Why don't you join me for breakfast? You need to eat." Sally started up the hill.

Zoe followed. "I'll pass on breakfast. I'm going after Alex if her father can't convince her to stay."

Sally stopped and regarded her. "All right, then. I'll count on it. At least grab a bagel or something from the camp kitchen. I don't want to worry about you too."

"If it's the last thing I do, I'm not going to let Alex get on that plane." Zoe's strength grew with the admission of her feelings. "Nothing in my life has ever mattered more."

# Chapter 22

The cab driver looked over his shoulder. "Where to?" He winked at Alex and looked like he intended to chat her ear off for the next hour.

"I'm going to the airport." Alex wished she could blink her eyes and be back in California now instead of enduring the hordes of people she'd have to wade through all day while traveling to the other side of the country and getting away from the toxic memories of her family. Under her breath, she said to herself, "Just get through the rest of the day before you come apart completely."

Her father's voice cut through the noise raging inside her head. "Alex, wait." He ran to the taxi and placed his hands on the open window's frame.

"I told you, I'm not staying. How else do you want me to say it so you'll finally hear me?" In the rearview mirror, Alex caught the driver peering at her. "Can we please go?" Daniel reached in and put a hand on her shoulder. The gentleness of his touch reminded her of when she was a little girl and still idolized him. She whispered, "Why can't you let me go?"

"You're all I have left. Please, stay."

Was it possible to hate and love a person at the same time? Would her soul be damned forever if she let herself feel hate, especially toward her father? The questions jammed her ability to speak. She could no longer tamp down her emotions and keep them locked in the deepest reaches of her heart. They remained on the surface, ready to burst free again. The pressure built to the breaking point. Her rage boiled. She was terrified that if her anger were truly unleashed, it would destroy her and her father for good. Ironically, she still protected him by keeping it at bay.

"I can't stay," she said.

Daniel clasped his hands together and pleaded, "What do you want me to do?"

A good thing about losing one's mind, Alex considered, was that she didn't care what the gawking driver thought of her or her crumbling father. Bystanders no longer meant anything. She rolled the idea around in her head. Jake had died because of what other people thought. Maybe this was the way to survive, to completely stop caring about other people's opinions, including the people she loved.

Thoughts of Sally, Claire, Chuck, and Zoe reminded her that was impossible, especially Zoe. They'd known each other only a short time, but she missed her more than she imagined she would. She put her fingers to her mouth and tried to touch the memory of Zoe's lips on hers. Anxiety raced to join the emotions plaguing her. It taunted her that the more she loved a person, the deeper it would cut when they were gone. Experience told her that people always left, even those she trusted the most, which was exactly what she intended to do. Leave.

She swallowed her anxiety and answered, "Nothing."

"You'll never see your mother again if you go," he said.

"Don't you know I see her every day in the void left by Jake? Not to see her hateful, angry face ever again is exactly what I need. Otherwise, she'll haunt me for the rest of my life. What difference would it make to see her one last time while she's still living?"

"You can't mean that."

Alex hesitated. An epiphany bloomed in her gut and over her body, slowing her thoughts as it took shape. This thing that manifested in what her mother had done to Jake consumed a piece of her every day that it festered. It was all she thought about, the only memory that came when she considered her mother. Maybe by seeing her one last time, she would find a way to extinguish the vision and put that awful memory away for good. Regardless of what she decided to do, her father didn't deserve to play a role. She let her rage loose. "I'll never forgive you for not protecting Jake. I can't pretend that it didn't happen, either. Every day I remember the things Mom said to him while you just sat there, paralyzed. Do you remember?"

His face paled and he didn't answer.

"Do you remember her calling him filthy? Do you remember her telling him what a disgrace he was? You and I both know Jake had the purest heart of all of us. He deserved so much more." Alex turned her eyes forward and stared at the back of the driver's seat. "Do you remember Mom telling him she would rather he be dead than gay?" She glanced back at him.

His body shivered. From what, she wasn't entirely sure. "I love you, Alex," he said.

"I wish I could believe you." Being honest about her hurt liberated her. With it came a new vulnerability, as if she'd been reborn, but as an infant without a home or family. She shook her head. "How can you say you love me now when you never did before? You don't even know me. Love in our family is nothing but a lie. It always has been. Love isn't something you barter with like you and Mom did. You don't say to a person, especially your own kid, that you'll stop loving them if they go outside the lines of your perfect, fake existence. I don't want anything to do with you ever again."

Daniel came apart at the seams, like pulling a thread from a sweater until the weave unraveled. He put his head in his hands and wept. Alex felt like throwing up. Instinctively, she wanted to run to him and put her arms around him to hold him together, but the rage living inside her took pleasure in seeing him feel the same pain she had felt every second of every day since Jake died. What was left of her rationality reminded her the rage was toxic, slowly and painfully killing her one piece of her soul at a time. She couldn't help it, though.

Her shadow on the seat next to her caught her eye. It resembled her mother. *Who have I become?* Tears welled in her eyes. "Please, just go, will you?" she asked the driver.

The driver fumbled to put the taxi in gear and pulled out onto the main road. His chatty expression was replaced by a determination to get her where she needed to go as quickly as possible.

Something caused Alex to turn back and look at the island one last time. That's when she saw the eagle, exactly the same as on her first day back in Glasgow. The enormous raptor kept pace with the taxi. She stuck her head out the window for a better view as it glided overhead. The eagle followed them over the next several miles. Its presence wrapped her in a desperate need to survive, as if her survival depended on the eagle, and its survival on hers.

"Please, stop the car for a minute!"

"Stop the car?" The driver lifted his head to glance at her in the rearview mirror. "You're going to have to make up your mind."

"Just for a minute."

"If you insist." He pulled the taxi onto the side of the road and parked. "Do you need something from the trunk?"

Alex opened the door and stepped outside. "No, there's someone I forgot to say good-bye to." She pointed at the sky. "I'll be right back. I'm only going to walk a little way down the road."

The driver looked at her as though she'd lost her mind. No matter, she had.

Now that the taxi had stopped, the eagle circled overhead. She must be crazy. No one but a crazy woman would believe that its focus was her. She kept her eyes on the sky, following the eagle's every move as she walked farther down the side of the road in the direction of the camp.

She heard the rumble of a vehicle before it appeared over the rise of the hill. Zoe parked her truck on the side of the road. Alex turned back in the direction of the cab, not wanting to have to face Zoe. She picked up her pace. She had suspected her father might try to follow her, but not Zoe. If he had, she was sure it would've felt like being chased by her demons. But seeing Zoe felt more like being rescued. She resisted turning around and running into Zoe's arms.

"Wait," Zoe yelled.

Alex stopped as Zoe's footsteps drew nearer. A hand covered hers. Instinctively, she turned her palm up and closed her fingers around Zoe's. Tears spilled down her cheeks. She was afraid to turn around and have Zoe see her as a tired, shattered person, unable to give anything to anyone. She felt Zoe's body so close to hers. She only wanted to turn and melt into Zoe, finally safe, but anxiety would come for her no matter where she tried to hide. Zoe would only get caught in the middle. She couldn't let that happen. She pulled her hand from Zoe's grip.

Zoe blocked her path and took hold of her shoulders. "I'm not letting you go." The still circling eagle called out a sound like a soft scream. "And obviously the eagles don't want you to leave either."

"I don't know how to feel better. I'll only hurt you," Alex said through her tears. "I'm so tired."

"I know." Zoe embraced her. "Let me help you, please. Stay for a little while longer. Don't run away. I'll do anything you need except let you go."

"Why?" Alex had to know. She craved having someone want her without expectation.

Zoe wiped a tear from her cheek. "You have the most beautiful smile I've ever seen. I'm afraid if you go now, that smile will disappear forever. Please, don't give up. I care so much about you."

Alex let Zoe fold her in her arms. For the first time since she was a little girl, she let herself be protected by another person. It felt good to let trust replace fear, if only for a moment. She rested her head on Zoe's shoulder. Everything about being in Zoe's arms felt good and right. She gestured at the eagle. "You and the eagle came when I needed someone the most."

"Mother Nature never leaves anything to chance. We were meant to cross paths this summer. I'm so glad that was her plan."

Alex pushed out of Zoe's embrace. "I am too. But I don't want meeting you to be ruined by the mess that I am."

"Listen to me." Zoe grabbed her elbows. "I have no doubt that Fate has a hand in what happens to us. Nothing you did, or didn't do, can change what happened to Jake. But you do have a choice in how you deal with it. He ran away, but you can choose a different path than he did. Find a way to let the past go and be happy. Stay and get help. Don't leave. Confront it. I'll stay by your side the whole way."

Zoe was right. Leaving Glasgow now was no different from what Jake did when he let go and slipped over the side of the canoe. If she left, her body might continue to live, but her heart would die. Zoe's touch gave her the energy to want to get better. She ached to finally break free from the despair and worry. "I'll stay through the summer. But then I have to go."

Smiling, Zoe put her hands on Alex's shoulders and shook her gently. "Will you do me one favor? When you do leave, please say good-bye in person."

"I promise."

"Let me get your bags from the cab driver. I'll take you back to the camp."

"I'm not ready to go back just yet."

"We'll go wherever you want to," Zoe said.

"I'd like to see Dac." Alex still felt the eaglet's heart beating as she had when she'd brought it across the lake in the night. A remnant of that energy pulsed with hers.

"I'll call Sally and let her know where we'll be so she can let your father know you'll be coming home." Zoe pulled Alex into her arms and held her close. "Thank you."

# Chapter 23

Alex followed Zoe into the office of the Lewiston Raptor Rehabilitation Center. The faces of Maine's most common birds of prey stared at her from photographs lining the entryway walls. She stopped to look at them more closely, the eagles, hawks, and owls of many different kinds.

"All of these birds have been visitors here at one time or another." Zoe pointed at a photo of an almost pure-white owl with yellow eyes. "This snowy owl was one of my favorites. She'd been hit by a car up in Bangor. We picked her up and brought her here. She was the feistiest bird I've ever known, except for maybe our Dac. Come hell or high water, that bird was going to fly free again. After several weeks of mending a broken wing, she was released. We tracked her all the way up into the Arctic over several years."

"She's gorgeous," Alex said. "I hope Dac can manage the same."

"He's in the best hands here. Nobody does raptor rehab better than Casey Stills and her staff."

"That's nice of you to say, Zoe." A tall, mocha-skinned woman wearing dark-green scrubs stood in the doorway of a room off to the side. She stepped into the office and put her arms around Zoe. "Good to see you, friend. Nice work getting that eaglet out of the water last night. You probably saved its life."

"I couldn't have done it without help." Zoe glanced at Alex. "Casey, this is my friend, Alex. Alex, this is Casey. She's the manager of the facility."

"Nice to meet you," Alex said.

A loud screech pierced the air.

Casey rolled her eyes. "That's Patch, one of our resident eagles. He knows the sound of his handler's truck. Rick shows up for work right about now, and you'd think Patch hasn't seen him in months. Rick is the bright spot in Patch's day."

"I wouldn't have thought an eagle would be so attached to a human," Alex said.

"Normally, we do our best not to let them get attached. Unfortunately, Patch is one of our birds who will never be released back into the wild. He can't fly anymore. The bones in his left wing were shattered when a poacher shot him." Casey shook her head. "Now, Patch lives for when Rick takes him on his arm out in the field. The two of them stand on the top of the hill. Rick lifts his arm as high as he can to let Patch spread his wings, letting his feathers get ruffled by the wind. I wonder if he imagines himself flying again."

Alex couldn't help thinking about Dac. She considered what would be worse: never learning to fly, or knowing how and having the ability ripped away by a bullet. Suddenly, the similarity between her situation and Patch's struck her. Having her childhood happiness torn away paralleled Patch's trauma from an injury. But Zoe was right. Unlike a shattered wing that couldn't be repaired, Alex still had a choice to mend her life and find happiness again. She tucked that thought away.

"Do you try to release the birds if there's at least some hope they'll fly again?" she asked.

"Definitely. Raptors are meant to fly. Don't get me wrong, Patch has a good life here, for the most part. He's loved and well taken care of. And he has an important purpose. Rick takes him to schools and events around New England to help educate the public about eagles. Patch seems to enjoy the attention and is always very well behaved. But if there's a chance to fly again, we'd rather the bird get it than not. Quality of life is more important than quantity for their wild souls."

"Speaking of chances, how's the eaglet we brought in last night doing?" Zoe asked. "Any idea as to whether, or when, he might be released?"

"He has a minor fracture in his right leg. The vet thinks it should heal fine without surgery. We're guessing it'll take about ten days to heal provided we can get him to eat. He's still a bit depressed this morning and hasn't been interested in food."

"That's not good for an eaglet," Zoe explained to Alex. "He should be eating nonstop. And if he's going to fly, he should learn from his parents. The longer he's away from them, the more remote that possibility becomes." To Casey, she continued, "I'd like to see him put back at the nest as soon as possible even if he's not a hundred percent. On balance, it'll be better for him. Every day he's here is one more day stacked against him living in the wild."

"I know. We have to get him to eat and heal first. We'll do it as quickly as we can, provided he's willing. Speaking of, that's where I was headed now if you're interested in joining me." Casey took a cell phone out of her pocket when it buzzed. "I'm sorry. I have to take this call. Zoe, you know the routine. If you and Alex want to give a shot at feeding the eaglet, that would help me out. Just keep an eye out for Star."

"Sure, no problem," Zoe said. She motioned for Alex to follow her.

"Who's Star?" Alex asked as she waved good-bye to Casey.

Zoe led the way outside to a separate building. She twisted the door handle. "She's a very old eagle who has been here almost ten years. Casey and the staff often put young, injured eaglets in with her to help them feel not so alone. Star has a strong maternal instinct even though none of the eaglets are her babies. She just seems to know when they need a little maternal care. The rehab center would rather they get it from her than humans."

"I never would've imagined."

"What's that?" Zoe asked, pushing the door open with her shoulder.

"Patch and Star, they've still found purpose even though they can't live in the wild."

Zoe winked. "Just goes to show that even wild creatures have it within themselves to make their lives matter despite their circumstances. There's a lot we can learn from them." She reached out and caressed Alex's shoulder. "Just like your life matters." She stepped into the room.

Alex let the statement sink in and followed Zoe into the room. She'd always believed that her work as a historian mattered, but she had never considered that *she* mattered.

She hesitated when they entered the room. Star stood on a perch and spread her wings wide, showing off her brilliant feathers. Her head and tail were snow white. Shiny black feathers covered the rest of her body. Her wings took up almost the entire width of the wall behind her. "Star is so regal," Alex said. "I feel like I'm in the presence of royalty."

Star tucked her wings against her sides, cocked her head, and seemed to study them. Her yellow beak and talons contrasted with her white and black feathers. Her large, pale yellow eyes locked on Alex and followed her every move. "I never realized how big an eagle's eyes are compared to the size of its body," Alex said.

"Eagle eyes are the same size as human eyes, yet the average adult eagle only weighs twelve to fourteen pounds. Believe me, they see everything."

"Like right into my soul." Alex was mesmerized, but out of respect for the bird, she didn't stare back. She was also humbled by a creature who'd had the most important thing in its world—its ability to fly—taken away, yet it held its head high and radiated life. Maybe the most important thing to Star wasn't flying, but being alive.

"She likes you," Zoe said softly. "If she didn't, she'd keep her wings spread wide in an effort to show off her size. She knows we aren't a threat. Star is both regal and wise. She's only curious about what we're up to and probably hoping she gets something out of the deal."

Zoe opened a drawer and got out two pairs of rubber gloves. She handed a pair to Alex. "You'll need these," she said as she put on the other pair.

"Where do you think Dac is?" Alex asked, putting on her pair of gloves

"Over there." Zoe pointed at what looked like a child's playpen, except its walls were about four feet tall and made of wood. She opened one of the two refrigerators in the room, took out several plastic bags, and tossed them on the countertop. "Casey said he's depressed. My guess is that he's huddled in the corner hoping no one notices him. Even though Star appears to be fine with us in the room, keep an eye on her and don't get close enough for her to grab you."

Alex meant to move, but her body remained rooted where she stood. Curiously, the overwhelming emotions suddenly welling inside her weren't driven by fear or anger. Star's palpable primal instinct to survive was the catalyst. Despite her circumstances, the eagle exuded an unconquerable will to live. She radiated a life that wrapped around Alex and filled her with hope.

Zoe took a step toward her. "Alex? I can take you back outside if you're afraid. I'll come back in and feed Dac after."

"I'm okay." Alex smiled and needed to say the words again to be sure. "I'm really okay. I love being here with you and Star. Tell me how I can help."

A grin spread across Zoe's face. "I hope you know what you're in for." She opened the plastic bags. The smell of dead fish filled the room. "Chopped salmon, an eaglet favorite. Why don't you grab a couple of pieces and let's see if we can get Dac to eat his breakfast?"

Alex made a face and scrunched up her nose. "If that smell stays in my memory, I'll never eat again." She picked up the fish parts and carried them to the pen. As she neared, she could see over the edge and spotted Dac sitting in a corner with his head hanging low. "He seems so sad."

Dac lifted his head and backed closer to the wall. Alex had the urge to scoop him into her arms and cradle him. She resisted, knowing it wouldn't be good for him to become attached to her. Besides, Star watched her every move, a good reminder that the eagle intended to be the only maternal caregiver in the room. Her shifting around on the perch made that abundantly clear.

Zoe tossed a chunk of fish near Dac's feet. He pushed himself even closer to the wall as if trying to disappear.

Alex's heart broke for him. She knew the feeling. "Come on, Dac. You have your whole life in front of you to soar around in the sky. Don't give up." *Don't give up.* The words were as much for her as for Dac.

"We should give him some space." Zoe removed the rubber gloves from her hands and tossed them onto the counter near the sink. "He's still too discombobulated to eat, especially with us around." She picked up a heavy leather glove from a nearby table and slipped it on. The glove covered her hand and arm up to the elbow. "Go ahead and toss what you have in with him. I'll feed Star the rest. I could show you the grounds afterward, if you'd like." She held out her gloved hand, filled with fish pieces, to Star.

"I'd like that." Alex watched Star take chunks of fish from Zoe with her talons and shred them with her knife-edged beak.

After Star had her fill, Zoe removed the leather glove while Alex did the same with her rubber ones. She and Zoe washed their hands and slipped out of the center into another steamy hot early afternoon. The dirt path they walked along was too dry and dusty for June. Up ahead, a bench sat next to a fifty-foot-wide raptor cage

"Do you mind if we sit for a while?" Alex asked when they approached the bench. "Being up all night might be catching up to me."

"You do look a bit pale." Zoe sat down. "Are you all right?"

"I feel a little light-headed."

"I'm not surprised. I'm sure the heat and the fact that you haven't eaten anything isn't helping either. We should get some lunch."

Several red-tailed hawks kept watch over them from perches inside the enclosure. Alex leaned against the back of the bench and studied them. "I'll need my strength, that's for sure. I'm glad you convinced me to stay a while longer. But I'm not looking forward to reliving what happened." She squeezed Zoe's hand. "I'm going to try harder this time to see it through to the other end, I hope."

Several seconds passed before Zoe spoke. "I'm sorry you have to go through it. But you'll get there. If there's anything I can do to help, let me."

Anxiety clawed at the back of Alex's throat, reminding her of its presence. She tried to gather strength from the hawks looking at her. "Remember when I told you I was in and out of the hospital after my brother died?"

"Yes."

"During that time, I saw a doctor who tried to make me understand I had to confront what had happened and not tuck it away. I wasn't ready to listen. It was just too daunting. The first chance I got, I went as far from Maine as I could go. I think it's time for me to finally listen to that doctor's advice. I know I can't keep running. The past is gaining on me. I'm too tired to try to stay ahead of it." She turned to face Zoe. "Part of me doesn't want to run anymore, even if I could. One of the reasons is because I want to get better. Another is because of you."

Zoe caressed the side of her face. "That means a lot to me, but you have to do it for yourself, not anyone else."

"You're right." Alex brought Zoe's hand to her heart. "I don't know what's going to happen. But I have nothing left inside to help me run. I can't do this anymore on my own. I know I need help." Some of the weight pressing on her fell away with the admission. "I want to live like Star and Patch, despite what happened."

Zoe pulled Alex into her arms. "You're the superhero."

# Chapter 24

The following morning, Alex watched Sally put the finishing touches on a sign she was making.

Sally looked tiny under a wide-brimmed straw hat while she sat at a picnic table under a blazing afternoon sun. Buddy slept soundly at her feet. She glanced up from her project and smiled. "Hello." She held up the sign. "What do you think, girlie?" She giggled.

"Puppy Fashion Show at the Camp Marcotte Barn on Saturday at Two PM." Alex finished making her way down the hill to the table. "I like it. The kids are going to be beside themselves. Do you need any more help to get ready?"

"No, this pretty much squares things away until Saturday, when I'll need loads of help. All those puppies and kids in the mix could get interesting."

Alex sat down. "I'll definitely be there."

"How did things go with your phone call to Dr. Kestler's office this morning?"

"Good. She's still in the same place and was able to fit me in for an appointment on Friday. I think she was pretty surprised to hear from me after all this time."

"And relieved, I'm sure." Sally patted her hand. "I'm really proud of you for taking this step. How do you feel about it?"

"I want to get better, that's for sure. I know this is something I need to do in order to get there, but I'm not looking forward to it." Alex shook her head. "I'll spend the next several weeks delving into things I've worked so hard to hide. It'll be like turning myself inside out and leaving all my vulnerable parts exposed."

"Ah, but who better to help you with that experience than Dr. Kestler? She knows you and all about what happened to Jake. You won't have to rehash things with a stranger. She'll keep you safe. In the long run, it'll be so much better for you to actually deal with those things instead of hiding them away." Sally waved a hand as if to brush away something bad. "Get rid of them for good. Who knows? Maybe then you'll want to stay here permanently."

Alex's father came from the barn. He chatted with Chuck as he pointed at the barn door. Most likely there was something he needed Chuck to repair. "I don't know about that," Alex said. "I sometimes wonder whether the only way for me to be free is to say good-bye to my parents for good. What they did and didn't do is at the heart of much of my trouble."

"What do I know? I'm just an old lady in a funny hat. But if you ask me, being free has nothing to do with what anyone else does." Sally tapped a finger to the side of her forehead. "It starts there." She moved her finger down and tapped her heart. "And ends there. The answers as to where you go rest within you and have nothing to do with your parents or anyone else. Trust me, honey. And trust Dr. Kestler this time."

Chuck and Daniel finished their conversation and came over to the picnic table. "The sign looks great," Daniel said to Sally. "Chuck has some time this morning to hang it wherever you like."

Sally picked up the sign. "Now works." She lifted her spindly legs over the seat of the picnic table and stood. On cue, Buddy did as well. "I'd like to take it over to Rita's General Store. Everyone in town will already know about the show. Rita's is the best place to advertise it with the out-of-towners. Come on, we'll take Hiccup." Sally kissed Alex on the cheek. "If you need anything at all, you find me." She left with Chuck and Buddy in tow.

"Age certainly hasn't slowed Sally down. It'll have to sneak up on her in her sleep to catch her," Alex said.

"I suppose so." Daniel stared at the lake for several moments. "You don't have to stay in the staff quarters. I'd like you to come back to the house."

Alex didn't answer right away. It was typical of her father to reach out without actually making a connection. Always the coward, not wanting to look her in the eye. Maybe because he didn't mean it. It occurred to her briefly that maybe he didn't know how to make a connection. "I'd prefer to stay where I am." Inside, she quarreled over whether she was being too hard on him.

"Is it because of Zoe?"

Frustrated, she rubbed her eyes. "With all that I said to you yesterday, why would you ask such a question?"

He finally turned to face her. "Because I practically begged on my hands and knees for you to stay, but you drove away as if I don't matter. It wasn't until Zoe went after you that you came back. Why her, not me? Is there something going on between the two of you?"

His words struck Alex speechless. Two sentences and two questions she'd spend some time grappling over. *Why not me? Is there something going on between the two of you?* It was as simple and complicated as that. She felt his hand on her shoulder.

"Maybe." Part of her wanted to confess everything in her heart to him. The other part despised him for asking.

He sat down next to her. "I don't want to lose you like I lost Jake." He folded his hands together on the picnic table. "I'm worried you might be in the same place as him. I'm so relieved that you agreed to stay and see Dr. Kestler before something bad happens."

Alex stared at him. Somehow, he always managed to say the things that hurt her the most. Her rational brain asked, what father wouldn't be worried? Her heart ached that he only seemed to be interested or care about her during a crisis. "Why do I only matter to you when you think something bad might happen?"

"That's not true," he said.

"Really? Since I've been home, you haven't asked me about my book or about school. You don't care to know whether I'm seeing anyone unless it negatively impacts you. When was the last time you asked me how I'm doing or whether I'm happy? The way you just asked me about Zoe felt more like an accusation than interest." Alex shook her head. "You make me feel as though I'm invisible, except for the parts you're willing to see."

"First of all," he said, "don't assume I have a problem with you caring about Zoe. You make a lot of assumptions for someone who's been gone for years. Second, you were the one who left. How am I supposed to get to know you when you're all the way across the country and refuse to come home?" Tears filled his eyes. "I don't know what I'm going to do without your mother. She's always been my whole world."

Alex contemplated her father in a way she never had before. Perhaps she was guilty of the same things she'd accused him of. For the first time, she saw him as other than a parent. The child inside her despised him for not letting his children share his heart in the same way their mother had. But the woman inside saw him as a human being struggling unsuccessfully with the impending loss of the person he loved more than anyone in the world. The clash between the two perspectives was one more problem she'd have to resolve if she had any hope of getting better.

"What does that have to do with me? I'm not her," Alex said.

"I need you in my life." He broke down. "I don't know what to do anymore."

The essential difference between her father and mother became clear. He was fragile, and her mother was hard like granite. Alex wasn't the only one who needed help. "Will you go see Dr. Kestler with me?"

"What are you saying? That I have a problem too? I'm not the one who needs a shrink."

"You have no idea what you just said, do you?" Alex shook her head in disgust. "Mom needed help for years, but you both saw therapy as a sign of weakness. Did you ever stop to think that if you'd insisted she get help, this whole thing might have turned out differently?"

Daniel slammed his hand down on the table. "Why do you always have to blame me?"

Alex struggled against her building anxiety and the impulse to run from him and the question. "You're right. Maybe it's time to stop blaming and figure out how to live free of it." Her anger at her parents battled against her desperate need to view what had happened in a different way. A way that was free from the bitterness that poisoned her, just like it had her mother and now her father. "Did you and Mom ever talk about what happened to Jake?"

"It wasn't something either of us wanted to think about, let alone talk about. We were focused on worrying about you."

"Maybe that's part of the problem. You haven't dealt with Jake's loss anymore than I have. You're still living it every day too. That's why you don't know what to do anymore. If you're serious about needing me in your life, then do this with me. I think it would help both of us."

"Will you stay at least through the summer if I go? I'll do it for you."

She got up from the table. "A very wise woman told me the same thing that I'll tell you: you have to do it for yourself first."

He sighed and seemed to weigh his options. "I'll call Dr. Kestler this morning."

"Thank you."

# Chapter 25

Alex leaned against the chestnut tree and let it support her weight. With her legs crossed in front of her and the buttress of the tree behind her, relaxation swept over her.

Dr. Kestler's quiet voice from their earlier morning session replayed in her head. "Let all the air out of your lungs, taking the negative thoughts with it. Focus on this moment. Feel every cell of your body."

She'd forgotten how meditation was like running. It offered uncluttered moments free from the messiness and worry of life. Unfortunately, it took discipline to find those fleeting instances of peace.

A light breeze wafted over her skin and evaporated the sweat from the day's heat. The air moved a loose strand of hair that tickled the side of her neck. She tucked her hair behind her ears and did her best to stay in the state of meditation until Zoe arrived.

Someone was coming through the woods, and Alex's heart skipped a beat. She opened an eye and smiled.

"I know I'm a little early. I hope I'm not interrupting." Zoe slipped her hands into the pockets of her cargo shorts. "I tried to make a lot of noise so you'd hear me. Should I go?"

Zoe only added to Alex's rare sense of calm. "No. I'm happy to see you." She patted the blanket spread beneath her. "Come sit with me. I was almost finished anyway."

"Were you meditating?"

"How did you guess?"

"You look like I feel when I'm in the top of the trees. There's nothing like escaping the troubles of the world by climbing above it. Sometimes I have to remind myself that I have to go down, that I can't stay up there forever." Zoe slipped the backpack off her shoulders and took a spot next to Alex. "How are things going with your therapy sessions, if you don't mind me asking?"

"I don't mind." Alex bit her bottom lip. "It's scary and cathartic. Right now, I'm mostly working on ways to relax, like the meditation. Dr. Kestler wants to make sure I have tools at my disposal to find calm before we really dig down into my family's past. Therapy can get ugly. Sorry for the analogy, but it's a lot like throwing up. Your brain begs you not to because it's so damned unpleasant, but the truth is, once it happens you always feel a million times better getting rid of whatever ails you."

"That's why I think you're amazing for being brave enough to do it." Zoe touched her shoulder. "Is your dad still going with you?"

"To my surprise, yes. He even agreed to see a separate therapist during the days we don't have joint sessions. Maybe he'll finally realize that this isn't only about me."

"That's a huge step for him." Zoe brought her knees up to her chest and wrapped her arms around her legs. "Will you let me know if there's anything I can do to help as you go through all this?"

"Just being willing to listen and not think I'm some kind of crazy person does wonders."

"I wish you wouldn't say that anymore. I've never thought that, and I never will."

"What *do* you think?" Alex asked.

"We all have things we struggle with. It's part of life. I'm short, but you don't hold that against me." Zoe grinned.

Alex ran a hand through Zoe's hair, entangling the strands in her fingers. "No."

"I saw Dac this morning," Zoe said with a quiver in her voice. She looked away.

Alex let go of her hair and sat up straight. "Yeah? How is he?"

"He's doing well. He's finally eating like he should, and his leg is healing perfectly. We're going to take him back to the nest next week. Do you want to join us? My guess is we'll shoot for Tuesday, if you're free."

"Oh, my God, I'd love to. Other than the camp and my therapy sessions, I was planning to go to the archives in Augusta one day to work on my book. But I can rearrange things. That's such great news. I imagine it won't be easy to climb the tree with him now that he's grown so much."

"We won't be putting him in the nest. It's too risky. We'll leave him on the ground and hope he can get back up there on his own."

"You're kidding, right? He can't fly. How is he going to manage that?"

Zoe stretched her legs out in front of her and crossed her feet at the ankles. "If he's going to get back into the nest, he's going to have to do it by himself, hopefully with the encouragement of his parents. He's ten days behind in his development. That's nearly forever for an eaglet."

"Why is leaving him on the ground to fend for himself better than putting him in the nest where he can at least be fed by his parents?"

"His parents or sibling might decide that after all this time, he's an intruder, and try to kill him. If he has to get into the nest himself, it'll force him to use his wings and instinct. It's going to come down to how good his instincts are and whether his family will accept him back into the fold."

"That's interesting to consider," Alex said. "It doesn't seem so different from what happened to Jake. He'd be alive if my parents hadn't rejected him. What do you think Dac's chances are?"

"Fifty-fifty. It's not only about being accepted. Dac's survival also depends on his will to live. He'll need both if there's going to be any hope for him. By the way, your parents rejected you too, but you're still alive. Let's hope Dac has a little of your grit."

Alex had often wondered about the disparity between her and her brother. They were twins and virtually identical in so many ways, yet their fates couldn't have been more different. "I always thought I was the coward. As bad as things got, I never could've taken my own life."

"It's not about being a coward either way. Jake didn't want to live anymore. You did. If you ask me, I think you were pretty fearless under the circumstances."

"I don't know about that. In fact, I dream of the day that fear is no longer a prominent emotion in my life." Alex turned her head and squinted against the sunlight so she could look at Zoe. "May I ask you a question?"

"Sure."

"Is there anything you're afraid of?"

"Everyone is afraid of something, even me."

"Like what?"

"When I climbed my first tree, I was scared out of my mind. I was sure I'd either throw up from nerves or pass out before I got safely on the ground. But I was too high up to back out. I had to go all the way. I'll never forget that feeling of getting past being afraid and making it to the top of the tree. Once I did, I had to go higher. It was exhilarating to be figuratively and literally on top of the world."

"I want to feel that someday."

"How about now?" Zoe pointed at a maple tree near the edge of the woods. "It's only forty feet high. You see that big branch coming off the trunk about fifteen feet up? I could rig a rope over it and teach you to climb."

"I'm not ready to climb trees."

"What's to be ready for?" Zoe stood. "Now's as good a time as any." She grabbed her backpack and extended a hand.

Alex looked up at her smiling face. Even though they were adults, Zoe made her feel like a kid, carefree and fearless. The nagging voice in her head reminded her she wasn't a kid and a lot could go wrong with climbing trees. "I really don't think it's a good idea." She paused. "You have a rope in your pack?"

"I never go anywhere without enough rope to climb a tree." Zoe grinned. "Come on. Indulge me."

Alex took Zoe's hand and let her pull her to her feet. "Do you have any idea how hard it is to say 'no' to you?" She followed Zoe to the maple tree. "What if I fall?"

Zoe dropped her backpack onto the ground and opened it. "I'll catch you." She pulled a long, soft, tightly woven rope from her pack. She made a knot in the end of it, tossed it over the large maple branch, and caught it as it came down.

"Are you sure that branch will hold my weight?"

Zoe put her hands on her hips and sighed. "That branch is probably ten inches in diameter. The tree is healthy, and *you* are a nervous Nellie. Yes, it will hold your weight."

"I just don't want to break my neck." Alex studied the branch for any cracks that would make it weak. "I don't think this is a good idea for me."

"The branch is only fifteen feet off of the ground." The tone of Zoe's voice hinted at exasperation. "Will you please trust me? Better yet, trust yourself. You can do this. It'll be fun. You said you wanted to be Batwoman, remember? Now's your chance."

Anxiety slithered along the back of Alex's neck leaving her queasy. Instead of letting it seize her as it always did, she fought back. She took a deep breath and slowly let it out. She would not let anxiety get the better of her. If she couldn't do it for herself, at least she could make the attempt for Zoe. "Okay, I'll try." Her throat went dry. Anxiety would not go quietly.

"Excellent." Zoe grabbed the ends of the rope hanging from the tree branch and tied them together to make two large loops with a tight knot above them. "This is a little tricky since I don't have my other climbing gear, but it's still doable." She untied the laces of her boots and kicked them and her socks off. She stepped through the two loops and slid them up her legs to the tops of her thighs. She glanced at Alex, who was watching her every move. "I've tied the rope so it serves as a harness."

"What's the knot for?" Alex asked.

"It's a special knot called a Blake's Hitch. It will hold you in place along the length of the rope and let you go up or down when you want to. You pull yourself up the rope and slide the hitch as you go. When you want to come down, you gently push down on it." Zoe pulled on the rope, hoisted herself off of the ground, and demonstrated the use of the hitch.

"Why did you take your boots off?"

"You'll see." Zoe pulled a few more times on the rope until she reached the branch. She climbed up onto it and wriggled out of the rope's makeshift harness. "Now comes the fun part."

When Zoe stood on the branch without the safety of the harness, Alex's heart fluttered. "What are you doing?"

Zoe raised her arms parallel to the ground. She put one bare foot in front of the other, pointed her toes, and walked gracefully along the branch like a gymnast on the balance beam. She pivoted before the branch narrowed and sauntered back to where she'd started.

Alex was mesmerized. She found herself smiling at Zoe's elegant athleticism even though her gut clenched in nervousness over her safety. Zoe was beautiful in more ways than she could articulate. "Don't fall."

"And now for the grand finale." Zoe stood on the branch about two feet from where it met the trunk of the tree. She bent her knees, threw her body into the air, and did a somersault to the ground.

A flood of instinct and fear propelled Alex to Zoe. She put her arms around her. "Are you okay?" Her voice shook. "What were you thinking? You could've killed yourself."

"Stop already. I didn't. It was a blast. Remember, I'm a gymnast. I know how to fling myself into the air and not get hurt. You have to try it."

"Are you out of your mind?" Alex stopped short of hugging and kissing her. A jumble of emotions ranging from awe, to affection, to fear jostled her.

"I'm not saying you should walk along the branch and jump off. But, trust me, there's nothing like the feeling of being in a tree. It's your turn to climb." Zoe made some adjustments to the rope and held the loops out to Alex. "Put a leg into each of the loops and pull them up as high as they'll go."

Alex hesitated.

Zoe flapped the loops toward her, gazed up at her, and said in a teasing tone, "Come ooon. I'll be right here."

Alex took another deep breath and wondered what the hell she was doing even thinking about climbing a tree. But she found it impossible to refuse Zoe's invitation. She stepped into the loops and pulled them up her thighs.

Zoe reached down. "I hope you don't mind." She grabbed the loops and slid them higher.

Her hands brushed along the skin of Alex's bare thighs. Alex admitted that attraction was among the mix of emotions rattling her.

"Okay, now hold onto the rope and lean your weight into the loops as if sitting down."

Alex was surprised that the rope held her. "Not exactly comfortable."

"I know. Next time we'll use a real harness."

"Don't be so sure there'll be a next time."

"Don't be so sure you won't love it so much that you'll be the one asking me for a next time." Zoe put her hand on the knot she'd called the Blake's Hitch. "Grip the rope with a hand just below this knot. As your body moves up the rope, slide the knot up with you. It will hold you in place if you take your hand away from it. To come back down, put your hand on top of the knot and slowly push down. Be careful not to go too fast."

Alex did her "breathing in deeply and slowly exhaling" routine. She pulled hard on the rope, amazed when her body lifted off of the ground. She pulled again and went higher. A smile spread across her face. "This is awesome." She felt free and pulled a third and fourth time until she was almost to the bottom of the branch.

Zoe laughed. "I knew you could do it."

The rope loops around Alex's thighs were uncomfortable, but she was actually doing it. When she glanced down though, her stomach did a flip and she froze. She gripped the rope tighter and closed her eyes.

"You're okay. Remember, you're only fifteen feet off the ground. Open your eyes and enjoy the view. Think about Dac. You're getting to experience being in a tree like he is. Climbing is like flying."

"I want to come back down." Panic edged through her words.

"Okay. Hang onto the rope with your left hand and slowly push down on the knot with your right hand."

Anxious to get to the ground, Alex put her hand on the knot and pushed down hard. She slipped down the length of rope so fast her left hand burned from trying to hang on.

Zoe caught her in her arms as Alex touched the ground. "You did great."

Alex struggled to get free from the loops her legs were in. She pulled each leg from them and stumbled in the process. "Damn." She fell backward onto her butt.

Zoe rushed to her side. She put a hand to Alex's cheek. "Are you okay? I'm sorry for pushing you to climb the tree."

Alex put her hand to Zoe's, and her entwined fingers tingled. A rush of desire overwhelmed her. She wanted to escape with Zoe from all that made her afraid. "I want to kiss you."

"Then do it," Zoe breathed.

Alex pulled Zoe to the ground and rolled on top of her. The kiss was gentle at first. Zoe stirred beneath her and pulled her closer. Something in Zoe's response rushed into her, summoning her to escape her burdens. To run, not with her feet, but by taking Zoe's body.

She pressed herself to Zoe and kissed her without restraint. The closer she got to Zoe, the less fear and sadness she felt. She desperately wanted to be free from those emotions, yet deep down, the thought of taking anything from Zoe in a bid to free herself felt selfish.

Zoe ran her hands along the sides of Alex's body, brushing her breasts as they went.

Wetness surged between Alex's legs, and her breasts ached to be touched again. "I need this," Alex whispered. Her words mocked her.

What was this need? Was it selfish? Was it that and so much more? She considered stopping what was happening before it went any further. Zoe deserved better. But fear threatened to dominate her once more. She wanted, needed, an escape.

She didn't stop. She ran a hand over Zoe's shoulder, feeling the solid muscle beneath the T-shirt's sleeve. "Your body is so hard." Her hand continued a path over Zoe's breast. It had been so long since she felt a woman's body under her own. Need crowded out her desire not to hurt Zoe's heart.

Zoe whimpered, put her hands on Alex's waist, and worked her fingers beneath her T-shirt.

Alex pressed her pelvis into Zoe when she writhed against her. Raw lust took over. She felt her clitoris swell with the need to be satisfied. She ignored the voice inside that begged her not to hurt Zoe. Her body's cravings drove her on. She rose off Zoe and put a knee between her legs before grabbing the bottom of Zoe's T-shirt and yanking it up to her neck.

She wasn't surprised to find that Zoe's stomach rippled with muscle. Even under the thick material of Zoe's sports bra, she could see the hardening nipples. She slid both greedy hands beneath the bra cups to fondle them. "So perfect," she whispered near Zoe's neck.

Zoe caressed her back and unclasped her bra.

As much as Alex wanted Zoe to touch her, not letting her might somehow keep Zoe at a safer distance, might prevent her from getting hurt. She removed her hands from Zoe's soft breasts and stiff nipples and took her by the wrists, bringing up her arms to rest above her head. "You're distracting me." She leaned down and kissed Zoe's stomach. "Don't." She fumbled with the button and zipper on Zoe's shorts and tore them open.

"Touch me," Zoe pleaded.

Alex put her hand inside Zoe's shorts and into her underwear. White-hot need exploded inside her when she felt Zoe's wetness. She thrust two fingers inside that warmth, in and out, again and again.

Zoe spread her legs. She brought her hands from above her head and dug her fingertips into Alex's back. "Faster," she whispered.

Her hurried panting encouraged Alex. She thrust harder and brushed her thumb back and forth over Zoe's swollen clitoris. Zoe's muscles tightened around her fingers, and her body tensed.

All of Alex's demons were blotted out. With each thrust, she extinguished them. She was startled when that little, carefree girl inside—whom she'd always hidden from—laughed.

Zoe cried out and her body trembled in climax. She hugged Alex tightly against her. "Oh, my God," she moaned.

Alex pulled away and covered her own mouth with her hand. The sweet smell of Zoe's fluids on her fingers made her heart hurt. She sat back and tried to catch her breath. "I'm sorry."

"What are you talking about? You just made love to me." Zoe sat up and scooted next to her. "Don't be sorry. I'm definitely not."

"I used you. That's not love," Alex whispered. "You were a means of escape."

Zoe bristled. "That's not what happened, and you know it. I wasn't an escape. You wanted to be with me as much as I wanted to be with you. What you did was panic like happened to you at the top of the tree." Zoe pounded a fist on the ground. "Maybe fear is a crutch you use so you won't have to face the things you don't want to. You don't want to admit you have feelings."

Alex considered whether Zoe might be right. Even if she were, Alex was angry that she'd had the nerve to suggest it. "It wasn't about fear." Was this another lie among the many she was so good at telling herself?

"Really? What was it then?"

Cold denial spread over Alex. "It was selfish of me. I don't ever want to use you. You deserve more."

"You're not the only one who gets to decide." Zoe stood. She pulled her shirt down and zipped and buttoned her shorts. "You asked me earlier what I'm afraid of." Her jaw clenched. Anger and hurt simmered in her eyes. "You coming close, and then pushing me away. That's what I'm afraid of."

Alex felt Zoe's anger and disappointment. "Then it'll never happen again. I tried to tell you I'm a mess."

"You don't understand at all," Zoe said. "I'm not sorry about what just happened. So much time to live, really live, is passing you by. You'll only have yourself to blame if you decide to spend the rest your time on earth letting fear dictate everything that happens to you." Zoe yanked the rope from the tree branch and coiled it up. "You lose, and so do those of us who want to be in that time with you." She placed the rope into her backpack. "I'd better go. I have more work to do at the island, and I want to paddle across the lake before it gets dark."

"I could take you back."

"That's okay. I need to be alone right now. I'll let you know about Dac."

Alex's heart pounded in her chest. She stood and reached for Zoe's hand. "Please, believe that I'm trying."

Zoe yanked her hand away, turned her back, and wiped her cheek. "I'll see you." She disappeared into the woods.

Alex slumped to the ground and put her head in her hands. She huddled alone under the chestnut tree, unable to move.

# Chapter 26

"He looks great," Zoe marveled.

The eaglet sat poised for his future of flight. His black feathers and gray beak looked healthy, and he'd gained a couple of pounds in the days he'd been away from the nest. With the leather hood covering his eyes, he sat motionless inside the pet carrier.

"It's his big day of freedom," Daniel said.

"He doesn't have any more time to lose. It's now or never for him to live. If he isn't able to get back into the nest within the week, he'll die not long after that."

"Why take such a chance with him, then?"

"Animals all want the same thing we do." Zoe dropped the corner of the blanket draped over the carrier, which sat in the back of her truck. She'd parked in front of the camp. It was early enough in the morning that the campers and their counselors had yet to stir.

"Which is?" Daniel asked.

"They just want to live free and be happy. If he has it in him to do so, we should let him try."

"So let him find his own way in the world, even if it turns out to be much more difficult?"

"It depends on what you consider difficult. From his perspective, I suspect difficult would be having to live in captivity. Trust me, he'll find his happiness flying free in the sky as opposed to sitting trapped on a perch all day with an unlimited supply of food." Zoe patted the top of the carrier. "I really appreciate your agreeing to keep things quiet about the eaglet coming back today. It's so important that we keep people away from him and the island if he's going to have any chance at all."

"I'm glad to do it. It's the only common ground Alex and I seem to have these days."

Zoe was relieved he had agreed to help bring Dac back to the island. His truce with Alex, as she considered it, was fragile at best. She was glad the three of them would take Dac home.

"Is she meeting us at the shore?" Zoe reached for a handle on the side of the carrier.

"Yes. She's getting the boat ready." He stood still, as if contemplating something to say. "You and Alex have become good friends, haven't you? I mean, you have to be. You were the one she listened to when it came to getting her to stay for the summer."

"I consider her a friend, definitely." Zoe let go of the carrier. She hoped he couldn't read in her expression that Alex was so much more than just a friend.

"You must know my family's dirty secrets by now. How do you think she's doing?"

"Mr. Marcotte, please. I don't think it's fair to Alex for me to talk about this with you."

"Did she tell you I've been going to therapy with her?" Daniel averted his eyes.

"She mentioned it, yes."

"I… I'm not a bad father," he blurted.

"Mr. Marcotte, you don't have to go into this with me. It really isn't any of my business. I care about Alex, but we can't talk about this when she's not here."

"I need for you to know something, though." He crossed his arms over his chest. "I never cared that Jake and Alex were gay. I still don't." He hesitated. "I just didn't know what to do. My wife was so upset, and I was afraid of what the world would do to Alex and Jake if they were gay. The kids at school had already tortured my Jake." He pointed at the carrier. "It's sort of like the eagle here. In a sense, we tried to keep our kids in captivity so they wouldn't be hurt by the world. What I'm learning now is that I wasn't protecting them by trying to convince them to rethink this whole gay thing."

Zoe bit her tongue. It wasn't her place to question his motives, but she found it impossible to believe that Daniel's only intent was the innocent desire to protect his son and daughter from a homophobic world. She could also see that he was in pain. "With all due respect, why are you telling me this?" She felt sorry for him despite what his paralysis had done to Alex and her brother.

"I saw the way she looked at you that night at the dance." He glanced away. "And the way you looked at her when you went after her. I may be inept as a father, but I'm not blind."

"Mr. Marcotte—"

"Hear me out. Will you?"

"Of course."

"When I asked Alex if there was something going on between you, she never answered me. Her silence spoke volumes." He swallowed whatever emotion caused his eyes to moisten. "If you're part of what makes her happy again, I don't want her or you to think I would ever stand between you."

"I'm relieved to know that. But it isn't me you should be telling. Please say it to Alex."

He shook his head. "I can't. It's been so long since I've known how to talk to my daughter." He breathed a sigh laced with sarcasm. "Or anyone else, for that matter. After all that's happened, I don't think she's able to hear me through the noise of our history. I hope you understand I'm not trying to make excuses. I still haven't figured out what she needs to hear from me."

"I mean you no disrespect by saying this, but if you don't know, you still aren't listening. You might start with something simple, like 'I'm sorry.' And, 'I love you.' Say what you feel like you just did with me." Zoe grabbed the handle on the side of the carrier again. "If you don't mind, sir, we really need to get the eaglet out of here before the day gets much hotter and the kids discover we have him."

"Thank you for listening." Daniel grasped the other handle and lifted the carrier in sync with Zoe. "Alex should be at the shore with the boat, ready to go."

"Perfect." Zoe struggled to hold the pet carrier level with the much taller man on the other side. She put her head down and ignored the pain in her shoulder from the heavy load. The lump in her stomach weighed her down even more. In the little time she'd spent with Alex since the day at the chestnut tree, Alex seemed to pretend they'd never been intimate, which broke her heart, but she refused to give up. Her anger had dissipated, but her desire to help Alex had increased.

Daniel said, "There she is."

Zoe lifted her gaze and saw Alex loading a dry-bag into the boat. Alex waved, hopped out of the boat, and jogged toward them. When she arrived, she reached for the handle on Zoe's side of the carrier. "I wouldn't miss this for the world."

Zoe let go, happy for the break, and even happier to see Alex. "I'm glad you're here."

"Me too." Alex carried Dac the rest of the way with her father.

Zoe slipped a couple of paces behind and watched Alex and Daniel working together to bring the carrier to the boat. Their familial resemblance was striking. They had the same facial features and tall slender build. Even their gaits were similar. The universe had a way of teaching lessons through its metaphors. There had to be a lesson in the fact that Alex and her father were taking Dac home. Maybe it was the other way around. Maybe Dac was taking them home.

Alex and Daniel carefully hoisted the carrier into the back of the boat and set it on the floor. Daniel stood at the controls. "Do you have everything you need, Zoe?"

Zoe slipped the backpack from her shoulders. "All set, thanks." She sat down near Dac's carrier.

"All right, then." Daniel turned the key and throttled the engine to back the boat off the sand.

Alex took a seat across from Zoe.

"I'm glad to see you." Zoe glanced at Daniel, whose attention was focused on the lake ahead of them. "I was afraid you wouldn't come."

"I've been thinking a lot about what you said about time. The summer's going to be over soon. I want to spend as much time with you and Dac as I can before I go back to California. If you'll let me, I'd love to help you keep watch over him in the coming weeks."

Zoe took in the sight of Alex. The need to memorize her face overwhelmed her. "I'd like that."

"Good."

They sat for the remainder of the ride in silence until Daniel rounded the back of the island and slid the boat smoothly up on the sand. Not only did he and Alex look so much alike, it was clear from whom Alex got her boat-operating skills.

Zoe took the binoculars from her backpack, zipped it closed, and put it on. She scanned the trees for the parent eagles. Dac's sibling, Terry, sat in the nest, looking curiously over the edge. He was big enough for his body to be visible in the nest, not just his head. Soon he would be perched on the edge of the nest with his wings spread wide, testing the feel of the wind against them.

"I don't see the parents," Zoe said. "I'm sure they aren't too far away. They're probably nearby hunting for breakfast. This is a good time to bring Dac home."

Daniel shut the engine down. "How can we help?"

Zoe pointed at a large boulder at the base of the tall pine holding the nest. "We're going to leave him next to that boulder. It's close enough to the lake for him to grab a drink of water if he gets thirsty in this heat."

Alex glanced from the boulder to the nest. "I still don't understand how he's going to get up there."

Zoe patted the underside of the backpack. "Remember that chopped salmon we tried to feed him at the rehab center? I'm going to leave a bunch of it on top of the boulder. When he gets hungry, he'll have to take the first step of figuring out how to get on top of the rock. Once he does that, he'll be close enough to go to the next level by getting himself from there to one of those lower branches on the tree. I'm hoping he'll hopscotch his way back into the nest."

"That would be remarkable if he's able to make it," Daniel said.

Zoe's gaze bore into Daniel's. "With some encouragement from his parents, he'll make it."

Daniel smiled for the first time she could recall since coming to the camp. "Let's get this little guy home." He reached for a carrier handle. Alex took the other. They toted the carrier the rest of the way to the boulder.

Zoe unpacked the plastic container with the salmon pieces. She grinned at Alex. "This could get stinky, remember?" She climbed onto the boulder and emptied the container's contents on top of it. She hopped off of the big rock. "Time for the moment of truth."

She pulled a large, heavy towel from the backpack. She slung it over her shoulder and unclipped the fasteners that held the carrier's top to its bottom. Alex helped her lift the top off. Dac must've noticed the sun on his body. He moved his head, clearly curious about his surroundings. The leather helmet still covered his eyes.

"I had no idea he would be so big," Daniel said. "I thought the heavy weight was all from the carrier. He seems even bigger than his parents. And he doesn't have a yellow beak or feet."

"They do look bigger because their feathers are different. But they don't weigh quite as much as their parents." Zoe put the towel over the eaglet and lifted him from the carrier. She set him down on the ground by the boulder and removed the towel. "When I take off his helmet, he might decide he needs to defend himself against us. Give him space. We'll grab our stuff and leave him to the business of getting on with his life." She reached for the helmet.

"Wait," Alex said. "Would it be all right if I touch his feathers one last time?"

"Sure," Zoe said.

Alex lightly stroked the thick, soft feathers on Dac's back. "Good luck, little one. We'll do our best for you." She stepped back near her father.

Zoe lifted the helmet from Dac's head. He blinked in the bright sunlight. He spread his wings wide, put his head back, and called out loudly.

"We should go." Zoe gathered the towel into her backpack while Alex and her father each grabbed a section of the carrier and headed toward the boat. "It's all up to him now."

Daniel stopped and looked over his shoulder. "This might be the most important thing that has happened to this camp in a long time. I intend to do everything in my power to protect this eaglet." He seemed to gather strength from Dac in the same way as Alex had.

Zoe saw an expression pass over Alex's face that she hadn't seen before. It reminded her of the way she'd looked up to her own father when she was a child.

# Chapter 27

Zoe noticed the subtle definition of muscle in Alex's slender shoulders as she held the binoculars to her eyes. Clad in a pair of shorts and a bikini top, Alex was impossible to look away from.

Zoe knew what it felt like to have Alex's lips on hers. She longed to know the rest. Unfortunately, dwelling on her desire was self-induced torture. She tore her gaze from Alex and scanned the island for any sign of Dac. She gripped the cockpit rim on Alex's kayak tighter to keep her close. The anchor attached to her own kayak kept them from drifting.

"It's been four days since we put Dac on the island, and we haven't seen him since." Alex lowered the binoculars. "That's a bad sign, isn't it?"

The question snapped Zoe back to the task at hand: looking for Dac. She weighed whether to answer from the optimistic peak in her heart or the pessimistic pit in her stomach. Every hour that passed with Dac on the ground increased the likelihood that his chances at life were quickly ticking away. "I'm worried. But I'm not ready to give up on him."

"Maybe we should land on the island and walk around in the brush to see if we can find him that way. He might be hungry and all he needs is a little more food." Alex pointed at the big boulder. "All the salmon we left for him is gone."

Zoe didn't have a lot of confidence that Dac had actually eaten the salmon. Any number of small predators or birds might have helped themselves to the easy pickings. She did intend to land on the island at some point to look for him, but she assumed that when she did so, it would be to locate his body. Given all that Alex was going through, Zoe didn't want her to have to witness finding Dac's carcass. But not letting Alex have a choice in the matter made her feel guilty.

"Let's wait a little while longer and let Mother Nature run her full course," she said. "We shouldn't interfere now."

Chirping came from the nest. Zoe gazed up to see Terry climb out onto its edge. He spread his wings wide and made his presence known with a long, strong call to the world.

"What's he doing?" Alex asked. "Is he trying to get his parents' attention? I haven't seen either of them since we've been out here."

"He's getting ready to fledge, which means he's ready to learn how to fly. See how he's keeping his wings spread open wide? He's testing to see how the wind feels. Eventually, he'll be brave enough to let wind gusts lift him from the nest and back down until he's ready to try flying from limb to limb in the nest tree, a little at a time until he goes for it."

"What do you mean, goes for it? It's hard to imagine he can learn how to use his wings hopping from limb to limb."

"I don't think it's as much about learning how to use his wings as it is about trusting them. Essentially, when he's ready, he'll stand on the edge of the nest, spread his wings wide, wait for a good wind, and take a leap of faith."

Alex switched her attention from Terry to Zoe. "That's how they learn to fly? They just let everything go and step into the wind?"

"Yeah, that's a great way to describe it. They simply step into the wind. What I wouldn't give to know how that feels. Maybe it's the same feeling a kid gets riding a bike for the first time without training wheels. They just do it because they know they can. All they need is faith. I'll have to keep that in mind for my presentation tomorrow on how birds fly." Zoe smiled at Alex. "I'm nervous. I don't really know how to talk to little kids."

"I'm glad Claire finally persuaded you to do it. The kids are going to love you. I saw how you were with Michelle. She was mesmerized by you. Besides, they're going to be on their best behavior since their parents will be there. I'm betting with your talk, and Patch making an appearance, followed by the puppy fashion show, they won't have time to misbehave."

"It was actually your father who convinced me. He said it would be a great way to win the parents over and get their buy-in about protecting the eagles. I was skeptical about making the eagles' location public, but he has a point. If more people learn to care about them, peer pressure might be enough to keep visitors away from the island, especially with the Fourth of July weekend coming soon. Your dad really seems to mean what he says about protecting the eagles and the island."

"We'll see how good his word is when it starts to hurt the camp."

Zoe gathered her courage. "Please don't take this the wrong way, but I have to ask: do you think you'll ever be able to forgive your father?"

Alex's gaze met Zoe's. "I hope so, if he asks. I'd love to let go of having a hard heart. It hurts to have it covered in stone all the time."

"Why not do it for yourself, then, regardless of whether he asks? Aren't you the one paying the price by letting your heart stay buried?"

"What if he's not sorry at all?"

"Why does it matter?" A large brown bird soaring through the sky caught Zoe's eye. She looked from Alex toward the sky.

"What is that?" Alex asked.

"It's a juvenile eagle, probably a couple of years old. I've seen it hanging around the past few days."

The young eagle soared high over them, circling in the updrafts of wind. It banked and flew in successively lower arcs around the island, heading in the direction of the nest.

Zoe searched the tree line on shore for either of the eagle parents. "Where are you, Mom and Dad?" This was not good.

"Do you think the new eagle's curious about whether the nest is occupied?"

"I'm sure it knows. Eagles may be majestic and inspiring, but like humans, they can be opportunistic invaders."

The invader screeched as it continued its tack toward the nest. Terry frantically climbed out of the nest and onto one of the anchoring branches. He scooted to the end of the branch as far as he could go, tucked his wings close to his body, and hunkered down as if trying to be invisible.

"He's terrified," Alex said. "What's happening?"

Zoe hoped the invader wanted whatever food it could grab in the nest while the parent eagles were away. It was a good thing for Terry that he had the instinct to get out of the invader's way. It wouldn't hesitate to kill him. She pulled Alex's boat closer and wished Alex wouldn't see the likely outcome if Terry's parents didn't show up soon to protect him.

Alex placed her hand over Zoe's and helped her hold the kayak steady. It was the first physical contact they'd had since the day at the chestnut tree. Alex's touch took her breath away.

The invader swung around to the front of the island and landed on the large boulder where they'd left the salmon for Dac. Zoe suspected that the invader had likely stolen the food and come back for what was in the nest. It may have already killed Dac. The invader opened its wings and flapped them together as it hopped from the rock to a branch low on the nest tree.

"That's a good sign," Zoe said.

"What is?"

"It can't figure out how to get into the nest by flying. Have you noticed how the parents always enter the nest from the back of the island? That's because there's a clear path they can take without getting their wings caught in the tree branches that hold the nest. This bird is going to try to climb the tree with its talons to get there. It's not going to be easy in all those thick, needle-covered branches. That ought to buy the parents some time to get here."

The invader hopped to another, higher branch that couldn't hold its weight. The branch snapped. The young eagle tumbled out of the tree and disappeared into the heavy brush.

There was still no sign of the parents when the tree's thick, bottom branches started to move. The dark green needles shielded the invader from her view, but Zoe knew there was no question of its giving up. With its talons locked into the rough bark, it continued to walk its way up the tree trunk instead of hopping from limb to limb. Occasionally, its progress would stall when its unwieldy wings got caught in the whorls of branches and it had to pause to untangle them.

Terry remained huddled as far from the nest as he could go. He must've sensed the danger in the invader's presence because his calls to his parents became more frantic the closer the invader came.

Alex twisted around in her kayak. "Come on, where are the parents? There!" She pointed.

Zoe looked over her shoulder and saw one of the parents gliding fast above the shore. It landed on a tree across from the island. She lifted her binoculars to her eyes. "It's the female." She could tell the parents apart based on the differences in their sizes. The female was larger than the male. She glanced at the nest in time to see the invader climb over its edge. It spread its wings and screeched, a sound that suggested its defiant victory.

Terry huddled in fear as his mother lifted off and flew toward the nest. Instead of entering it from the back, she went straight for the front where the invader faced. As she attempted to land, her wings tangled in the branches. The invader lunged at her, pulling her into the nest with it. The two raptors clawed at each other with their razor sharp talons and beaks.

Zoe's heart sank. If the invader couldn't be stopped, or if it seriously injured or killed the mother, the entire eagle family would be doomed. "Don't let him get the better of you," she yelled, turning her hand palm up to squeeze Alex's.

The battle in the nest continued. Finally, the mother freed herself from the invader's clutches. She flew off the back of the nest toward the opposite shore and disappeared in the trees.

A tear slid down Alex's cheek. "No," she whispered.

Zoe reached over and put her arm around Alex as best she could, considering they sat in separate kayaks. "Don't give up on the mother yet." Her hope was fading, but for Alex's sake, she held onto it.

Alex pointed. "She's coming back."

Relief flooded Zoe as the mother tore along the shoreline back toward the island. The strength of the eagle's flight betrayed no evidence of any crippling injuries. She flapped her wings again and again, picking up speed as she moved out over the lake, heading straight toward the back of the nest.

The invader appeared oblivious to her approach. It faced the opposite direction, ripping and tearing at the stolen food. When about thirty feet from the nest, the mother tucked her wings in close and pointed her head straight. She was a missile locked on her target. She rammed full force into the invader's back. It tumbled out of the nest and down into the tree branches. The mother clawed the edge of the nest and kept from going over the edge too.

The invader somersaulted down the branches. It disappeared again in the thick brush below. The mother eagle stood tall in the nest and called to Terry. He scooted tentatively along the branch, back toward safety, and tucked himself close to her body.

"She did it," Alex yelled.

Zoe's relief was short lived.

The invader flew out of the brush, back toward the nest. The mother launched into the air and met it in the sky. The two eagles locked talons high over the water and battled for dominance. Locked together in combat, they hurtled toward the lake.

The mother managed to right herself. She was above the invader, driving it headfirst toward the water below. Almost ten feet from the surface, she let go, flapped her wings hard, and caught an updraft. The invader splashed down and sank. It popped back up and churned the water with its sodden wings. Finally, it managed to lift itself out and flew fast and far away from the lake.

Zoe grinned. "I have a feeling it's not coming back any time soon."

Alex clapped their hands. "Mama eagle rocks!" she said as her boat drifted away from Zoe's.

Zoe laughed, reached out, and took Alex's outstretched hand. She pulled Alex's kayak next to hers and put her arms around Alex, almost tipping over. She gave way to a fit of giggles. Suddenly the branches at the bottom of the tree started to move.

"I'll be damned," Zoe said, stunned by what she realized was happening. "Our little Dac was paying attention to how the invader got into the nest without flying." She pointed to a tangle of boughs bouncing under Dac's weight as he clawed his way up one branch at a time toward the nest.

Alex wiped tears from her eyes.

"I hope those are tears of joy."

"They are, for Dac and for me. He managed to claw his way back up. There's a lesson in that."

"Yeah, what is it?"

"You asked me why it mattered whether my father ever apologizes so I can let go of my anger. Dac just showed me that maybe it doesn't. Even though his parent chased the invader away, he had to climb the tree all on his own. Nothing his parent did or didn't do would've mattered if he hadn't."

Zoe rubbed Alex's shoulder. "And he did it one step at a time." She pointed to Dac, now sitting in the nest with his family. "Dac had lots of help along the way, but the biggest reason he's still alive is because he wants to be."

# Chapter 28

Alex found the step stool next to the tool chest in the barn where her father said it would be.

Zoe had insisted on having something to stand on behind the podium during her presentation to the camp about how birds fly. She was afraid the kids wouldn't take her seriously if they realized she wasn't much taller than they were. Alex smiled. Zoe was larger than life despite being so small in stature.

When Alex slid the stool out of its resting place, she noticed the dark-brown leather of her brother's prized possession—his baseball glove—on the back of the tool chest. She let go of the stool and reached for the glove. She could feel Jake near. The glove had been one of the last things he touched before he died.

The barn door slid open. "Your dad said I'd find you in here." Zoe paused. "Nice old glove. Did you play ball when you were a kid?"

Alex ran her hand over the leather. "No, this belonged to Jake. He loved playing baseball." Her eyes misted over. "Unfortunately, even that was taken from him by the kids who bullied him. They forced him to quit. If he was going to play, he'd have to endure their abuse. He couldn't. It was too much."

"Where the heck were the adults when this was going on?" Zoe came into the barn.

"Making excuses that kids will be kids. Looking the other way, or being too caught up in other things to see what was in front of them."

"We all do that to some extent." Zoe came closer.

"What's that?" Alex asked.

"Not see the obvious. We get so bogged down with what happened yesterday and what we're going to do tomorrow that we forget to see or feel things in the moment. That's where the obvious is."

Alex replaced the glove where she'd found it. She crossed her arms over her chest and leaned against the tool cabinet. Several seconds ticked by. "Thank you, Zoe."

"For what?"

"When I saw my brother's glove, I could only think about how angry I am at my father for what happened all those years ago. But thinking about it here and now, I think I know why my father still keeps the glove with his tools. Maybe it's his way of keeping Jake close because he misses him every bit as much as I do."

Zoe closed the distance between them. "I'm glad you're finding a way to look at the world from a different place."

"I'm trying hard to see things in a forgiving way, like we talked about." A lump caught in Alex's throat. "Maybe my father and I share the same pain." She bit her bottom lip. "There's something else about this moment." She tugged the bottom of Zoe's T-shirt, pulling her even closer. Everything about Zoe felt like life. She noticed Zoe's breathing getting heavy. "No matter how hard I fight it, the need to touch you overwhelms me. Right now, I don't want to think about tomorrow and what might happen next. All I want is this moment." She put her hands on Zoe's hips. "Here, with you."

Zoe moved to Alex's side, put her palms on the workbench, and lifted herself into a sitting position. "I want to be face-to-face with you."

Alex stood between Zoe's legs. With Zoe on the bench, they were eye to eye, only inches apart. Riding on a building crest of desire, Alex put her hands on Zoe's backside and slid her to the edge of the bench. "Are you still afraid of me?" she asked.

"I want this moment too. I want whatever you'll let me have." Zoe glanced at Alex's lips before leaning forward and kissing her.

The kiss was gentle and sweet, like sunrise on a summer day. A whimper escaped Alex's throat. She pushed closer to Zoe. Their tongues touched as she slipped a hand under Zoe's T-shirt. She pulled back and looked into Zoe's eyes.

Zoe smiled and guided Alex's hand to her breast. "You aren't using me. You're giving me what I want."

Alex felt Zoe's nipple harden under her touch. She tried to ignore the sound of voices outside the barn.

Zoe must've heard them too. She pulled Alex's hand from under her shirt and rested their foreheads together. "It might not go over too well if a camper barges in and catches us."

"No." Alex put her hands on either side of Zoe's face, kissed her quickly, and moved away.

Zoe hopped down and smoothed her T-shirt. Her face was flushed. "I should see if Patch and his handler have arrived. I'll meet you in the main building. People are starting to gather outside under the tent for the presentation and puppy fashion show." She took Alex's hand on her way out, holding it until they exited the barn, when she let go to continue on her way.

Alex called after her, "They're going to love you." *I do too.*

"I hope so," Zoe answered. "See you soon."

Zoe slipped her cell phone into her pocket. "That's not good."

"What's that?" Claire checked her watch. "Everyone's ready for the show to start. Is there a problem?"

Zoe glanced from Claire to Alex and Sally. "A major brush fire broke out not far from Lewiston. They had to close the highway because of smoke and the proximity of the fire, which has taken off and is merging with other, smaller fires. Sounds like it's getting out of control. Rick had to take a detour. He and Patch are going to be late."

"That's all right. We have you and the puppies." Sally clapped her hands. "The show must go on." She cocked her head. "You look a little pale. You're not nervous, are you?"

"Truthfully, I am. I was looking forward to Rick and Patch being the stars of the show."

"Honey, enough worry. There's too much of that going around." Sally winked at Alex. "We're on a mission to do away with that sort of thing. Aren't we?"

Alex wanted to hug Zoe's worries away but had concerns about what Claire would think. A question that her therapist asked recently played in her head. *Why not test whether your fears are legitimate by doing the thing you think you're afraid of?* Besides, in this moment, giving Zoe a hug seemed the thing to do.

She put her arms around Zoe. "You have nothing to be worried about. You're amazing, and it'll only take two seconds before everyone out there figures that out."

Zoe returned the hug. "You know how to talk a girl off the ledge."

Claire laughed. "We're all going to have to go over to Hawk's Leap some afternoon." She patted Alex's back. "No one was better at talking a kid off the ledge than Alex when it came to getting them to jump. I'm glad to see a little of that fearlessness again in her."

Daniel popped his head into the room. He looked long at Alex and Zoe in each other's arms before his gaze fell on Claire and Sally. Alex couldn't read his expression. For once, it didn't matter if he thought less of her. Being in Zoe's arms made her happy. To her surprise, he smiled at Zoe. "Time to get this show on the road. I'm going to announce you now."

Alex and the rest of the group followed him out of the main building and in front of the crowd of kids, parents, and counselors gathered under the big tent set up to shade them from the sun during the show. He picked up the microphone lying on the podium.

"Good afternoon and thank you all for coming. We have a real treat for you. Zoe Kimball, a wildlife biologist we've been lucky enough to have stay with us this summer to look after our eagles on the island, is here to talk with us about how birds fly." Daniel paused while the crowd clapped. "Let's show Ms. Kimball how grateful we are for her time with a proper Camp Marcotte greeting."

The children rose to their feet, blew kisses at each other, and yelled, "Welcome to Camp Marcotte, where kids learn to love to play outside!"

Alex grinned, in part because the greeting always made her laugh, but mostly because her father had suggested it for Zoe. She joined in with the kids and counselors when they continued, "You'll always be a friend of Camp Marcotte."

In unison, everyone blew a kiss to Zoe.

Zoe took the microphone from Alex's father, who stepped away. "Wow, that was the nicest greeting ever. Thank you. Let me ask a question. Does anyone know how hummingbirds fly?"

Whatever nervousness Zoe felt certainly didn't show. The kids seemed mesmerized by her. Alex also noticed that Zoe never stepped behind the podium onto the step stool. She stayed in front of the crowd like she'd been doing this her whole life. Zoe was a natural and didn't know it.

A child in the back answered, "They flap their wings really fast. They come to my mom's bird feeder all the time, and I see them."

"Have you ever seen a helicopter fly?" Zoe asked. "Hummingbirds are like that. With their short wings, they can hover by flapping forward and backward instead of up and down." She moved her arms to show the crowd what she meant. "Did you know that hummingbirds go to sleep at night like they're hibernating? They do that because it takes so much energy for them to fly fast like they do. They need to eat three times their weight in food every day."

A different child joined in the conversation. "That's a lot of pizza."

Zoe laughed. "Yeah, you look like you weigh about eighty pounds. I wonder how many pizzas it takes to equal three hundred twenty pounds, which would be three times your weight."

"Maybe we'll have to try to get that many pizzas before you kids leave here," Daniel teased.

The campers shouted their agreement with the idea. Seeing her father play to the crowd like old times tugged at Alex. This was the father who had loved her and Jake with all his heart when they were growing up. He was also the father she loved to her core. Now, she felt a bittersweet understanding of how much he loved this camp but couldn't love his son and daughter as much. Despite the laughter in the crowd and the smile on his face, sadness threatened to pour out of her.

"Be sure to invite me for the pizza," Zoe said. "How about eagles... does anyone know how they fly?" The little girl she'd met on the beach a couple of weeks ago raised her hand. "Yes, Michelle. Can you tell us?"

"They have really big wings that they flap up and down. But not as fast as a hummingbird," Michelle answered.

Alex noticed that the grin on Michelle's face wasn't nearly as wide as the one worn by the woman sitting next to her, whom she assumed must be her mother. She suspected it had been a big deal for her mother to make it since Michelle had mentioned that her mom worked two jobs.

Seeing her beam with pride at her daughter and knowing Michelle had learned some valuable lessons about life during a few weeks at the camp reminded Alex of its importance. The camp meant the world to a mother on a limited income and a kid like Michelle, who'd had the opportunity to spend time in such a beautiful place. She proudly gave her father credit for making that experience happen for so many children.

"That's right. Good job." Zoe smiled. "They do flap their wings but not forward and back like a hummingbird, nor as fast. They don't have to. Because as Michelle told us, they have very long wings, and they use them to soar and glide. The hummingbird's wings look more like oars. But an eagle's wing is long and wide with slotted wingtips." She held up a model of an eagle.

Alex thought Zoe was doing a fine job of showing the kids the parts of an eagle, even without Patch. The replica combined with Zoe's explanation did the trick. She had the audience captured.

Zoe pulled the model eagle's wing out straight for the kids to see its shape and size. She set the model down on the table behind her.

"Eagles flap their wings up and down to get momentum for flight, but they use the wind to go long distances without having to flap their wings constantly like a hummingbird. They can go lower in the sky by gliding on the wind without flapping their wings. Or they can soar higher by riding updrafts in the wind. All without moving their wings."

She paused and looked into the air. "You're so lucky to see this." She clapped her hands and pointed upward. "Look there, that's one of the camp's eaglets flying now. That's Terry!"

The eaglet soared above them. The crowd gasped in awe at *their* eaglet. Terry bobbled in a gust of wind, got his bearings, and flew off into the distance.

"Did you see him practicing in the updrafts?" Zoe asked.

A dark-haired little boy in front jumped to his feet. "What does updraft mean?"

"The wind comes in different temperatures. The warm ones rise while the cooler ones stay close to the ground." Zoe accompanied her words with hand gestures. "The updrafts are the warm winds rising. They can carry the eagles far because of the way the eagles' wings are shaped. The eagle simply spreads its wings and lets warm air currents carry it high into the sky."

Again, Zoe pulled the model's wing out for the kids to see. "Based on the shape of the wing, the layers of air above the wing flow faster than the ones below it. This difference in pressure lets the eagle be lifted by the wind. Pay attention in science class when your teacher tells you about Bernoulli's Principle because that's how eagles fly." She pointed toward the back of the crowd. "Guess what? The star of our show has arrived."

Everyone turned to look over their shoulders, including Alex. Rick strolled in with Patch held high on his arm. Gasps of delight came from the kids as well as adults. Patch couldn't have seemed more proud. He turned his head from side to side as if to make sure they all got a look at his profile.

Zoe laughed. "Ladies and gentlemen, girls and boys, it's my pleasure to introduce you to Rick Watkins and a most incredible eagle named Patch." She stepped down from the stage and went to stand next to Alex.

Rick placed Patch on the perch that Zoe had set up earlier. "Thank you, Zoe, for the introduction. Sorry we're late. Patch and I had to dodge a forest fire to get here. But like Patch always does, he found a way." He proceeded to tell the crowd about eagles and about Patch in particular.

Alex leaned over and whispered to Zoe, "You were great. I told you they'd love you. And you didn't even have Patch for backup." She slipped her hand into Zoe's. No one paid attention to them with Patch in the room. "Look at them. They're all smitten by Patch, even my father."

"Patch has that effect on people." Zoe nudged Alex and jutted her chin in the direction of James. "Except maybe him. He looks like a pouting two-year-old."

"That's because he knows after today he's lost the battle over the island. It belongs to the eagles now."

"Thank goodness. Dac and Terry are going to need all the quiet they can get, especially Dac. He has a lot of catching up to do with his brother if there's any hope he'll be on his own by winter."

Daniel went to the front of the room after Rick and Patch finished their presentation. "What a wonderful morning this has been. Thanks again to Zoe, Rick, and Patch for teaching us about eagles. We're so lucky to have eagles on our island. If you learn anything this summer here with us, I hope it's to always respect wildlife and do your best to protect them. The world would be a very sad place without such beautiful creatures as Patch."

Patch cocked his head at Daniel and chirped. Everyone laughed.

Daniel waved his hand. "On that note, it's time for lunch. We have a big spread for everyone down by the water. Let's go enjoy some great food and meet back here at two o'clock for the puppy fashion show."

Alex squeezed Zoe's hand tighter before letting go. "I can't remember the last time I had such a great day. I should try to live in the moment more often. Shall we get something to eat? The camp always has yummy food, especially for Parents' Day."

# Chapter 29

Alex finished the last bite of her veggie burger. "Did you enjoy lunch?" she asked Zoe.

"I did. Then again, a grilled hot dog with the works is impossible not to like." Zoe nodded at the crowd of adults and kids enjoying their lunches. "I'm in good company."

Alex smirked, leaned in close to Zoe, and whispered in her ear, "You do know what they put in those things, don't you?"

Zoe put up her hands. "Don't say it. Please don't ruin hot dogs for me." She smiled. "Let me continue to enjoy them in my naiveté. There are just some things a girl doesn't need to know. The contents of a hot dog are one of them."

Something about Zoe made Alex want to tease her, kiss her, and love her. The last emotion sat heavy in her heart. "All right. We'll leave the hot dog mystique intact."

Daniel approached. "Excuse me. I hope I'm not interrupting."

Zoe took a step away from Alex. "Not at all. In fact, I was eyeing the sodas over there and thought I'd go grab one. Would either of you like one as well?"

"No." Daniel seemed uneasy. "I have something to say."

"Okay," Alex said.

Zoe started to walk away.

"Wait," Daniel said. "I want you to hear this too."

Zoe turned around.

"You were fantastic with the kids today, Zoe." Daniel motioned toward the crowd. "I have to be honest. Not since before Jake died has this camp had a more perfect Parents' Day." His voice quivered. "Thank you both. If this turns out to be the last year that a Marcotte owns the camp, we'll have gone out on a high note. I have you to thank for that."

His comment came out of the blue. "Dad, what are you talking about?" Alex asked.

"I didn't necessarily want to get into this conversation now, but maybe you're right. Perhaps it's time for me to let the camp go. I—"

Sally's voice booming from a megaphone drowned out whatever Daniel was about to say. She bounded up onto the presentation stage. She wore a Dalmatian costume, white with black polka dots. A short tail protruded from her backside. She slipped the costume's hood off her head and yelled, "Who's ready for the puppy fashion show?"

The kids went wild as Chuck came from the main building holding the leashes of seven puppies in fancy collars.

"Ladies and gentlemen, I give you the Camp Marcotte puppies. Each is wearing a collar and leash made by one of the children from the camp," Sally said. "All the kids made one and a panel of counselor judges chose the best seven examples for the show. As you know, this show is part fundraiser for the Glasgow Humane Society and an opportunity for these puppies to be adopted into good homes. The first-place winner for the best collar and leash will have the opportunity, should his or her parent's wish, to choose which puppy to adopt."

"Ouch," Zoe said. "I think Sally may have put a parent or two on the spot with that one."

"Fortunately, no." Daniel grinned. "I wouldn't want a puppy to be adopted because a parent felt cornered by their child's excitement. I've spoken to all the parents up front and stressed that they shouldn't bid on any puppies unless they're absolutely sure they can and want to provide a good home. They've also been told that where the puppies go is up to the Humane Society's ultimate approval."

Alex mulled over her father's comment about the possibility of this being the last year the camp was owned by a Marcotte. It was what she wanted, wasn't it? The camp had become too much for him to handle alone. Yet the camp made a difference. Her father made a difference.

Taking Zoe's advice about living in the moment allowed her to see the perfection of this day. She also saw a glimmer of what she had always loved most about the camp: her parents and Maine. Her *parents*. Despite all that had happened, someplace deep inside, she questioned whether it was possible that she missed her mother too.

"Who won?" Zoe asked Daniel.

He glanced in the direction of Michelle and her mother. "Michelle won. I pulled her mom aside to let her know ahead of time. Unfortunately, she can't afford either the time or money for a puppy. Understandably, Michelle is heartbroken, but we both talked to her and she understands. She's an amazing little kid. She said if she couldn't have the puppy, she at least wanted me to make sure it went to a good home. Her mom got a little choked up over it. Most kids would've put up a fuss. Instead, Michelle consoled her mother. She's a special kid."

"Poor thing. Not only can she not have a puppy, the surprise of having her name announced as the winner had to be taken from her too," Alex said.

"I didn't want to put her in the position of being in front of all those other kids and having the rug pulled out from under her," Daniel said. "Not to worry. She and I worked out a solution."

Sally took the leash of the first puppy from Chuck and marched it in front of the other puppies. "I give you Rascal. He is wearing a leash made by Kelly Brown of Saco."

The crowd clapped and cheered.

Sally introduced the next five puppies and the children who'd made their respective leashes. The last puppy to be introduced was the runt, black and brown with a white dot between her eyes. Sally patted the puppy's head as it wriggled with excitement.

Alex studied her father. His expression reminded her of her family's playful times before their world came apart. When she pulled back all the layers of negativity, at his core he was a decent man. Instead of despising him, she wanted to find a way back to him, even if it meant slogging through the hurt to get there. *I still love you.* Some of the taint was washed away by the admission. It was as if the warmth from the sun shined past her skin and onto her heart.

Michelle squealed when her name was called.

Sally waved at her to come up in front of the crowd. "Our first-place winner, folks! And wearing the first-place collar and leash is Penny."

Michelle joined Sally and giggled when Penny licked her face when she hugged her.

"Congratulations, Michelle. As the winner, you get first dibs on one of the puppies. Is it going to be Penny?"

"Yes. But I want Penny to live with Mr. Marcotte. He promised me I could come see her anytime I wanted, and he would take the best ever care of her."

Daniel smiled at Alex and went to join Penny, Sally, and Michelle onstage.

Zoe leaned closer to Alex. "What your dad just did was really nice."

"It was, wasn't it?"

Daniel ruffled Michelle's hair and gave Penny a good scratch behind the ear. "I'm honored that you would choose me to take care of Penny."

Chuck interrupted by stepping onstage. He leaned next to Daniel's ear and covered his mouth with his hand when he spoke to him. Daniel's face went white. He said to Sally, "If you'll excuse me." To Michelle, he said, "Would you mind looking after Penny for me until I get back?" He handed her the leash and moved quickly through the crowd toward the main building.

"Something's wrong," Alex said.

"Let's go find out." Zoe pulled Alex along with her. They caught up to Daniel as he slid the main building's glass door open.

"What's the matter?" Alex followed him inside.

He took a deep breath. "The wildfire near Lewiston is completely out of control. The facility your mother's in has decided to evacuate the patients just in case. They're moving her to Augusta. Come with me."

All the moisture in her throat evaporated. "I can't."

"Alex, please stop this. Just stop long enough to say good-bye. I know your mother better than anyone. She won't survive this move." He put his hands on her shoulders. "This is your last chance to see her."

Anxiety found its opening. Her body vibrated with the pounding of her heart. The back of her neck felt hot, and she instinctively darted her gaze around the room, looking for an escape. Nausea rode on a wave of conflicting emotions. Her thoughts began to swim. A parade of horribles descended on her like a rolling fog over Maine's rocky shore.

A hand in hers calmed her. She let her fingers curl around Zoe's and kissed the back of Zoe's hand. "Will you be here when I get back?"

"I'll be wherever you need me to be."

# Chapter 30

Thick, black smoke billowed on the horizon. The day looked more like dusk than late afternoon. Alex had never seen anything like it, as if everything to the west of them was ablaze. Her father turned up the volume knob on the car radio as he drove.

The radio announcer said, "The wildfire burning toward the city of Lewiston is growing by the minute. Neighborhoods in its path are being evacuated as well as the Lewiston Nursing Home on the outskirts of the city. The weather service has issued a severe fire danger warning for all of Maine south of Augusta. Stay tuned for details."

Daniel turned off the highway at the exit sign for the nursing home. He hadn't spoken a word to Alex during the entire drive.

She didn't know what to say to him. She wasn't sure how to articulate her feelings. Besides, it was all she could do to keep her anxiety at bay. She sat quietly in the passenger seat and concentrated on her breathing. She found equilibrium in her emotions by meditating like she'd practiced with Dr. Kestler so many times in the last several days.

A mile down the road, Daniel turned onto the well-kept grounds of the nursing home. It seemed peaceful enough. Someone had made an effort to keep the flowers in bloom despite the drought. Alex looked again at the smoke-filled horizon. If the fire wasn't brought under control soon, the smoke and devastating heat would kill the fragile flowers before the fire even touched them. Jake's death had been the fire that destroyed her fragile family. She wished she could be anywhere but here. Her mother had set the flame. She thought about darting from the car when it came to a stop and running as far as she could to get away.

Daniel parked the car. He kept his hands on the steering wheel for several moments and stared straight ahead. "She'll be happy to see you. I'm sure of it."

Alex nodded and reached for the door handle. She wondered whether the statement was more of Daniel's delusional thinking when it came to her mother, or his heartfelt wish. Deep down, she held on to a glimmer of hope. She refused to let her anger crush it this time.

Ambulances were lined up in front of the building. "We should hurry. They're going to be moving everyone within the next couple of hours." Daniel got out of the car, seemingly on autopilot.

She was relieved by his lack of desire or inability to talk about what was happening. She couldn't bring herself to look at him, let alone talk to him. The anger she held at her core had traveled to just below the surface, simmering and threatening to boil over. She followed him inside the building, so tired of the anger.

When they entered the lobby, the worried receptionist said, "Hello, Mr. Marcotte. I'm glad you could make it. Carolyn isn't doing well."

"Is she lucid?" he asked.

"Yes, in and out."

"Thank you." He turned right and hurried down the long bleak hallway of rooms.

Alex kept pace with him. The place depressed her. She thought of her mother tending to her flower gardens every spring. There were few places Carolyn loved more than being in the sun at the camp surrounded by flowers. Despite Carolyn's unhappiness, Alex was glad she'd had something in the world that she loved without strings attached.

Her stomach did a hard flip when Daniel paused in front of room 128. She tried to moisten the inside of her dry mouth so she could speak.

He glanced at her and stepped into the room. He went to Carolyn's bedside, sat down, and took her hand. "Honey, it's me, Daniel." He brushed the side of her cheek. "Alex is here too."

Alex moved closer. The facility's institutional scent invaded her senses: bleach, antiseptic, and sadness. She stopped to take in the sight of Carolyn, a ghost of a person lying in a bed, waiting to die.

Carolyn was half the size Alex remembered, and her hair was completely white. Her skin was pale and loose. The woman who haunted her thoughts and dreams was really no more than a frail, defenseless person. It hurt to see her like this. Alex found it impossible to be angry with someone so weak and in poor health. Tears welled in her eyes. Carolyn needed to be protected. So had Jake.

Daniel stood when Alex came next to the bedside. He put a hand on her shoulder. "Would you like to speak with her alone?"

"No." She was still terrified of her mother. She didn't want to be alone with her. Not because Carolyn could hurt her physically. The old woman trapped in this bed couldn't physically harm anyone, and she'd never laid a hand on her or Jake. She didn't have to. She used words to wound instead. "Please stay." Carolyn could still crush her with a look or a word. She needed her father near.

She sat in the chair next to the bed, and Daniel stood close by. She reached up and took one of his hands in her own.

Carolyn's eyes opened. She stared straight ahead for several long moments. A single tear slid from her eye when she tried to say something.

Alex took her mother's hand. It felt cold and impossibly small. She wanted to cry away all of their pain. More than that, though, she wanted to be able to forgive.

"My beautiful Alex," Carolyn said in a barely audible, scratchy voice. She turned her head. Her gaze locked with Alex's. Her blue eyes hadn't aged. They were the same clear, midnight blue they'd always been. Her face softened. Then her expression hardened. "I don't see you anymore, nor do I want to." She rolled her head away.

A garbled sob lodged in Alex's throat. She put her hand to her mouth, refusing to let her mother see or hear her cry. Stunned, trapped again in the darkness, she couldn't move. She closed her eyes and tried to imagine the sun and Zoe, but they were shut out by the rage still burning in Carolyn's heart. Like the flames from the wildfire miles away that threatened to descend on the city of Lewiston, her mother's anger had clearly flared out of control, resorting to the rejection.

Alex stood and took in her father's shocked expression before she bolted from the room.

He called to her as she went, "Don't go. She doesn't know what she's saying."

Alex left the room, ran down the hall, and exited the building. She stopped to sit on a bench outside. Everything she'd worked through over the past several weeks crumbled under the heavy weight of Carolyn's words. She'd tried her best, but it hadn't worked. Memories of what Carolyn had done to Jake still hurt too much for her to stay in Maine.

She waited for her father outside, but he never came. Just like before, he abandoned her in favor of her mother. The sob she'd choked back earlier broke free, and she cried alone on the bench outside as the flames and smoke from the fire came closer. All around her, a flurry of people continued the process of moving the residents to safety.

What seemed like hours later, she saw Daniel emerge from the building next to someone wrapped in blankets and lying on a gurney. Her mother, she thought. He walked alongside until the gurney was about to be lifted into a waiting ambulance. He leaned over and kissed Carolyn good-bye. Alex knew the same thing he must know: this was the last time they'd see Carolyn alive.

Daniel's shoulders slumped when the doors closed and the ambulance drove away with his world. When the ambulance was finally out of sight, he sat next to her on the bench. "I'm so sorry."

He'd never said those words to her before. Alex expected to be angrier, but she wasn't. Maybe she was too tired.

"I'm sorry I didn't keep Jake safe. I'm sorry I let you run away without going after you. For not trying to make you understand I never chose Carolyn over you, despite what you think."

"But you did. You heard what she said to me. Why didn't you say something? Why couldn't you ever stand up to her?"

"Please try to understand." He hung his head. "She's been sick a long time. The thing I wish more than anything is that I could've convinced her to get help. Her sickness consumed her and Jake, and it's trying to consume us with it. I don't want it to take you too. I always knew that out of all of us, you'd be the one who would be okay. That's why I didn't go after you. Your mother needed me in a way that you didn't. I do love her with all of my heart. She wouldn't have been okay without me. For what it's worth, I just said good-bye to my best friend in the whole world."

Alex stared at the dry grass under her feet. The only thing she felt was numb.

# Chapter 31

Zoe pressed the gas pedal down farther. Her truck's engine raced as she sped around a curve in the road. Embers from the fires blew across the pavement and onto the hood. The heat and the smell of her soot-covered clothing tempted her to open the window, but she didn't dare.

"Come on." She pushed the truck to its limits, unconcerned about getting a ticket for going over the speed limit. With the number of forest fires that had broken out in the area, and everyone racing around trying to stop them, a police officer wasn't likely to pull over a state vehicle.

A sign ahead indicated another sharp curve in the road. She let up on the gas. Ticket or no, she didn't want to end up in an accident. Alex needed her.

Shortly after Alex and Daniel left for the nursing home, the decision was made to cut Parents' Day short in light of the fires. Everyone was sent home early. The camp had been quiet.

The cell phone call from her boss came while she helped the camp staff with cleanup. "All hands on deck," he'd said. She had been needed to assess whether to evacuate some of the raptors' nests in harm's way. Once that was done, she was let go for the evening but instructed to be on call.

Now she continued to speed southeast toward the camp. About an hour later, she pulled onto the dirt driveway. Daniel's car was parked in the lot next to Hiccup. She flew out of her truck and met him as he stepped from the main building with Sally. They each wore the same grave look. Penny stood protectively at their heels.

"Where's Alex?" Zoe asked. "Did something happen?"

"She went to the chestnut tree," Daniel said. "She said she couldn't be here right now."

"Mr. Marcotte, what happened today?"

"I never should've pressured her to go. Carolyn rejected her, and I couldn't do anything to stop it. I didn't know how to do it and protect them both." He seemed paralyzed.

Zoe glanced into the sky just as Terry soared above the camp, still testing his fledgling wings. One of his parents flew nearby, teaching him. Some eagle parents were innately good at teaching their young, some weren't. No one knew why. Human parents were the same. Fortunately for Dac, his parents had so far proved top of the line. If he had it in him to fly, they would see to it that he learned all he needed to know.

"I'll call her cell phone and tell her I'm coming to find her," she said.

"She doesn't have her phone with her," Sally said. "I think she left it here on purpose so she couldn't be found. Do you want us to take you over in one of the boats?"

"No." Zoe pointed at the western horizon. "There's talk of evacuating several more towns. Glasgow may be one of them if the winds shift, which they very well might. The boats might be your best means of escape. I'll take my kayak. I'm assuming Alex has one of the camp's boats already, right?"

"She does," Daniel said.

"Don't take any chances. If they tell you to go, you go," Zoe said. "I'll find Alex and stay with her." Even though night had yet to fall, the heavy, ominous smoke hanging over the fires raging in the hills had blocked out most of the remaining daylight.

"Well, let's get you loaded up with a couple of sleeping bags and food in case you have to spend the night across the lake." Sally headed toward the main building. "You be sure to call us one way or the other."

"I will." Zoe followed Sally into the building.

Not long afterward, Zoe pulled her kayak onto the dock along the shore that led to the chestnut tree. She was relieved to see the camp's boat tied there too.

The evening was pitch black now that the sun had set and smoke covered the moon and stars. She unclipped the flashlight attached to her kayak and grabbed the backpack that Sally had made ready for her. She ran down the dirt path through the woods toward Alex and the chestnut tree.

Alex must've seen the flashlight. In the darkness, her silhouette stood as Zoe approached. "Who's there?"

The sound of Alex's voice washed over her. Somehow, the wall of despair that threatened to silence Alex's voice had to be brought down once and for all. She picked up her pace. "It's me, Zoe."

When she was a couple of feet from Alex, she tossed the flashlight and backpack down on the ground next to the blanket spread beneath the chestnut tree. Four large citronella candles in metal buckets spaced around the blanket kept the mosquitoes at bay. She threw her arms around Alex.

Alex hugged her. "I prayed you'd come. I was so worried when Claire said you'd been sent to the fires." She kissed her cheek. "My mother…"

"I know." Zoe wiped away a tear running down Alex's face, and another. "Stop being afraid of the past or things in the future that haven't even happened yet. Stop long enough to just be with me in this moment." She cupped Alex's face in her hands. "Let it all go and be with me." She pulled Alex's face down to meet hers and kissed her.

Alex opened her mouth and pressed her tongue to Zoe's in an uninhibited kiss. "Make love to me," she whispered when the kiss ended.

Zoe caressed Alex's breasts and closed her eyes, relishing the feel of Alex's nipples hardening under her touch. Heat surged between her legs.

Alex stepped out of her reach.

The sudden separation sucked the wind out of her. "Please, don't pull away again."

"I couldn't if I tried." Alex grabbed the bottom of her tank top, pulled it over her head, and tossed it near the blanket. She reached behind her back and unclasped her bra, leaving it loose. She reached for Zoe. "Come here."

Zoe stepped to within inches of Alex. She slipped her fingers underneath the straps of the silky bra and slowly slid them from Alex's shoulders. The bra fell to the ground. Her breath caught. Alex stood motionless, naked, tempting. Zoe's mouth watered at the thought of tasting her.

Alex's breathing grew heavy. She placed a hand to the back of Zoe's head and pulled her in.

"You are so beautiful." Zoe marveled at the body in front of her. Alex's lovely breasts were hers for the taking. She sucked in a nipple and kneaded the other with her fingers.

Alex yanked at the bottom of Zoe's T-shirt and pulled it free from the waistband of her work trousers. "I want to feel your skin on mine." She undid the pants' button and zipper.

A whiff of smoke reminded Zoe how filthy she was from the fires. "I'm hot, wet, and dirty. Maybe I should rinse off in the lake first." She jumped a little when Alex's hands slid into the back of her pants.

"I don't want to wait. We can rinse off together later." Alex rubbed her buttocks. "I'm just as hot and wet," she breathed. "I think that's a good thing, don't you?"

Zoe kissed her hard with an open mouth. She pushed Alex's shorts down the length of her hips as far as she could reach, and Alex pushed them the rest of the way down and stepped out of them. Wearing only her underwear, she lay down on the blanket beneath the chestnut tree. The flickering candles illuminated her beautiful body.

"I want to touch every inch of you." Zoe bent over, untied her boots, and kicked them off. She took off her shirt. Her bra followed. Her nipples hardened as Alex gazed at them. "If you keep looking at me like that, I might come before you even touch me." She grinned and removed her trousers and underwear. Standing naked in front of Alex, she was hotter than the fires blazing in the hills.

Alex pushed her underwear off. "Please, Zoe." She spread her legs invitingly.

Zoe knelt down next to her. She brushed her hand between Alex's legs, determined to go slow. She kissed Alex softly as she ran a fingertip between her breasts, down her belly to the wiry hair wet with desire. She rested up on an elbow and scooted down until her fingers brushed the swollen clitoris.

Alex trembled. "Go inside me."

Zoe pushed two fingers inside of her. Slowly, she thrust her fingers in and out, letting Alex set the rhythm. Without stopping, she massaged the slippery clitoris with her thumb. Alex groaned. "That is heaven."

Zoe continued, edging Alex closer to climax. She needed to have all of Alex. She pulled her hand free and nestled her body between Alex's legs. "I want to taste you." She kissed Alex's neck, then each breast and her belly before she dipped her head and put her tongue where her thumb had been. She pushed Alex's legs farther apart and thrust her fingers back inside while savoring the sweet, salty taste.

Alex didn't try to hide her pleasure. She moaned and panted while holding Zoe's head tightly in place. Her hips thrust and her body quivered. Entangling Zoe's hair in her fingers, she screamed when her climax came. Her body jolted in aftershocks.

When she let go, Zoe rolled onto her back. She found Alex's hand and held it tight as they lay on the blanket, trying to catch their breath. "I love you," she said.

Several seconds of silence passed. Alex rolled toward Zoe and caressed the side of her face. "This time with you has been perfect. I don't want anything to ruin it." She cupped Zoe's breast.

The pleasure of having Alex make love to her blunted the sting of rejection. Zoe closed her eyes and moved Alex's hand down lower on her body. If she couldn't have a life with Alex, if she couldn't have Alex's love, at least she could have this time.

She and Alex continued to make love to each other long into the night, together under the dark sky and the protective canopy of the chestnut tree. A warm wind, no doubt kicked up by the fires raging across western Maine, snaked over their bodies.

Zoe fell asleep in Alex's arms.

Sometime later, she stirred and wondered where she was. The smell and feel of a warm, soft, naked body spooned against her back refreshed her memory. This was definitely not a dream. She pressed the arm draped over her waist more closely to her. She breathed in deeply. The air was heavy with smoke. She coughed.

Alex whispered, "Are you all right?"

Zoe opened her eyes. A thick wall of smoke, much bigger than the day before, hung over the western sky like an ominous wave threatening to overtake them. Flames rose from the hills in the distance. The cell phone inside her backpack rang. As painful as it was to extricate her limbs from Alex's, she sat up and reached for the phone. "The fires must be a lot closer. I'd better answer this."

Alex fumbled for her clothes while Zoe took the call. She let her head fall back in frustration at what she heard from the caller. "I'm not in Glasgow. I'm across the lake with Alex." She pounded a fist on the ground next to her. "Oh, my God. Okay." Her mouth dried.

"What's happening? Who was that?"

"It was Rob. He was wondering where I am." She put a hand on Alex's shoulder. "We have to go find your father and Sally. Glasgow's being evacuated."

Alex stood and tugged on her clothing. "Will you call my father and tell him not to worry? Tell him we're coming to help."

"Sure." Zoe tugged on her dirty clothes. They'd missed the rinse in the lake. She didn't mind. Alex's scent lingered on her skin.

Once Alex left Maine, and especially if the camp burned, she'd probably never see her again. Alex's non-response to Zoe's declaration of love spoke volumes. The most perfect summer of her life would soon end. Unlike the summers of Maine to come, she couldn't look forward to Alex's return. It would always feel like winter without her.

# Chapter 32

Sirens blared in the distance. As her boat neared shore, Alex realized the air was thick with smoke—not only from trees burning, but also from the acrid smell of chemicals in buildings being ravaged by the fire. She saw Zoe crane her head in the direction of the nest tree. "Any sign of Dac?"

"I can't tell through the haze. I was hoping I'd hear him or his parents, but there's nothing."

"Maybe he flew away with them to get away from the smoke and fires."

"I don't know. But after we check on your father and the camp, I'm grabbing my climbing gear and coming back out here. I need to get him out of the tree if he's still up there. He's been spending a lot of time on the edge of the nest and nearby branches, but I haven't seen him fly at all. I think he's still up there and doesn't know what to do."

Alex throttled back the motor. "I'm coming with you. We'll keep your kayak tied to the back of the boat so we don't have to leave it here."

"Good, because I need you."

Alex glanced from Zoe to the shore as the boat slid onto the sand. Frenzied people were taking things out of the main building and loading them into trucks at James's direction. She jumped over the side of the boat and ran toward them. Anger welled inside her. "What are you doing? Shouldn't we be trying to save the building instead of taking everything out of it?"

"There are fires all around us now," James said. "The wind is spreading embers everywhere. We can't save the building. All we can do is save what we can carry and pack into those trucks."

"I don't believe you."

Sally interrupted. "He's right, Alex. We can't save the camp this time. In fact, Glasgow is being sacrificed to stop the fire. If the firefighters can keep the fire moving in our direction, it'll run out of fuel when it hits the lake."

"Where's my father?" Alex asked, already moving toward the main building before Sally could answer.

James blocked her path and put his hands on her shoulders.

"Don't you ever fucking touch me," she said in a grating tone.

He put his hands up and took a step back. "I'm sorry. There's something you need to know before you go in there. I'm only trying to help."

Alex rubbed her eyes and tried to make sense of what was happening.

Zoe put a hand on the small of her back.

"Really? You're trying to help. Don't you have any clue what you've already done to my family? How dare you."

"Listen, Alex. You can hate me all you want. But it isn't going to do any of us any good, especially not your father."

"Since when do you care about my father?"

"Unlike you, I always have." James glared at her.

Alex's hands balled into fists. She took a step forward to strike him, but Sally and Zoe each grabbed one of her arms.

"I'm sorry for what happened." James's face contorted into a mask of grief. "Remember my dad, Alex? The town drunk? Everybody hid from him when he came around because he was so goddamn mean. While everyone in this town looked the other way, he beat my mother and me relentlessly. My only escape was this camp. Daniel Marcotte was the father I always wanted." He hung his head. "I love your father. I always will."

Alex lunged at him and banged her fists against his chest. "Why did you do what you did to Jake? You destroyed my family."

Zoe pulled her away from him. "Alex."

"I was jealous." James's tone was flat. "I wanted what you and Jake had. If I could take it all back, I would."

Alex put a hand to her mouth to stifle a cry. A veil lifted from her eyes. A memory flashed in her mind. James as a boy. In her anger, she'd forgotten, but now she saw an image of him coming to school with a black eye that he'd blamed on wrestling with his dog. The bully and the bullied weren't all that different, she realized. She, Jake, and James had been crushed by their parents, who were supposed to love them unconditionally.

"What do I need to know before I see my father?" she asked him.

"Your mother's dead. She died last night," James answered.

The words echoed in her head. *Your mother's dead.* An eagle screeched. Alex looked at the sky. Dac's parents circled the nest, calling to him, coaxing him to fly. No doubt they sensed the imminent danger. She let everything sink in, the ground seeming to vibrate under her feet. It hummed with the memories of so many things she held dear, happier times during her childhood with Jake. She saw her mother's smile before it was buried under years of bitterness and sickness. The brightness of her father's eyes before they were dulled by the things he couldn't fix. She ached to free them and herself.

She studied the camp's buildings, trying to memorize them. They would be gone in hours. Only scorched ground would remain.

"I wish you could forgive me." James's voice was quiet.

"I do." Alex never imagined it would be so easy. Maybe because she understood that he'd been a victim too. The burden of hate left her. Her body felt lighter, free of its weight. "I'm going with Zoe to save Dac. Make sure my father and Sally leave here soon and are safe."

"I will, and, Alex? Thanks for understanding."

Alex hugged Sally, who whispered into her ear, "Don't worry about us, honey. You stay safe too, and we'll all meet up again soon."

"Where's Buddy?" Alex asked.

"I sent him off ahead of me with Doc Parsons. He's safe and sound," Sally answered.

"Will you do me a favor?" Alex asked.

"Anything."

"Please make sure that the pictures of my family hanging on the wall by the staircase get safely out of the house."

"You bet." Sally turned to Zoe. "Don't let anything happen to you or my girl." She hugged her too. "Now get going. We need to get to work like we did in '47. There's a whole lot to be saved."

"Don't you want to see your father before we go?" Zoe asked Alex. "We might not be able to come back this way."

"I can't." Alex battled over whether to see him or not. She desperately tried to hang onto the feeling of numbness that had come over her earlier, which was better than the alternative. Her anxiety seemed to have gone quiet. "I'm afraid if see him right now, I might come apart."

"Okay." Zoe turned to Sally. "I'll have my cell phone with me. Assuming the towers don't go out, I'll try to call. Or you call me."

Alex took a last look at the camp. In the chaos and frenzy, she saw everything that had ever been good about it. Glasgow would never be the same without the camp, and neither would she or Daniel.

This wasn't the way it was supposed to end. For all the bad things that had happened, the camp was a magic place that she loved from the bottom of her heart. Zoe was right. She'd lost too much time staying away, time she couldn't have back.

Alex turned to Sally. "Please tell my father I love him, and I'll see him in a little while."

# Chapter 33

Alex pointed the boat in the direction of the island. Her heart broke when she thought about Dac. He'd yet to learn how to fly. With the fires closing in, his hours were numbered. She wept for him. Like Jake, he would die before he ever really learned to live.

The wind drew the fires further into the town. The fires also kicked up the winds. The lake churned into froth as the boat bounced toward the back side of the island.

Dac stood alone at the edge of the nest and cried. He flapped his wings wildly. A gust caught him and threw him back into the nest. He tumbled over, flailing.

"Where do think the parents have gone?" Alex asked.

"They may have decided to cut their losses and leave with Terry. The winds are bringing the fires closer."

Alex looked toward shore. There were no more people coming and going from the camp. "James must've left with my father and Sally by now."

"They're going to be okay. How about you?"

"I don't know how I feel." Alex landed the boat on a small swath of sand on the island. "Are you sure it's safe to climb the tree?"

"It isn't," Zoe said. "And as much as it hurts to leave Dac up there, things have changed for me."

"What do you mean?"

"I don't want to take the chance. I'm not going up there. The winds are too heavy."

"I'm so relieved, but has being around me made you afraid?"

"No. It's made me know exactly what I want, and I'm making the choice." Zoe embraced her. "I don't know what's going to happen to your family's camp or to Dac. I told you last night that I love you. When you didn't respond, I figured I had to let you go. I can't, not unless you tell me to my face that's what you want. Life is precious and can be gone in an instant. I don't want to have to live with doubt about whether I tried hard enough to get you to hear me." Zoe took her hands. "I love you. I want to be around for you, however things turn out. If you'll stay."

Alex laid her head on Zoe's shoulder. She felt like Dac. Not sure how to fly or brave enough to try as the world around her burned. She had Zoe. That made the difference. He was alone.

Dac cried.

Alex looked up and saw him standing on the edge of the nest. He flapped his wings wildly.

"Don't give up, Dac," Zoe yelled. "Trust your wings."

He tumbled again and struggled to claw his way back to the edge of the nest. He spread his wings in the smoke-filled wind and screeched. He clearly wanted to live.

"Please, just let go. You can do it," Alex said to herself as much as to him. "Step into the wind and fly."

Zoe urged him on. "Come on, buddy, it's all you. Don't be afraid. Let go and fly."

An eagle's cry came from behind them. A dark speck emerged from the smoke. Terry. He circled the island and called to his brother.

Dac stood on the edge of the nest with his wings spread wide. Several gusts lifted him and slammed him back into the nest. Each time, he climbed back to the edge. He craned his head in the direction of his sibling, who continued calling to him. He spread his wings and stepped from the edge.

A gust lifted him high above the nest tree. He wavered and fell. Suddenly he flapped hard and gained altitude. He soared higher toward his brother. They circled around the island together and flew off into the distance.

Tears spilled from Alex's eyes, taking the hurt, anger, and fear with them. "He did it. He just let go. That's all he had to do to fly."

Zoe hugged her. "We have to go. Embers are falling on the lake now."

"Let's go to the chestnut tree." Alex turned the key in the ignition and backed the boat off the island. She glanced toward shore. One of the bunkhouses was on fire, and the camp was deserted. She wondered why, as her world came undone, it felt like the beginning. She looked at Zoe and turned her eyes away from the camp. She'd never see it again.

Alex sat huddled with Zoe under the safety of the chestnut tree. She could no longer see it, but she knew from the smoke and repeated sounds of explosions rocking the night that everything her family had created was burning to the ground.

"You've lost so much tonight," Zoe said.

Alex breathed in deeply and let her breath out slowly. "Out west, there's a tree called the jack pine. Do you know of it?"

"I do. Its cones won't release seeds unless they're exposed to extreme heat."

"That's the one. It takes a wildfire to destroy everything for the jack pine to survive." Alex folded her knees to her chest and wrapped her arms around her legs. "I always wondered whether I needed for my parents and the camp to finally be out of my life for good in order to be happy. Did moving on from Jake's death require extinguishing everything that made me sad or afraid?"

"Do you know the answer now?" Zoe asked.

"I do. I won't be happy simply because the bad memories are gone. The truth is, they'll always be part of my life. My history can't be erased. History never can be, no matter how hard we try to bury it. It is what it is. You and Dac taught me the answer to living happy and free in spite of my past. Now that my mother's gone, I have only one wish for her. I'm hoping she's in Heaven, finally free of her burdens, holding my brother in her arms."

Zoe brushed the hair away from her eyes. "What did you learn?"

"To be brave enough to let go, step into the wind, and fly. It's funny. I never imagined that I'd ever be able to forgive my father. Or James, for that matter. I still don't know exactly what it means to forgive. But it does feel so much lighter to let it all go. To leave it behind, like Dac left the nest behind to live his life. That's what I intend to do by staying in Glasgow."

"You're staying!" Zoe kissed her cheek.

"I love you, Zoe. And I love Maine. I always have and always will. What I learned from James tonight is that he was a victim of bullying too. I want to help my father rebuild the camp and change the course of it. I want to help kids learn a different way of living where there are no bullies. I want to teach them what Dac taught me. To be brave enough to embrace life no matter the circumstance or outcome." Alex squeezed Zoe's hand. "And I want a life with you."

"Somewhere out there," Zoe said, "our Dac has a smile in his heart almost as big as mine." She cupped Alex's face in her hands. "I will love you for the rest of my life."

"I'm going to hold you to that. Will you fly with me?"

"Wherever the winds take us."

Author Bev Prescott

# About the Author

Bev Prescott shares her life with her beautiful partner of 23 years and their clever calico cat, Lilliput. They live at the edge of a meadow in New England.

When Bev isn't working as an environmental attorney, or writing stories about everyday lesbian heroines who make a difference, she's picking berries or flowers from the meadow, hiking in the woods or playing on the water.

# Make sure to check out these other exciting Blue Feather Books titles:

**www.bluefeatherbooks.com**